QUEEN

OF

DESIRE

QUEEN
OF
DESIRE

A NOVEL

Sam Toperoff

HarperCollins*Publishers*

QUEEN OF DESIRE. Copyright © 1992 by Sam Toperoff. All rights reserved. Printed in the United States of America. No part of this book may be used or reproduced in any manner whatsoever without written permission except in the case of brief quotations embodied in critical articles and reviews. For information address Harper-Collins Publishers, 10 East 53rd Street, New York, NY 10022.

FIRST EDITION

Designed by Alma Orenstein

Library of Congress Cataloging-in-Publication Data

Toperoff, Sam.
    Queen of desire : a novel/by Sam Toperoff.—1st ed.
      p. cm.
    ISBN 0-06-016611-8
    1. Monroe, Marilyn, 1926–1962—Fiction. I. Title.
PS3570.06044   1991
813'.54—dc20   90-56372

92 93 94 95 96| AC/RRD   10 9 8 7 6 5 4 3 2 1

For Lily

THE DEATH OF MARILYN MONROE

The ambulance men touched her cold
body, lifted it, heavy as iron,
onto the stretcher, tried to close the
mouth, closed the eyes, tied the
arms to the sides, moved a caught
strand of hair, as if it mattered,
saw the shape of her breasts, flattened by
gravity, under the sheet,
carried her, as if it were she,
down the steps.

These men were never the same. They went out
afterwards, as they always did,
for a drink or two, but they could not meet
each other's eyes.

    Their lives took
a turn—one had nightmares, strange
pains, impotence, depression. One did not
like his work, his wife looked
different, his kids. Even death
seemed difficult to him—a place where she
would be waiting,

and one found himself standing at night
in the doorway to a room of sleep, listening to a
woman breathing, just an ordinary
woman
breathing.

        SHARON OLDS

QUEEN
OF
DESIRE

CHAPTER ONE

A Rape, a Whisper

LIGHTS

LIFE: In so many interviews you've given, you allude frequently to your childhood in a way that makes one think of an unwanted waif. Could it really have been as bad as all that?

MONROE: It wasn't pleasant. Sure, there were times when individuals treated me well, but they were few and far between. A child knows when she's unwanted—my God, how could I miss it? One month I was hustled off to this so-called "relative," the next month in a foster home, and then back with my mother whenever they let her out of the mental hospital. I won't even mention the Los Angeles Orphan's Home. It wasn't pretty. You see kids who are loved, who have stability and normal human affection, so you know exactly what you are being denied.

LIFE: Heavens, that conjures visions of Dickens, *Oliver Twist*, beatings with a cane, bowls of gruel, dirty-faced street urchins. Surely it couldn't have been that bad.

MONROE: I don't really want to get into specifics. What's to be gained? It sounds like you're complaining or looking for sympathy. Almost like a "Tell me how hard your life was" deal. It's too depressing.

LIFE: But it would help people understand what makes an individual tick, especially when the individual is talented and widely admired. Isn't it possible, for example, that the events that marked your childhood, unpleasant though they may be to contemplate, actually had the effect of shaping you into the creative personality that has emerged?

MONROE: Funny you say that, because it's the question that's on my mind all the time these days. Sometimes I believe in my heart I would have become what I did even if I had an "apple pie" childhood. Then there are times when I'm one hundred percent certain I became an actress and have driven myself to be better precisely because of the childhood I had. I know it forced me deeper into myself, made me develop an imagination— I know it drove me to want to prove to the world I was somebody, that it couldn't beat me down.

LIFE: Well, which one was it?

MONROE: Probably both . . . and neither. Or is that too
Zen?

CAMERA

*Marilyn was at the Alcott and Murchison Funeral Home in
Santa Monica. She wore a tailored suit, black linen, a black
straw hat with a wide tilted brim, pulled taut by a tulle veil
that tied under her chin. She had flown in from New York,
where she was studying with Lee Strasberg at the Actor's Studio, preparing, as the columnists were all speculating, for her
stage debut.*

*In the open casket, "Aunt" Ana Lower, the aunt of her
mother's best friend. "Aunt" Ana was indeed a great woman.
Norma Jean lived with her in a large rambling house in Santa
Monica for thirteen months when she was ten. Ana Lower offered the girl the purest, most nourishing love Norma Jean
would ever have in her life. Now Marilyn gazed at the wonderful woman, whose tiny, shriveled body offered fraudulent evi-
dence of what once had been.*

*Relatives and friends were, for the most part, keeping their
distance. The wife of a cousin sat down alongside Marilyn and
asked for an autograph for her children. Marilyn looked for help
while she signed. Mr. Murchison came to her aid and led Marilyn up to the casket.*

*Ana's eyes were closed. Marilyn recalled eyes as gray and
clear as a pencil sketch. The face was spotted and deeply lined; it
used to have a soft pink glow Marilyn took for a standard of
good health. This was not the person who saved Marilyn's san-
ity; this was the dry husk of what was left when that person
had given out.*

Norma Jean was brought to live with the sixty-two-year-old spinster lady after her tenth birthday. The child did not consciously decide to stop talking, as her mother, Gladys Baker, believed. Gladys was certain her child was being purposely difficult. It was as though one day she was a bright and active little chirper; the next, a sick, silent bird.

The man with the mustache had been one of her mother's friends. They had gone on nice picnics with him, to the zoo, even on a trip to Santa Monica to visit Ana Lower.

As Marilyn tried to look into the woman in the coffin, she considered touching the back of the dead hand. Had she thanked her enough for saving her soul? The man's name came to her just then. For the first time in more than twenty years. Harley Lowes.

It was 1935. Gladys was home again, working at the studio after a brief hospitalization for a nervous breakdown. Marilyn saw the room clearly too—the wallpaper in aqua tints, the stuccoed ceiling, billowing white curtains, Grand Rapids maple furniture, and mirrors: a mirror running the length of the closet door, another on the face of the armoire, and a three-way makeup mirror on the dressing table. Her mother loved mirrors; once, when Norma Jean asked why, she said, "Mirrors make more light. Let there be light," and then something in French.

Marilyn remembered another strange thing in the room: a single silver candlestick on top of the armoire. What had happened to it? Where was it now? Where was any of that stuff?

He was a young man, she realized now, in his mid-twenties perhaps, but she was so young all adults were old to her. Why, why in the world would her mother leave her alone with him? She began to see it all again through childish eyes. Even in death, "Aunt" Ana had helped her to understand. Marilyn touched the dead hand.

As she leaned near the body in the Alcott and Murchison Funeral Home, Marilyn whispered the first thing she'd ever said into "Aunt" Ana's sacks. "I don't ever want to be in the world without you, Gram." She had said it into the "Good Things" sack.

ACTION

Norma Jean keeps her gaze on his wispy mustache. It is very different from the photograph her mother showed her once, which she associated with the word "father." She knows this man isn't her father, but her mother likes him so much. Cleaned the apartment all morning, gave him two cups of coffee, even let him put his feet up on the fancy ottoman. Walked him through the sickroom, saying, "It's nothing, just a fever, a runny nose. I'm taking precautions. You think I'm too much of a doting mother?"

"No, not at all. It means you love her. Doesn't she, Norma?"

Norma Jean is selecting a crayon. If her mother likes him, she likes him too. She likes that he's never tried to play up to her or talk to her in a fake voice. But she keeps watching him, curiously, from her cluttered bed, where she is coloring pictures in *Ben, the Firehouse Dog*. She colors the fireman's red slicker aggressively, not bound by the outline. When she turns the pages, she peeks at the man till the moment she senses he's going to look at her. Then another mad scribble.

"Why don't I drive you?" the young man tells Gladys.

" 'Cause I don't want to leave her alone."

"But what could happen? Nothing."

"That's not the point. You just don't leave a sick nine-year-old alone. You just don't do it."

Norma sees how naturally he places his hands on her mother's shoulders and how she smiles back.

"So why," he says, "don't you let me drive to the studio and pick up the stuff? Just call so they'll expect me."

Gladys makes her sourpuss face. Norma knows nothing can change her mind. "No one but employees in the cutting room. Studio rule. It'll take twenty minutes. No more." Her voice softens and gets childish, a mannerism Norma Jean has noticed only when there's a man with her. "What's the matter, Mr. Lowes, a problem letting a woman drive your precious automobile?"

Mr. Lowes smooths his mustache with a thumb and forefinger.

Gladys's eyes bulge peculiarly. "Just as well. I'll call a cab."

"Don't be silly." Mr. Lowes digs in his pocket for the keys. "It pulls a little to the left when you brake. Just ease them, don't come down too hard."

Gladys is more than coy as she takes his car keys: "Tell me, when've I ever been too rough, Harley?"

Norma bites her lip, making it seem as if her choice of crayons puzzles her.

"Mommy's got to leave for a little while, honey. Mr. Lowes is going to stay with you till I come back." Gladys Baker hasn't ever referred to herself as "Mommy" in Norma's presence. The "honey" has never been used very much, and never so sweetly as this.

Since her mother believes she's ill, Norma obliges and manufactures a thin cough.

"I'll pick up some cough drops while I'm out. And how about some vanilla ice cream? It's good for your throat."

Norma doesn't respond. She puts her red crayon back in the place reserved for it in the tin. It's time to start on Ben himself, the firehouse dog. He's sitting in the seat next to the driver of the engine. Like Ben, Norma has her tongue pointed intently out of her mouth.

"I said, should I pick up some ice cream?"

Norma heard the offer the first time. She hates vanilla. That's the flavor her mother likes.

"Sure," Mr. Lowes says, "get some ice cream. Here." He takes a roll of bills out of his pocket and pulls off a dollar, and another.

"I've got money. It's Norma Jean. She hasn't said she wants ice cream. Have you?"

Norma bites her tongue and begins to color Ben. Because she has never seen a Dalmatian, she reverses the coloring. The black spots she leaves white, the white background she strokes in black, deep gray actually. "Uh uh."

"Is that a yes or a no?"

"Don't like vanilla."

"That's what's good for a cold, vanilla. That's what they give you in the hospital, vanilla."

Mr. Lowes says, "The flavor don't matter. Just that it's cold. It soothes the throat. Here." He flutters the bills. "Get her what she wants. You and me, we'll have vanilla."

"So what kind?"

Norma Jean does not look up from her work. "Something with fruit."

"Other kids, it's vanilla or chocolate. My kid, it's something with fruit." Almost casually, she takes the money.

"And why don't you get us a pack of Camels too," he says.

Gladys Baker goes into her bedroom to select shoes and a hat. Mr. Lowes wanders around Norma's bedroom, first peering out the window at his Studebaker, then shaking her piggy bank—to which he adds a quarter—and reordering her blocks alphabetically. He leans over Norma to inspect her coloring. He says unconvincingly, "That's very good."

Norma smells him. He is wet wool and caramel. He smells her. She is warm grass and cough medicine.

Mr. Lowes wanders out of the bedroom. Norma hears his voice coming from her mother's room. She darkens Ben's coat to a deeper gray, aware of their distant voices. She cannot discern words; the tone, however, is new. Her mother's laugh is unusually rough. Mr. Lowes speaks softly and slurringly, like a radio that isn't tuned in properly. Norma is still, holding her breath, listening.

Then her mother, completely dressed, buttoning her pale yellow Easter coat, comes into the bedroom. Mr. Lowes stands in the doorway and smiles like a friend at Norma, as her mother places a hand on her daughter's forehead and scowls.

"Fever?" Mr. Lowes asks.

"A little warm."

"Got a thermometer?"

"Norma Jean hates it."

"Which kind?" He places his finger in his mouth and then behind his rump.

"That kind," Gladys says. "Okay now, young lady." The "young lady," too, is only for guests. "If you need anything, just call Mr. Lowes. Some juice. You're supposed to drink lots of juice. Where's your handkerchief?"

Norma pulls an unused, neatly folded handkerchief from the sleeve of her flowered nightie.

"Okay. Don't be ashamed to go to the bathroom."

Embarrassed, Norma Jean looks to the visitor for help. He indicates a secret alliance with pursed lips and a faint nod. She immediately turns to her coloring book and reaches for a yellow crayon to color number 74 on the fire engine.

Gladys kisses Norma Jean's forehead. "I'll be right back with the ice cream. And don't be such a sourpuss."

"We'll be fine, Gladys," he says.

Her mother moves past Mr. Lowes, and he runs his

hand across her back and follows her out to the living room. Norma hears the front door close. Then a snap that might be the lock. After a minute or so, music comes from the big cabinet radio in the living room, Russ Columbo singing "Prisoner of Love."

He steps into her doorway. "You like that music?"

She strings out her answer, trying for the same coyness she's heard from Gladys: "Yeah."

Stroking his mustache, he comes alongside her bed. "You don't really have a fever, do you?"

"I might," still coy with her eyes and her tongue. "I usually wear a bow in my hair. The yellow one."

"You want your bow now?"

"Yeah."

Lowes brings the ribbon to her.

"I don't know how to tie it." Even while speaking, Norma turns in her bed, putting her back to Lowes. "She puts it under my hair and ties it up like on a package." Norma lifts her soft brown hair and bends her neck forward. It is long and slender and very white. He is reminded of a swan. He sits down on the edge of her bed and places the ribbon flat against that neck. She drops her hair over it.

At just the moment he is pulling the second loop through the ribbon, Norma Jean looks back at him in a curious way. Her hair smells like perfumed soap. There seems to be a warmth coming off her vulnerable little body. He feels as though he is doing something terribly wrong. He ties a large, irregular bow high in her hair.

He realizes he is in an inviolate place; it frightens him. It excites him.

Norma Jean asks, "Do you have a sister?"

"Why?"

"Just want to know."

"Why?"

"I just thought . . ." The rest of the thought is dismissed with a fetching shrug.

Harley Lowes knows he is aroused, has been since he saw and then touched her delicate neck. He won't actually do anything wrong, but it's too soon to leave her bed. He tells himself he won't let things go too far.

"So what do you like to do when you're not drawing?"

"I'm not drawing. I'm coloring."

"Oh, coloring. Yeah."

"You're not supposed to say 'yeah.' You're supposed to say 'yes.' "

Like a child himself, he says, "I heard you say 'yeah.' "

"You like my mom?"

"Sure. Why?"

"No reason." For the first time, Norma looks directly into his eyes and lets the glance linger. Lowes becomes conscious of the fact that the child is extremely beautiful. He catches his breath. There is still room to maneuver; he has not gone too far. He knows he ought to leave.

"Let me see your fingers." He very much wants to touch her hand: that's all, touch her hand. She puts down the crayon and offers her hand to him palm up. He treats it as something rare. It feels warm and begins to quiver as he squeezes it slightly. She starts to pull it away. He looks into her face; her tongue is folded over her lower lip. His breath catches in his chest. He squeezes her hand tight. He has an erection pushing down the leg he has angled on the bed by Norma's side. Their eyes meet again and he looks down, trying to draw her gaze to the swelling on his thigh. His temples throb with his heartbeat.

Norma Jean's voice is a whisper. "I know what that is."

"No you don't."

"I do."

"How?"

"I won't tell."

He doesn't want it to be his voice, so he removes himself from the words. "You can touch it."

"No."

"There's nothing wrong." He brings her hand to his leg and brushes her fingertips along his swollen penis. Norma has no expression on her face. She feels only the texture of the wool. Excitement pushes him to the edge of control. He closes his eyes and breathes through his mouth in rhythm to the stroking.

She tries to withdraw her hand. The breathing, though, and the baring of his lower teeth have frightened her. The pupils of his eyes appear to have darkened, appear tinged with red. She tugs her hand suddenly, and he lets go.

"You shouldn't do that. You're not allowed."

He's reluctant to look at her face. "Why not?"

There's no answer. He hears the rippling of crayon on paper again. The radio is playing "Sunny Side of the Street." When he stands, the swelling in his crotch hardens again. Norma Jean says, "What are you doing?"

He intended to leave the bedroom, but he says, "I'm looking for the thermometer. I told your mom I'd take care of you."

"I don't want that."

"Where's the thermometer?"

"I don't like it."

On a shelf in the bathroom, the thermometer is next to a small jar of Vaseline. "Nothing to worry about. You're probably normal."

"You're not supposed to do it."

He comes back into the bedroom, shaking down the thermometer. They look at each other. Lowes says, "Let's surprise your mother. We'll prove to her you don't have a temperature."

"I don't."

"We have to be sure. We don't want to lie. You'll have to take off your panties."

"I don't have any on."

"Fine. Then pull back the cover."

Norma Jean shakes her head. Lowes pulls the patchwork quilt easily out of her hands down to her ankles. *Ben, the Firehouse Dog* and a handful of crayons fall off the bed. Slowly, she pulls her knees to her chest; it is a protective reflex, which Lowes perceives as inviting because the child's calves and the back of her thighs are revealed as the hem of her nightgown is lifted. Her face is quizzical. She looks exactly like her mother.

Lowes begins to speak and abruptly catches himself. He unscrews the Vaseline and rolls the tip of the thermometer in the lubricant. Norma Jean doesn't move. He rescrews the cap and sits down on the bed.

Norma says, "Don't look."

Lowes turns his head away slightly and guides the thermometer into the darkness beneath her nightgown. He can feel it brush the inside of her thigh. When it touches her vagina, Norma Jean tenses. He does not stop. He probes the area delicately. The thermometer enters the tight fold. "Not there," Norma says.

Still he probes. He feels it continue into the girl. She squirms slightly and says, "Not there."

He waggles his wrist and it enters deeper still. For the first time, there's insistence in her voice. "No. Don't."

He stops, but he doesn't withdraw the thermometer. "I have a sister. I did this with her. When she was sick in bed. It was okay to do."

"It isn't. Stop or I'll tell."

"You won't. You better not."

"I will."

Lowes withdraws the thermometer slowly. His expression perplexes Norma Jean: he looks like the one who's been insulted. He picks up the Vaseline jar and goes into the bathroom. She hears the water running, the medicine chest open and close. He emerges, patting his face with wet hands.

Pulling her cover over herself again, Norma begins to frown. He takes it for the onset of tears. "Don't cry. Your temperature is normal."

"You didn't take it. I know what you did." But her frown is caused by the book and the crayons out of reach on the floor. Lowes bends and picks them up, putting them gently next to the girl.

"Remember, I'm the one who got you the kind of ice cream you wanted."

Norma seeks the page she has been working on. "It's only ice cream."

"*Only* ice cream. That's a fine thing to say. You ever hear the saying 'Looking a gift horse in the mouth'?"

"Nope." She's coloring the fire engine again.

"You're supposed to stay inside the lines."

"If you want to." Her manner is coy again. Her tongue comes out.

Lowes takes a thin black comb from his rear pocket and runs it straight back through his light hair, which falls neatly in waves on his head. Norma watches, impressed. So he does it again. "You have nice hair too," he says.

"My mother says it's mousy."

"It's not. She's wrong."

"It used to be real light. It's turning. I'm gonna tell Mama what you did."

Lowes leaves a long silence. Norma colors and hums so

softly and intermittently it might not be humming but the breeze or another, more distant, radio.

"I was worried about your cold. I took your temperature."

"Oh, sure."

Her tone scares Harley Lowes. He walks out of her bedroom and peers from the front window for his car coming down the street. Before he sees it, he unlocks the door and walks out on the front steps. He lights a cigarette. He is ashamed and frightened.

His car turns into Grove Street. Gladys is driving too fast and too far in the center of the road. Lowes looks for cars coming from the other direction; there are none. She turns too sharply into the driveway and hits the edge of the curb jarringly. Lowes scowls and forces a smile when Gladys waves.

He approaches and helps her out. She has a pile of folders and a film canister. "The ice cream?" he reminds. She picks two hand-packed containers off the floor.

"How'd it go?" she wants to know.

"With Norma Jean? Fine. We took her temperature."

Gladys Baker looks a little surprised. She says, "Oh."

"She was normal."

They all have their ice cream, Norma Jean in her bed. Lowes and Gladys talk for a while out in the living room. Then Lowes leaves, earlier than planned. He doesn't say goodbye to Norma Jean; she hears him tell her mother, "I think she's sleeping. She needs her sleep."

Norma Jean didn't tell her mother anything the next day, or even the following week. The two spoke so little, Gladys didn't realize for months that Norma had developed a worrisome stutter. Finally, a note came home from school saying that Norma Jean was acting strangely and could she please make an appointment to come to school. She didn't respond, and the school contacted her again.

Norma Jean refused to speak when she was asked a direct question by her teacher. There were rare occasions when she spoke, softly and briefly, but most of the time she just shook her head. Eventually, she didn't speak at all. She did everything the teachers asked. She did all her homework. But the teachers were concerned because Norma Jean had been such a normal, outgoing girl. This was all very strange; they were worried. What had happened? Gladys certainly didn't know.

The girl wasn't exactly choosing not to speak; either something was blocking the process from thought to word or it was broken. She had thoughts, she had a few things she wanted to say; there was simply no reason to say them, no impulse to propel them, no desire to share them.

Hardly anyone in those days understood psychological trauma, although the school principal mentioned the word "psychiatrist." The word, the suggestion, offended Gladys Baker. Her daughter would not be crazy. The problem did not keep Gladys from seeing Harley Lowes. He came to the house for dinner one night and brought Norma Jean a box of chocolates. Norma took it into her room. Rarely after that did he come to the house; he picked Gladys up at the studio. Those nights, Norma made her own supper.

At school, the assumption was that her stutter was the reason she didn't speak. She was assigned a speech teacher for an hour each day. Norma spoke haltingly with the teacher for a while and then stopped speaking entirely. The teacher advised that nothing be done: when the child wanted to speak again, she would. This was a reasonable assumption, which Gladys did not have the patience to allow to run its course. She would go a few days without badgering the child and then suddenly explode at dinner,

insisting that Norma Jean drop the damn act and start talking.

Those nights Norma Jean cried herself to sleep. Gladys
believed the weeping was better than the silence, a step on
the way to speaking again. Speech didn't come while Norma
Jean lived with her mother.

One night, Gladys did not come home from the studio. Norma opened a can of tuna fish and toasted bread for
a sandwich. At the kitchen table, she drew a map of Africa
for her geography homework. The telephone rang after she
was in bed. It wasn't her mother; it was Grace McKee, her
mother's best friend at work.

Gladys had been hospitalized again. Norma stayed a
short while with Grace McKee and her husband. Then she
stayed with Grace's aunt, Ana Lower.

When Norma Jean arrived at "Aunt" Ana's house in
Santa Monica, it was one of the largest farmhouses in town.
Its east facade still looked out over sloping farmland with a
view that stretched to distant mountains. Times were very
hard; Ana had turned the place into a rooming house. There
were five or six families sharing the premises, but most of the
men were looking for work far away and were never there for
more than a day or two. It was a house of women and children. Meals were shared; so were the tasks and chores.

Norma was happy there, especially when she came
home from school and the large kitchen was quiet for about
an hour while Ana baked a pie or prepared muffins for
dinner. Norma loved to help the woman she called "Gram."
She had been there for three months and had become a
happier child, but changing schools twice had been difficult. She had stopped speaking again.

Norma keeps the screen door from slamming and tiptoes
across the linoleum. All the familiar baking paraphernalia is

on the table. Ana, in a pinafore apron, has her back to the door.

Ana knows her sweet girl is approaching and holds in a laugh while letting the child near. She begins to hum while wiping an already dry plate with a dish towel.

Ana hears Norma's soft breath and then feels cool hands on her cheeks just below her eyes. "Oh, my, who's that? It can't be . . . ?" She spins. "Oh my, it is. It's the Princess Casamassima." Ana curtsies. Norma dips even lower. They hug.

"I've got a tiny piece of pie left. And some chocolate milk. The Princess would like?"

Norma nods.

Ana takes a cold plate with a slice of peach pie and a bottle of milk from the huge gas refrigerator. Norma sits at the kitchen table. Ana fetches a tall glass and a tin of chocolate syrup. The sounds of pouring, the clinking of the spoon against the thick glass, are especially distinct.

"I've been doing some thinking, Princess. It isn't good for you not to talk. Not good because you have to hold too much inside yourself. You might explode."

There's a frown on Norma's brow.

"See what I've got." From below the table, the old lady elevates two paper sacks. She has printed in bold blue crayon letters the words "Good Things" on one sack and "Bad Things" on the other.

Norma's frown gives way to interest.

"Here's what I figured. Of course, it may be a very foolish thing. You don't have to talk to me, not to anyone. But if you have something to get off your chest, something that's bothering you or something you're really happy about, why not just whisper it in the sack. I'll have them here every day when you come home. Your secret sacks. Anything in your heart you can whisper in them."

So simple, so profound an idea. Ana Lower understood the mysteries of the human heart; she was the saving psychologist in a time and place where there was no one else.

The very next afternoon, Norma comes into the kitchen with a secret smile on her lips. The sacks are on the table. Ana, at the sink, turns and folds her arms. Norma puts her books on a kitchen chair. Their eyes lock. Norma kneels on the chair next to her books and leans her chin into the "Good Things" sack.

The whispered sounds come to Ana's ears like lovely music.

Every day for a month, Norma spoke into her sacks. Ana also brought them up to Norma's bedroom every night before bed. Soon after, the girl whispered to her directly. A while after that, she spoke softly at dinner to some of Ana's boarders. It took longer for her to speak at school, but eventually she volunteered to spell the word "friendly" in class. Then it was over: Norma Jean spoke quietly but as normally as any of the girls in her class.

Norma Jean would have stayed with Ana for years, but Ana's health had begun to fail; she was living in constant pain.

Marilyn Monroe never forgot the majesty of "Aunt" Ana. Or her debt to her. The two paper sacks were the end of insult and humiliation, of shame and guilt. Ana was also the midwife of her imagination, of confidence, of the breathless Marilyn whisper.

CHAPTER TWO

With Mickie Woody
in the Woods

LIGHTS

PSYCHOLOGY TODAY: We all know—and if we don't we're
sure to learn—that all things in life are a trade-off.

MONROE: And it's a lousy deal, most of the time.

PSYCHOLOGY: So what did Marilyn Monroe lose when she
became a world-class celebrity?

MONROE: I know what I'm supposed to say, or, rather,
what people expect me to say. I'm supposed to complain about the price I have to pay, how great the cost
of fame really is. But the truth is that in most of the
ways that count, a celebrity can still have as much
privacy as most people really need in the world. Look

at [Greta] Garbo; she had all the privacy she ever wanted. The real problem is that everything becomes unnatural. You even have to go about trying to have a normal life in an unnatural way. That's the part you don't understand until you're in it for a while.

PSYCHOLOGY: If you could have had a more ordinary life . . .

MONROE: I said *natural*, not *ordinary*.

PSYCHOLOGY: "Natural" then. What natural things are missing from your life?

MONROE: A normal family. Children. Naturally.

CAMERA

So many black-and-white movies, especially in the '40s, used to open with shots of a street almost like this one—tidy white houses, well-tended lawns, no refuse anywhere, none of the cars parked by the curb; they were standing in the short driveways instead. Neat, ordered homes, reflecting neat, ordered lives. Nothing fancy; very few of the houses with porches, merely brick steps leading up to a nicely painted front door.

The house numbers were in black, clearly visible from the road. The houses on the south side of Vista Street were even. Norma Jean Dougherty lived in number 38.

It was early on a sunny Saturday morning. The movie would have begun with a paper boy biking down the empty street, tossing the local paper toward the steps. He would miss, and the paper would wind up under a shrub. Someone, a kid

*most likely, would come out of the house and fetch the paper; the
camera would follow him back into the house, and we're into the
story.*

*There was no paper boy. There was nobody until a black
Plymouth rolled down the street and stopped in front of number
38. Norma got out wearily. She wore slacks and a gray
sweater; a red bandanna tied like a turban covered her head.
"Thanks a lot, Marge," she said into the car before she slammed
the door.*

*As she approached the front door, a long rectangle with
glass panes, she noticed with pleasure the small flag. The red
banner with a blue star in the whitened center indicated this
house had someone in the service. In this case, her husband, Jim
Dougherty, whose ship had sailed for an unknown destination in
the Pacific three months before.*

*Norma had gotten a job at the aircraft factory in Burbank
the week he left. Every day for the first two months, she wrote a
V-mail letter to him; recently, she'd begun to miss occasional
days, and now, she was down to three letters a week. She'd been
moved to the night shift, so it became much harder for her to do
her daily tasks.*

*She loved the sense of well-being she got from meeting her
patriotic obligations. She had become the admired image on the
posters, on the radio, in the movies—the young American wife,
standing behind her serviceman husband, making sacrifices on his
behalf, on behalf of all the brave young men who were risking
life and limb to keep the yellow barbarians from all the Vista
Streets in all the towns across the country.*

ACTION

Norma is beginning to have a sense that sacrifice is for her not a natural or an enduring trait. But when she sees the flag mounted on her front door, she quivers with weary pride.

While she digs through her bag, looking for her key, the telephone begins to ring. A ringing phone always signifies possibility. She thinks it might be the modeling agency, an unlikely thing on a Saturday morning, but maybe. Still she can't find the key. The phone rings even as Marilyn unlocks the door.

Must be serious, she thinks. "Hello. Hello." Disappointed, she puts the phone back on the hook. *They'll call again*, she hopes.

She takes the cover off the canary cage, and the tiny yellow bird begins chirping joyfully. "How the hell do you do it, Jimmy boy?"

The phone rings again. "Hello."

"Oh, Norma." It's Mickie Woody, her best friend at the plant. "Oh, Norma," she says again. What makes the voice so worrisome is how bone dry, how almost rusty it is.

"What's the matter, Mick? When you didn't show up last night, I thought . . ."

"Oh, Norma. I don't know what to do. I'm pregnant."

For a few seconds, Norma Jean Dougherty doesn't know what to say. "Okay, okay. It's not the end of the world."

Mickie Woody squeaks, "Norma." It is the hopeless plaint of a friend. Mickie was always such fun, someone Norma Jean could talk with about her deepest feelings, someone really lively she could go out with and who knew just how far they could fool around with some of the guys after work. When Mickie was sober, she never let Norma get into trouble. Mickie was tough, smart, a little wild but not crazy, not the voice cracking on the telephone now.

There are dumb questions to be got out of the way. "How'd you find out?"

"I guessed. Then I went to my sister's doctor out in San Bernardino. Yesterday. I took the bus. He said yes."

"So what . . . how . . . are you going . . . ?"

"I really need some help, Norma."

"Sure, Mick. I'll help."

"Mostly what I need is a ride out to near San Bernardino, this side, Fontana. Today. It's arranged for later today. I could take the bus again, but . . ."

"No bus. I can get Jim's car from his mother. I'll take you. Don't worry. Is it the same doctor?"

"No. No." There's a long pause on the line. "He won't do it. My sister set up something else. She had to use this guy once. But she doesn't want her husband to know, so she can't take me. She's afraid to be involved, but it's all set up safe, she says. It's nothing to be scared about, she says. But I don't want to, I just can't, go alone." There is the hint of a sob, not at all characteristic of Mickie Woody. "I'll explain it."

Norma wants to know more, much more, but she says, "I'll see about the car and call you right back."

Mickie Woody squeaks into the phone something unintelligible that Norma takes for "I think you're great."

Norma's wisdom tells her there will be complications. But now she must just respond.

There are complications sooner than expected. When she calls Mrs. Dougherty to borrow the car, Mr. Dougherty answers. Of course, it's Saturday. "Mr. D., hi. I've got me a little problem. One of the girls at the plant, you don't know her, well, she's married to a sailor whose ship is coming in today at Long Beach. She has no way to get down there, so I told her I'd take her."

"So."

"I mean I want to borrow Jim's car, just for the day."

"It's up on blocks. Changing the brake pads."

"Oh." He's not going to offer one of the other cars. "It's really important, Mr. D." She doesn't know anyone else who would leave silence after such a statement. "I need a car is what I'm saying." He senses a challenge in her voice.

"You can have John's Chevy around noon. It don't have much gas, and I don't have coupons for it."

"I'll get the coupons. Be by to pick it up at noon."

Then she dials Mickie's number to be sure noon is okay, but the line is busy. She puts on some coffee, digging the thermos out while waiting for the water to start to perk. If she needed an abortion, who could she turn to? Not to Mickie. Not to anyone.

She dials again. This time Mickie picks up. "I can't get the car till around noon. Is that too late or anything?"

"I got to be at this motel in Fontana by five at the latest."

"We'll make it easy. It's way less than a hundred miles."

"Norma. I'm going to need some money too. I've been making some calls, and maybe I'll get some more, but . . ."

"How much?"

"The guy charges thirty-five. And we're going to need a room. I've only got fifteen bucks."

"I've got some saved. You can pay me back whenever."

Norma expects Mickie to gush gratefulness. She doesn't. The coffee on the stove bubbles loudly twice. "Thanks."

"I'm gonna need some gas coupons. Any ideas where I can get some?"

"I've got plenty."

"You don't even own a car."

"I've got plenty, I said."

"Fine, you've got plenty."

Norma considers how to spend these few hours. A bath. A nap. How to dress. "What do you wear to an abortion, Jimmy?" The bird chirps a response, then puffs and preens. "Feathers? No, I don't think so." Norma pours her coffee and watches the sun climb up her kitchen window. She looks at the banner on her front door and wonders if she'd tell him if he were here. "Maybe," she tells Jimmy, "when it was over. If it went all right." She knew she would not. They once talked about people who did it, and he went a little nuts, got that same bulldog look as his old man.

The aroma of coffee fills the kitchen, the whole house; rouses her other senses. Smell becomes touch and taste all at once. For some reason she is more alive than at any time in weeks. She puts on a coffee-flavored robe. The first sip is a warm, internal coffee kiss that lowers itself slowly down the axis of her body and pools warm in her stomach, where it tingles.

In a vague way she knows that what Mickie is asking her to do could be dangerous. Not just illegal; that is nothing to her now. But things could go wrong for Mickie, dangerous in that way. She vows not to let that happen. She is unusually alert.

Mickie's line is busy again, so Norma runs her bathwater. She watches herself undress in the narrow mirror behind the bathroom door, sipping from her mug after discarding bandanna and robe.

Standing in panties and bra, Norma leans her shoulders far back and distends her stomach as much as she can; she moves her hands slowly, searchingly, over its soft smoothness.

Something told her the phone would ring as soon as she stepped into the tub. It rings when she puts her second foot in. Naked, she runs downstairs, cupping her breasts.

It isn't Mickie. "Norma Jean? Mrs. Meyers."

"Oh. Hi."

The "Oh" warns of complications. "Norma Jean, we've got an assignment for you. Bathing suits. A desert shoot. Leaving from here tonight at seven-thirty, returning tomorrow afternoon, evening, can't be sure. It's Lyle Tasman; he's one of the best, as you know. He didn't really know your work, but I showed him your book and, well, he wanted you. They'll pay fifteen dollars an hour."

"Gee, Miss Meyers."

"Thank me later, Norma Jean."

"I can't do it."

"Can't?"

"Something's come up. Important. A family thing."

"He especially selected you."

"Maybe I can be back by then." She tries to figure out the timing. If an abortion takes twenty minutes . . .

"No maybes. I need a yes. This is a professional."

"I'm afraid I just can't."

"If you're doing this for a man, Norma Jean, you're making one hell of a mistake."

"No, it's no man. No man."

"I swear I don't understand you girls. You tell me, you beg me, please just get me work, get my foot in the door. And when I do . . ."

"Any other time, I promise."

"Of course, any other time."

"Miss Meyers? Is this going to go against me?"

"God. Spare me."

The bird chirps like crazy. Norma notices dry skin on her kneecap; she picks away small particles of skin with her thumbnail. She doesn't realize she's mumbling.

When she leaves her house—rather, her husband's house (since it is in his name only)—she has a sense of well-being growing in her. And she knows precisely why. Her overnight things are packed neatly in a small valise, as are four sandwiches, some fruit, and a thermos of coffee. She wears a pink blouse and a short, pleated tan skirt she bought with last week's paycheck and never wore before. And sandals whose thongs tie halfway up her calf. She is dressed and packed for adventure.

There is secret pleasure in the fact that she is not the one pregnant, not the desperate one, not the one in jeopardy. She is only the loyal friend; she can participate without having to risk any of the actual, physical effects, all of which have to be unpleasant.

As she nears her in-laws' small house on Bueno Pico, her mood changes. She becomes edgy, combative. Norma hates the place.

The house is perfect. Not a fleck of paint peeling. The lawn is a rich green and cut to perfection, with a border so clean it defines the property more forbiddingly than a wall. The mailbox is a vivid red marvel. The walk is three-colored flagstone laid in a Moorish design. All the other houses in the neighborhood have Roman numerals on their front door. The Doughertys have script. Even the service flag in the window is special: the same blue star on white with a red border, but larger, with the words "Our Son" hand-embroidered in gold at the bottom.

Norma knows that behind their compulsion to be

unique, distinctive, their drive for perfection, is an obnoxious sense of superiority. So smug they are. Norma knows
there's a perfect word for them and worries it up from the
depths; when it comes, she feels comfortable again. *Con-
temptuous.* Being able to label them correctly before she sees
them gives her the weapon she needs.

The first time she entered their home she knew they
disapproved of her. It took no great sensitivity to make that
discovery: they wore their disappointment on their faces—
in his cold eyes; on the curl of her lip. At least he didn't try
to be polite. Mrs. D. faked interest from time to time, a
hateful pose as far as Norma was concerned. In high school,
she had read parts of a Dickens novel that had a character
exactly like her: she'd forgotten the name of the novel and
the character but not the description.

Norma walks around the side of the house and raps
loudly on the screen door. There's no response. The garage
doors are open. The Chevy isn't there.

She calls, "Mrs. D."

"Up here." The bedroom window upstairs is filled
with Mrs. Dougherty. She wears a dust cap on her head
and a yellow pinafore apron. "Just cleaning." Said with the
subtle suggestion that her daughter-in-law ought to be doing the same. Her eyes fasten on Norma's valise.

"I came to pick up the Chevy."

"Yes, of course. Milton's giving it a little test run."

Mrs. D. doesn't invite Norma in. That both suits and
upsets her. She vows not to say the next word. She sets
down her bag and waits. Mrs. D. closes the window. Under her breath, Norma repeats, "Hateful, hateful, hateful."
She imagines this woman lying next to her husband every
night. The thought is repulsive, but it strikes her as such
perfect justice that she smiles.

An immaculate black Chevy comes up the driveway

and stops alongside the valise. Dougherty glares at Norma and then down at the suitcase. "Long Beach?" he questions.

"Long Beach. A picnic."

She notices Dougherty glancing at the mileage meter. *Jeez, what a bastard.* Would he report this to his son? Of course, but indirectly, through the missus.

He kills the motor and gets out of the car. "Told you about the gas," he says.

"I've got coupons, don't worry."

"I lock up the garage every night. When you getting back?"

"Oh, don't worry about me. I'll bring it back when I bring it back."

He glares at her.

Norma throws her bag in the back seat. She doesn't intentionally grind the gears backing out to the street. It just happens, precisely because she didn't want it to happen. The sound causes a flash of pain on the old man's face, followed by disgust.

His odor is in the car even after Norma turns the corner. When she opens the window, all vestiges of her father-in-law fly out into the street; a soft breeze blows in, carrying with it a great breath of freedom. She is still absorbing it when she runs a stoplight on San Fernando Road. A car coming from the left honks and brings her to her senses.

Mickie Woody has an apartment in South Pasadena, a walk-up atop a wood-frame three-family house. Norma gets there a few minutes early. Mickie wears a polka-dot halter and blue shorts; she's pulling on a bottle of beer. "Hi, Norma. Thirsty?"

Norma is a little surprised—and disappointed—by how casual Mickie seems. "Nooo, I'll pass."

"I'll bring some for the trip. Okay?"

Norma shrugs.

"So maybe not. What's a matter?"

"This isn't something I do every day, you know."

"And how many abortions you think I've had?"

"That's what I mean. It's not like we're gonna meet some sailors down at Long Beach. This is serious stuff."

Mickie puts a forlorn look on her face. "Is this better? Wait, I'll go get a long black dress."

"You crazy nut. Let's go."

At the corner garage, not one but two guys come over to pump the gas. But they don't get to the gas or to cleaning the already spotless windshield very quickly; they both know Mickie and want to fool around. The one she calls Glenn comes to her side of the car and leans in the window all the way to his belt buckle. "Can't stay away, eh, babe?"

Mickie runs her fingertip down his nose. "How about you show your appreciation by a fill-up and I'll give you the coupons tomorrow." She squeezes his nostrils. "Promise."

"Duke. Top it up for these girls."

Duke has been intending to lean in on Norma's side, but he glares over at Glenn, licks his lips, and goes to the pump. He leaves a strong odor of sweat around Norma. She's both repelled and attracted. That upsets her.

While the needle in the gas gauge elevates slowly, Mickie's fingertips run over Glenn's lips. "You mind very much if I pay tomorrow when I give you the coupons?"

Her fingers don't let him answer. He bites them.

Duke hangs up the hose. Before he can get in the window, Norma rolls up the glass. He walks in front of the car and looks menacing. Norma throws the stick into reverse with a grind and backs slowly. Glenn is still partially in the car. "Hey, watch it, girl." He's laughing, though, so Norma gives it a little more gas. Glenn runs alongside for a few more steps. Before he breaks away, he manages to pull Mickie's halter open. She screams and giggles. He hollers, "Shit, I missed." Mickie leans out and shouts, "Thanks, Glenn. Tomorrow." She blows a kiss.

Norma has been quiet through Arcadia and Azusa. The car is very hot. Mickie has opened a bottle of beer. She turns on the radio. War news is being read in a flat, irritating voice. She changes stations until a rumba comes in without static. She shakes the beer bottle like a maraca.

"How'd you know exactly?" Norma says.

"When? At first?"

"Uh huh."

"You know me, Norma Jean. I never miss. So when I missed the second time, I said, 'Uh uh, you better check this out.' I went out to my sister's, and bingo, bango, bongo, there came the news."

"So who was it? If you want to tell."

"I got it narrowed down to a dozen guys."

"A dozen!"

"Only kidding. You're so easy to get a rise out of." A long pull on the beer. "It could be a couple of guys. But in my heart I know, I just know."

"So, who?"

"Eaton."

"Eaton! From Personnel? God."

"Why 'God' in that voice?"

" 'Cause he's so old."

"Old don't mean anything, Norma. He's a good guy. That's what counts with a man. That's *all* that counts."

Although Route 66 runs straight as a string from Glendora to Fontana, Norma suggests an alternate route. Up the Cucamonga Canyon and down to Fontana from the north. "Sure," Mickie says. "We got the time, and the gas is free."

Within minutes of leaving the highway, the road begins to fold back on itself and the terrain becomes a little like a moonscape. It's also a lot cooler. "Did you tell him about being pregnant?"

"I thought about it for a while. Like I said, he's so good, he would have gone along with anything I wanted. Even if I wanted to have the kid. But I didn't think it was right to tell him. Why give him a headache he don't need?"

A rabbit shoots across the road, causing Norma to hit the brakes.

"Would he have helped you get the abortion?"

"Sure. Paid for it and everything."

"You must care about him."

"You could say that."

The hum of tires on the road, even with the need to remain alert—maybe *because* of the need to remain alert—begins to dull Norma's brain. She's been working midnight shifts for two weeks and really didn't have more than a string of catnaps this morning. Suddenly, she feels extremely weary. She turns up the volume on the radio. It is Mickie who curls up and closes her eyes. Norma drives on, fighting the temptation to drowse.

Eventually, coming down through Deer Canyon, she passes a sign that says FONTANA—29 MI. Ten minutes after that she sees a roadside restaurant, so she taps Mickie and says, "Coffee." She pulls into the restaurant, having completely forgotten about her thermos, the sandwiches, the fruit.

The coffee revives her. It also makes her realize how hungry she is. She orders a BLT, french fries, and a Coke. Mickie seems to have lost some of her nonchalance about the abortion. She gazes dumbly out the window into the hills beyond. The cup of coffee she ordered does nothing but warm her hands.

Norma says, "Tomorrow this time, it'll be over. That's

what I always tell myself to get through tough times."
Time was, after all, just a state of mind, or you could
imagine it to be. Past, future, just opposite ends of the same
piece of string, slipping away.

Mickie's lip curls into a sneer. Her voice is hollow.
"Why a tough time? This is no coat hanger deal. It's all
done natural. With a fluid. You pass it yourself. Completely natural. My sister said nothing to it. The fluid, the
whole thing, just poured out of her after a couple of hours.
No pain, nothing. He's a dentist. She said he could have
been a doctor if he wanted. Treated her with such respect.
Everything so clean and proper."

If she didn't know Mickie well, she'd never have
thought the girl was frightened. Even knowing her, Norma
couldn't be sure.

"God," Norma says thoughtlessly, "I hate doctors."

"Needing them or not needing them?"

"What?"

"Do you hate them all the time or only when you don't
need one? 'Cause I've got to tell you, I'm sure glad this guy
is there for me. You could get yourself infected real bad or
even killed if you go to a butcher."

"I guess."

Mickie's eyes register extreme disappointment. "Remember that party, the one at the photographer's attic?"

"A loft; they call it a loft."

"I swear I wouldn't mind getting high tonight after it's
all over."

"It's not a party you want. You just want a couple of
reefers."

"That too, heh, heh. Don't you?"

"Tell you what," Norma says. "If we get out of this
safe and sound, I'll give him a call."

"You're on."

Back on the road, the girls rediscover their compatibility. They both realize there is a situation to be got through. As the Chevy crosses the Fontana city line, they discuss directions.

"It's on the far side of town," Mickie explains, "almost when you're in San Bernardino. On Rialto Avenue. The . . . the Air Ease Motor Hotel. My sister reserved for me."

"Then what?"

"Then we wait. He'll call our room. Then I think he just comes by and does it. . . ." Mickie snaps her fingers. "He's got to watch himself. They catch him, they'll hang his ass up in the breeze."

Rialto Avenue takes them through Fontana, and there is no Air Ease. Well into San Bernardino, Norma says, "We go too far?"

"I sure as hell didn't see it."

They double back on Rialto and do see a motel—the Aries. "I thought you said Air Ease."

"That's what my sister told me."

The Aries Motor Hotel is not as terrible as Norma expected. Relatively new and surprisingly clean. Norma parks the Chevy in front of the small lobby. The girls look at each other for a long moment; Norma sighs without realizing she's made a sound. Mickie Woody sets her mouth pugnaciously and nods with emphasis.

The carpet in the lobby is plush. The girls walk self-consciously over it toward the desk. Mickie swings her hips aggressively. Norma follows her, eyes on her own sandals.

At the desk, an old man in a beige sweater reads a newspaper deliberately, only looking up a long while after Mickie has established her presence. His eyes peer over the top of his glasses. Sharp hollows form from the corners of his lips down to his chin and give his face the look of a ventriloquist's dummy, a mean one.

"You got a reservation for Marilyn Woody?"

He thumbs through a dog-eared notebook.

Norma whispers, "Marilyn?"

Mickie whispers back, "That's my factual name. I just never use it."

There is indeed a reservation for Marilyn Woody, and a problem as well. "Reservation for one for one night," the patriarch says meanly.

"There's two of us."

"I can see that. Costs three-fifty more. Eleven-fifty to fifteen dollars." His face sets in a comic sneer.

"No problem, sir." Sarcastically.

"In advance."

Mickie fishes ten one-dollar bills and a five out of her bag deliberately. She finishes by placing both elbows on the desk and cradling her broad face. It's a small triumph.

He tosses a key on the desk and turns the guestbook around for her to sign. Simultaneously, both girls think it's dumb to sign real names, but Mickie's sister made the reservation under her real name. Mickie says, "I'll sign for both of us, Carla."

Norma and the desk clerk stare at each other. His pale eyes are completely dead. She vows not to break off the staring first, but she does.

"This place is respectable. I don't want no trouble." His gaze penetrates Mickie.

"Then keep your fly zipped, Pop. Where's the room?"

He points with his chin down the central hallway.

The room is a small square done in leafy lime-green wallpaper. Two narrow beds face a tiny bathroom, immediately occupied by Mickie, who squeals, "I gotta pee something awful." The door cannot be closed completely. After Norma falls backward on one bed, she can hear the force and duration of the fierce stream. She realizes the room is unbearably stuffy but is too tired to get up to open the window.

"You come out, open the window, Mick?"

"I might be a while."

"You okay?"

"Yeah, sure."

The window, when Norma tries it, can only be opened two inches. She tugs on it, then bangs under the handle with the telephone book, to no avail. She wants to smash it. The day's emotion builds in her chest. "Goddamned shit."

"What's the matter?"

"Window won't open."

"Turn on the fan."

For some reason Norma hadn't noticed a large over-head fan. "It'll just blow the hot air around."

"No. Try it. I'm taking a shower. You want one?"

"No."

It's a nasty "no." Mickie says, "Relax, for god's sake. We made it, didn't we? Take a shower."

"Maybe later."

"What time you got?"

Norma hears the shower water running before she can answer. She knows she won't be heard, but she says anyway. "Twenty to five."

The telephone rings twice and twice again. Norma has no choice but to pick it up. A male voice says, "Marilyn?"

"Oh. No, she's in the shower. This is her friend. Carla."

"Oh. Can you get a message to her?"

"Sure. She's just in the shower."

"Will you tell her it's Dr. Smith. I've got her molds with me. I'd like to come over for a fitting."

"A fitting?"

"Right. Is that room 108?"

"Yeah, I think so. Wait, I'll check."

"It should be right there on the phone."

"Oh, right . . . 108."

"I'd say about ten, fifteen minutes."

He's already hung up when Norma says, "Fine."

The shower whines noisily as Norma goes to the door and hollers, "The doctor. He just called."

"What?"

"He's coming."

The water goes off abruptly. "What's he sound like?"

"Nice-sounding. Young-sounding." She realizes that what she really means is sexy and surprises herself with the observation.

Mickie comes out wrapped in a pale blue Aries towel. Her skinny legs drip water into pools on the soiled rug. "I'm just glad," she says, "that it'll be over soon."

"I'm glad there are guys who'll do something like this."

Mickie looks heavenward. "They don't do it out of the goodness of their hearts. They do it for the damned money."

"Maybe not this guy. His voice sounded real kind. And he's taking such a big chance."

"For—the—money."

"It's not worth it. If he loses his license, he's completely out in the cold. He's risking too much for it to be just the money. It's got to be more."

"Hah."

"I'm glad there are guys like him around."

"Why? You got nothing to worry about. Husband away. You don't take the same risks some of us do."

"It's not just a question of taking chances, Mickie. What about getting raped? What happens to you then?"

"Raped. What are the chances? One in a million, maybe."

"I was raped."

Mickie Woody stops patting her stomach with the towel. "What d'you mean, raped? When? How?"

"When I was nine."

A scream. "Nine?"

Norma knits her fingers in her lap. Mickie sits on the bed, her arm across Norma's shoulders. The towel has shifted across her knees. "Nine. Who? Your old man?"

"A friend of my mom's."

"The son of a bitch. Nine?"

There are two soft raps at the door. Mickie shouts, "Just a minute," and runs into the bathroom.

Norma opens the door on a thin, light-skinned black man. He wears a striped seersucker suit and a dark tie. He has a trim mustache, piercing eyes, and a face a lot like a young Duke Ellington. Norma doesn't get past his skin. Her mouth remains open.

"Miss Woody?"

"No. She's in the bathroom." He looks back into the hall. "Come in."

Only when he's standing inside the door does she notice his black bag. "He's here, Mickie."

"Right out."

Norma says, without quite knowing why, "You're real nice to come out here to do this for us."

"It's not far. My practice is only a few minutes away."

"Still, it's nice."

Mickie Woody, again in halter and shorts, her wet hair wrapped in a towel, comes out of the bathroom. Her breezy "Hi, Doc" strikes Norma as especially dumb.

Dr. Smith smiles. He seems very cool, even though it's a tense situation. He's done this before and exudes experience, confidence. "It won't take long," he says, "and I'd like to get to the fitting as soon as possible." He moves past the girls, opens his bag, and places various dentist's tools and a large plaster of paris mold of teeth on the bedspread. "Since this is my final visit, I'd also like to complete payment before we begin." He raises his eyebrows as he looks around the room suspiciously.

"Payment. Norma."

"Uh, how much do we owe?"

"Thirty-five dollars, I believe, is still outstanding on your bill."

Norma wonders if he's nuts talking about all this teeth business even here inside the room. "Sure, I've got it." She opens her bag and takes out four bills folded into a neat V—three crisp tens with a five tucked inside.

He places the money in his pants pocket while taking off his jacket and folding it on the bed. "I'd rather," he says, "have done this fitting at my office, but this shouldn't take very long. It's a procedure virtually without pain." He signals Mickie toward the bathroom with his eyes and picks up his bag. Mickie precedes him in. He attempts to close the door but manages only about three quarters. Water runs loudly in the sink while the two talk. The conversation continues for quite a while. Finally, Dr. Smith leans out of the bathroom and asks Norma to please hand him the towel. He adds, "We probably won't need you, but I'd appreciate it if you come when I call. She may want to hold your hand or something."

"Sure."

Norma can see Mickie stepping out of her shorts. She sees Dr. Smith's hands cleaning out the sink with soap and a washcloth. She hears the word "organic" twice. She hears "least violent means" and "matter of hours but could be sooner." He empties a bottle of blue fluid into the sink, then some clear fluid from a dark bottle. He tests the mixture for temperature on his wrist. Having heard horror stories about abortions for years, Norma is surprised by how moderate Smith's procedure seems to be. That's when she sees the hypodermic and begins to feel sick to her stomach.

The tube is immense, about the size of a roasting baster; the needle his rubber-gloved hand attaches to the end is about the size and length of Norma's little finger. Norma watches as Mickie, following Smith's instructions, leans back and spreads herself over the edge of the tub. She can see his elbow and one of Mickie's legs up to the thigh. She can't see the tube entering. He instructs Mickie to bend her body slightly, first one way, then another, then still another. The hypodermic slowly disappears in Mickie Woody.

Instead of feeling sympathetic, or even sicker to her stomach, Norma begins to feel just the opposite. A coldness sets in. She feels suddenly unrelated, unconnected to everything, to everyone else in the world. She is isolated. Absolutely alone.

The sounds come to her from a great distance now, as though a glass wall separates her from the bathroom. Mickie's giggles are sounds of pain; there is no pleasure in her whispered moans. His melodic voice never varies—directing, explaining, calming, warning. Norma just wants it to be over. She leans back on her bed and closes her eyes.

"I'm worried." The words come from very far away. "Norma. I'm a little worried. Wake up."

Mickie's face is out of focus, inches away from her own. "What?"

"I heard these cars drive up. There were voices out back, and when I looked out I saw cops."

Norma, jolted awake, sees faint red lights flashing on the ceiling. She jumps to the window and sees patrol cars parked in front of the motel. "Where is he?"

"He left."

"When?"

"A few minutes ago."

"We better get out of here." Norma grabs her valise. Mickie runs into the bathroom and comes out clutching two slightly bloodied towels.

There is an exit sign at the far end of the hall. Norma leads Mickie quickly to it, out the door, and into a wooded area behind the motel, from where they can see some of the activity in front of the place.

Mickie holds a small tree. She is bent at the waist, wincing in pain. Norma puts her arms around Mickie and holds tight. "It'll pass," Mickie murmurs breathily.

The lights in the room they've just vacated flash off and on a couple of times. Norma can make out Dr. Smith standing with a cop out front. The cop holds his black bag. "That old shit at the desk," she says. "He set the whole thing up."

Mickie, still in pain, gasps, "We'll come back and set him on fire."

"Yeah, right."

Mickie slowly slips to her knees, and Norma goes down with her. "Did he hurt you bad?"

"No, no. He told me this could happen. Supposed to happen. He . . . he injected some kind of salt solution way up me. It'll feel like a bad period, he said. And when . . . when it pours out, it'll be over. Maybe if we drive home, Norma. Or we could stop somewhere. . . ."

"We can't now. We got to wait. They'll see us. The car's too close to them."

For the better part of an hour, Norma Jean embraces Mickie Woody in the woods, patting her, rubbing her almost naked back in circles, talking about the people at work, about herself and her plans to become a singer, an actress. She's talking without any clear focus, but there is some logic, so it's not completely crazy talk. What bothers Norma Jean is that nothing she says, although she means every word, has any conviction behind it. Norma still feels unconnected.

She feels the goose bumps under her hand as she tries to rub some heat into her friend's quivering body. "I promise you we're gonna laugh ourselves silly soon as this is over. Crazy as can be, the whole thing. Most people get pregnant in a motel—we go to one to get unpregnant. Then this nutty dentist shows up talking about his molds. Some molds, I say. And he's this colored guy you'd like to jump in the sack with. Man. Then, next thing, cops and hiding in the woods. Listen, Mick, next time you want to call me for help, do me a favor—don't."

Still her words seem lifeless to her, as though she's saying what ought to be said instead of what she feels. But she wants to feel it; she almost does feel it.

Mickie's spirit ebbs and flows. Together—talking, hugging, simply breathing hard in unison—they pass another hour without any consciousness of time. Norma watches the police cars leave, one at a time. It's not until the multicolored neon ARIES MOTOR HOTEL sign flashes on that she feels it's safe to try to get to the car.

"Mickie. I can run to the car and bring it close to here."

Mickie shakes her head emphatically. "Don't leave."

"Can you make it to the car?"

"In a while. Feels like my insides are on my outsides. I'm cold as hell, Norma."

"You can waddle. Come on, let's give it a try."

Norma helps her friend to her feet, and in a not very straight line, they tread down out of the woods, across the lawn, and to the parking lot. Norma opens the door on the passenger side and folds the towels on the seat before Mickie edges in. She throws her bag in the rear and comes around to the driver's side. Inside the motel, the desk clerk is still leaning over his newspaper. He doesn't look up as the Chevy's motor starts. Norma rolls down the window and honks the horn. Now he looks. She makes a fist, crosses her hand over the crook of a bent elbow. Her lips mouth a distinct, silent "Fuck you." There isn't the pleasure the gesture should give her.

There are almost no cars on the route back to L.A. The radio plays big-band dance music live from the Wedge-wood Hotel; it fades in the valleys. Mickie says at last, "It comes and goes. I feel almost okay, and then it's like I've got to pee and crap at the same time and my stomach muscles get weak and watery."

"We'll get you home."

"No you won't. I think you got to pull over."

The Chevy rolls to a stop on a site very much like the terrain behind the motel: a thinly wooded area, slightly elevated, just off the road. As Norma walks Mickie up the incline and into the shelter of these woods, she sees the front of her friend's shorts become soaked. Watery, rust-colored liquid runs down the inside of her legs. Norma notices her sandal thong is unlaced; her new skirt is mud-died and torn. She has no idea how that could have hap-pened.

Even before they're fully hidden from the headlights of cars on the road, Mickie pulls off her pants and squats. Her eyes appear glazed; she doesn't seem to be aware she's mak-ing rhythmic, squealing noises. Norma is temporarily helpless—there doesn't seem any way to get close enough, so she takes a similar squatting position facing Mickie.

"Yeah. Yeah. This is it. Oh. God."

Rising slowly from the squatting position but still bending at the waist, the two girls join hands, Mickie squeezing mightily. Their legs remain spread. Mickie

Woody is making sounds like a squeaky gate, followed by sighs that are almost pleasurable.

Norma sighs quietly in sympathetic unison. But she is still hatefully, shamefully detached.

"Oh . . . oh . . . oh . . . okay . . . okay . . . here . . ." What has been a trickle of liquid becomes a flow, and as Mickie emits a cry, a bath of milky water rushes out of her. Some silvered tissue has rushed out with it and glistens momentarily on the ground.

It's over.

The girls remain in their peculiar position, bent forward, legs spread, fingers interlaced. Mickie Woody does nothing but breathe heavily. Time passes, measured by the rough friction of wheels on the road below them.

"God. I'm starving."

"I got sandwiches in the car."

"Thanks, Norma."

"And coffee. It's probably cold."

They unlace their fingers. Mickie Woody pulls on her shorts. In the distance, Norma sees headlights approaching. She freezes, almost hypnotized by their expanding beams.

CHAPTER THREE

Billy Bam and Marilyn Darvey's Baby

LIGHTS

DER SPIEGEL: You have many detractors . . .

MONROE: As anybody would who takes artistic risks.

DER SPIEGEL: Yes, of course. But in your case there seems to be a special venom in their censure.

MONROE: Oh, you've noticed.

DER SPIEGEL: It would be difficult not to. However, we wonder how you manage to keep criticism from eroding your belief in yourself.

MONROE: To be perfectly honest, I don't always. But mostly, it's the belief in my talent that gets me through times of doubt. If that sounds arrogant, I don't mean it that way, it's just that finally I believe in this something that's in me and that lets me act and sing and . . . well, you know.

DER SPIEGEL: You seem surprisingly self-conscious saying you have a talent.

MONROE: I don't want to be smug about it. Also, it is something I've had to nurture for so long I sometimes get the feeling that talking about it might cause it to go away.

DER SPIEGEL: Is there any other reason for your reluctance to discuss your talents?

MONROE: I just don't want to offend the gods.

DER SPIEGEL: Gods? As in those old-fashioned Greek gods?

MONROE: As in those studio big shots, those newspaper columnists, and those radio and television people.

CAMERA

By 1946, most of the men who had enlisted in the merchant marine had been discharged. Not Norma Jean's husband, Jim. He had been back in L.A. on leave three months earlier. And now, unexpectedly, he was home again, on shore leave for a week. For the first two days, the two of them never left the Vista Street house.

They talked a lot about the future—when he would get out, what he would do, what she would do. That last one fig-ured to be a bit of a problem. Jim wanted a family. There were lots of articles in the papers telling young wives not to expect their returning husbands to slip into the old patterns too easily. Wives were advised to be patient, things would work out.

When the war had ended the previous year, Norma Jean quit work at the aircraft plant and tried for every modeling assignment she heard about. She had worked as a model during the war too, but without the same commitment she felt when she was free to pursue a career. The Doughertys had written their son regularly, always mentioning their daughter-in-law's activi-ties. Jim defended Norma, saying he was glad the world could see how beautiful she was. Still, it bothered him that his wife was in the presence of other men so much. When he had come home earlier, he asked her to quit. She cut back for a while. On this visit, he expected the modeling to have ended.

Norma had taken singing lessons while she was in high school and only the previous year paid $135 for six months' worth of classes at the Glendale Music Academy. Manny Bonito, the owner of the Cork and Flask in West Alhambra, an old speakeasy redone to look like a new speakeasy, hired her as his Wednesday night singer a few weeks before her husband came home. Norma thought Jim would approve, since it wasn't mod-eling. Jim was only passively against her working there. He figured she'd give it up when nothing happened with her career.

Weekends at the Cork featured rising young jazz players— they drew customers and didn't cost Bonito much. Gerry Mulli-gan, Chet Baker, a few players from Stan Kenton's band, drew big crowds.

Norma Jean Dougherty worked under the name Marilyn Darvey, the brainchild of Mickie Woody, who convinced Norma to go with Marilyn—Mickie's given name—and whatever name turned up in the Glendale-Pasadena telephone book. The first one was Caniglio. The second was Cannon. Darvey was the fifth.

She started out as a typical mid-1940s torch singer, doing classics like "My Man," "It's Been a Long, Long Time," "These Foolish Things." She worked with the Billy Bam Trio—drums, piano, bass—and developed an easy friendship with the drummer, a small, baldheaded black man. Billy Bam wasn't his real name; it was bestowed by Lester Young in honor of his power and skill on drums.

At the Cork, Billy Bam was the resident musicologist, historian, and philosopher. He played with bands Norma Jean had never heard of, but everyone, including Manny Bonito, gave him a measure of respect you couldn't miss.

Billy Bam and Marilyn Darvey often talked backstage between sets. Norma wanted to sing on weekends. Bam told her she wasn't ready, that she'd have to have some jazzy, uptempo numbers.

They worked for a few weeks on some jazz and scat tunes. Norma Jean couldn't really handle the rhythms. Bam decided on going the other way, taking fast numbers and singing them slow and sensually, having some fun with them. He had convinced Manny to let Marilyn try some numbers Saturday night between regular sets.

Norma invited Jim, who had only two more days in port. He agreed to come. Mickie Woody invited herself.

Norma Jean dreamed about stepping onto the small stage, singing her songs, being discovered, and starting on the road to another, more glamorous life. Should such a dream come true, living with Jim would be difficult. She knew that. Difficult but possible, she thought.

She didn't have to go to the doctor to know what her missed period and the nausea she'd had for the last three weeks meant. That, too, could be taken care of later.

She'd never been to the club on a Saturday night. The card with her name and picture was nowhere to be seen. The Art Pepper Trio had the billing. She was equally surprised to see the place packed.

ACTION

Mickie Woody, sashaying ahead, blows through the door like a star. Her manner, her strut, is comical until Manny Bonito, who is greeting a well-dressed party of six prior to showing them to a reserved table, notices Mickie and rushes over to her. "Hey, kiddo, they didn't tell me you'd be in tonight."

"I don't tell *them* everything, Manny dear." Mickie makes sure everyone hears.

Behind her, Marilyn Darvey slips in almost unnoticed, a remarkable feat since she looks gorgeous. Tangerine cashmere sweater that shows every contour of her body above the waist; forest green pleated skirt; a string of cultured pearls; patent-leather heels. Her hair is combed straight back and shines like new gold beneath a black ribbon. Her pale skin is almost unearthly in its purity. She slides along the wall past the coatroom, where the hatcheck girl chirps hello.

"Hi, Natalie. Busy night."

Natalie is one of Manny's girls. She dislikes Mickie Woody but fights the instinct to dislike her friend also. "Yeah. Manny's talking about taking a wall down and enlarging the place. Gets one crowd and he thinks he's going to conquer the nightclub world."

"That's why we love him. I guess."

"Sure. Love. Hah."

"Anyone backstage?"

Natalie shrugs.

Just before she ducks through the curtains, Marilyn hears what she doesn't want to hear. "Hey, Blondie. Blondie."

Most nights, but tonight in particular, she doesn't want to be bothered by the bartender. Randy Hagan is what Mickie calls "a beach hunk." Naturally, Mickie is interested. Randy Hagan has eyes for Marilyn. He calls after her, "C'mon, Blondie."

Marilyn ducks through the curtains and down the dark, narrow, brick-walled hallway that runs behind the bar to the tiny cubicles where the musicians leave their personal stuff. Just before she gets there, a side door opens and a glowingly tanned, muscular man blocks her way.

"Randy, don't. Please. I feel punk tonight."

"Heartsick, probably. Because you're fighting it. I say don't fight it, sweet face, it's bigger than both of us."

"The only thing bigger than both of us, Randy, is your idea of yourself. No kidding, I don't feel so good. I need to sit down."

"Want me to bring you a drink? The regular?"

She considers her nausea. "Make it a ginger ale."

"You got it."

Marilyn slips into an empty room cluttered with pork-pie hats and instrument cases and laden with the dry, pungent odor of reefer smoke. She looks at herself in the cracked and flaked mirror, concerned about the puffiness around her eyes, the extreme flush of her cheeks. She examines her face, drawing her cheeks long and taut by extending her jaw. Her eyes, too, disturb her. Small and red. With her fingertips she stretches the skin taut around them.

Billy Bam finishes his solo. The crowd applauds. The

trio comes together for a final melodic chorus of "Love for Sale," slowing the tempo so the song will almost exhaust itself as it ends. Bam kills the tune with a series of rim shots and soft fading brushwork on his cymbal. The jazz buffs guffaw and applaud; the rest of the crowd appreciates it too.

She hears Billy's rolling voice in the echoing mike say, "Pleasure, pleasure, playing for y'all. We're gonna be cooling out for a while, but the music's gonna get real hot. Pepper hot, you might say." He chuckles. "Yeah. Right, right."

Marilyn realizes how much she likes Billy Bam's smooth voice, the sliding style. She feels comfortable with most black men.

Bodies squeeze past one another in the narrow hallway. Randy is bringing her a soda while the featured players are making for the stage.

"So without further ado, ladies and gentlemen, the Cork and Flask proudly present, the distinguished, the exalted . . ." Marilyn silences Randy with a finger across his lips; she wants to hear Billy's intro.

". . . the prodigious . . ." He waits a beat. ". . . the mon-u-ment-ally trans-cend-ent . . . Art . . . Pepper . . . Trio."

Pepper's virtuoso sax comes from offstage. It's a song Marilyn doesn't know. She'll ask Billy.

Billy Bam's pianist, a silent, very dark-skinned man known as Roscoe, comes into the dressing room first. The bass player, whose name she's never heard, follows. She nods to them but isn't sure they recognize her.

"He-ey, sly hips." Billy Bam most assuredly recognizes her. He kisses her cheek lingeringly. He is too old to be a diminutive, a "Billy." She prefers him as "Bill."

She puts a soft hand on his face. Billy Bam thumps his heart with his fist. "Glad you're here. We got some talking about your music."

"That's why I came a little early."

"Hey." He leans back and examines her face. "Something's wrong. Love troubles?"

Marilyn shrugs. "Not particularly. It's everything troubles."

"Great for mood. We'll open with the blues number tonight. Blow them right away."

"Sure."

"You want to talk, right?"

Marilyn sips her soda and nods slightly.

"So you guys need a little walk. Meet you out back when we're done with business."

Roscoe and the bass player glide out of the room, making a point of not looking at Marilyn as they pass.

"Want one?" Bam holds a pack of Chesterfields under her chin.

"Nope."

"Not to worry, ducks. There's writing on them."

"Not before I sing."

Billy Bam lights one and sits in a battered armchair directly in front of Marilyn. Their knees almost touch.

"So tell the doctor."

"It's everything, but mostly it's that things were supposed to be getting so good, with my man back and everything, and they're not."

"The malaise of unfulfilled expectations. Gets us all, sweetheart, just when we think we're in for a smooth ride. The bumps, I call it. You got to know, bad as it gets, it's usually better than dying, which is the only real alternative we ever have. You know, to be or not to be, that's the big knot in the pine."

When Marilyn talks to Billy Bam, she sometimes doesn't understand all the words; she always understands what he's saying. "Well," he says, "things'll open right up for you after this gig. White girl sings suggestive like you, looks like you, moves like you, should be able to write her own ticket."

"That's the problem. Ticket to where?"

"To anywhere, sugar. Radio, sing with a band, movies, you name it."

Marilyn Darvey murmurs, "I've thought about the movies."

"So make it the movies. Why not? It's your choice, but even for a sweet thing like you, the movies is the scurviest deal. All the fine lookers are going for the same gold ring, and the guys who own that ring, they call the tune. I've done some movie work; seen it on every level."

"Can't be rougher than modeling."

"Maybe not, but I've seen some real heartbreakers spending a hell of a lot of time on their knees."

Marilyn leans forward, cutting the space between them in half. Her face is flushed. Art Pepper is playing something with a Latin beat. Billy's hand comes forward and touches her cheek; the hand is callused and feels like a foreign object. With his other hand, he places his cigarette directly in the center of her lips. She draws on it clumsily.

She smiles into his sharp, glistening face.

"Yeah." He appreciates the moment. He suspects it foreshadows something better for him. But he's a little concerned that she doesn't understand how things really work. He takes her chin. "They could devour someone like you."

"Don't worry. Once I decide I want something, I'm willing to . . ." She doesn't have to finish the statement.

Billy Bam holds her chin in his hand, studying her

face. He sees a wave of mulish strength move across the eyes. An uncertain, self-conscious smile chases it away.

"You mind?" he says, and takes Marilyn's left hand, palm up, to read its mysteries. He's absolutely serious. He notices a wedding band, which he's never seen before, but says nothing. Marilyn touches it with her thumb.

"Sure. I love stuff like that. Only don't screw me up for tonight."

"No way, no way." He immediately concentrates on his task, making humming sounds of which he is completely unaware.

She says, "What, what?" and "Is it good?" Questions to which he is equally oblivious.

Billy believes he is reading her soul with his fingertips. He traces life and love and health lines, the rough field of creases at the base of her thumb, the pattern on the meaty part of her hand. He murmurs, "You actually learn more about someone from the shape of the hand, the fingers, than you ever do from the lines."

"What're you trying to tell me?"

"Here, look at the shape of your fingers. They're square at the tips. Every one. And look how little they taper down to the knuckle."

"So what's it mean?"

"See how wide, how thick and square at the base."

"But what's it mean?"

"Your lines, though, are emotional. There's tremendously powerful feelings in those lines." Marilyn pulls her hand away. "It means good things and bad things."

"Thanks loads."

"It means you can go either way when you have to. You can be realistic and you can be real emotional. You'll be okay, if. *If.*" He stares at her through marbled eyes. "*If* you can keep the two things separate. If you can't, it means the practical side and the feeling side will always be trying to kill each other."

Marilyn stares at her own hand, trying to release its mysteries. She can't and tosses it into her lap.

"No, no, great people have had that same kind of hand."

"Like who?"

"Napoleon. Florence Nightingale. George Washington Carver."

"How the hell do you know that?"

"I read about their hands. In a book when I first got interested in the subject. Let me tell you what makes a hand like yours so special. You got the artistic secret."

Marilyn wants to change the subject, wants to talk about her songs, but she is curious about this secret.

"It's tension. Just like setting a drumskin. You want it tight but not too tight." He's lost her. He chuckles, laughing at his own obscurity. "Look. There's always two things pulling against each other." He sets his tapering fingers in opposition. "In all art, I mean. Color and form. Rhythm and melody. Meaning and sound. You name it, there's always two things pulling. That's the secret of jazz but not only of jazz. Of everything. Say I set up a rhythm, the singer got to know to come in a tick late to pull the rhythm, or early to push against it. That's the soul of jazz. It's the soul of all art."

He takes a slow breath to recharge his passion and says, "The biggest tension is between what's expected and what you never expect. The thing to do is set things up, have it lead people a certain way, then, *wham*, ring the change on it."

He's touching Marilyn's knees lightly. She takes it as an expression of his intense interest in what he's saying. She doesn't mind being touched by this Svengali.

"That's why you people are the lucky ones. You got all the tensions within yourselves. You got more possibilities, more variety. And you got one combination you don't see very much. You got innocence—that's what you show— but deeper down there's a sense that you're real shrewd."

It's taken a while, but Marilyn finally feels flattered. "Is any of that gonna help me tonight?" she says.

"That's what I've been trying to tell you. You've got the power to go lots of different ways with a song. The most powerful tension you got, once you get those hips rolling and the sex dripping off you, is to come in with something a little funny." He has cupped her kneecaps in his hands. "I'm saying, go with a little more of the comic tonight."

From the doorway, a raucous voice. "Hey, you two. If you ain't got it together by now, you better hang 'em up." Manny Bonito, the moody club owner, wearing a full-house satisfaction, enters the dressing room. His plaid-jacketed arm hangs over Mickie Woody's shoulder like a colorful cut of meat.

Mickie Woody's contribution is, "Nervous? Don't be. They're gonna love you."

"Yeah, of course," Bonito says. "But remember who we're featuring tonight."

Bam slips into a slight drawl: "What you saying, Manny? You don't mind if a star is born in your club tonight— you just want to make sure she gets born real fast and gets her ass offstage?"

"Don't get sarcastic with me, Billy. Just play your world-famous music to order drinks by."

"You see, baby, Manny here is a perfect example of what I was telling you. He's a great artist because he can make jokes and threaten your ass at the same time."

Furrows form on Manny Bonito's sloping brow. Mickie pats the back of his ham hand and says in a calming voice, "C'mon, Manny. I wanna get out front." She manages to start the thick man moving out the door. She calls, over her shoulder, "Break a leg, Norma."

Billy Bam says, "Norma. I thought your name was Marilyn."

"That's just my stage name."

"Norma what?"

"Norma Jean Dougherty."

"Dougherty's your old man?" He looks again at her wedding band.

"Uh huh." Marilyn takes off her ring and squeezes it into the palm of her right hand. "He's supposed to come tonight."

"You should have just stayed with Norma Jean." She doesn't understand. "Your stage name. Just Norma and Jean alone."

"I don't know. Doesn't it sound too much like a child star?"

"Yeah, maybe. Anyway. We're going to open with 'Paper Moon.' Features Roscoe; he's got his people here tonight too. Then I'll introduce you. You want the hand mike?"

"I do better with the stand-up."

"Fine. You want to introduce the song?"

"No; I'll just look over at you and wait for the beat."

"Sure. Gate flies open. And we're off. But think what I told you about working against the rhythm. And listen for the changeover. I'll clue you with the cymbals."

"You think we rehearsed enough?"

His response is an are-you-kidding smile.

Art Pepper is wrapping his set with a reckless, virtuoso

solo on "Hindustan." The crowd has applauded the solos of the piano player and bassist; there are footstomps and whistles building as Pepper finishes. The applause continues as the trio comes together for a slower, final melodic chorus.

In the dressing room, Billy Bam stands and places his large, tapered hand across the dark ribbon on Marilyn's head, trying to infuse her with his certainty. Marilyn picks up her warm ginger ale as Billy leaves. She is unaware of her nausea, unaware of nerves, unaware of anything but how she's going to walk out onstage—in the flouncing, tight-heeled walk she's practiced in front of a mirror for days—how she's going to phrase that first line: "Baby, won't you . . . please come . . . home."

She's unaware of the voices in the hallway, the lingering applause out in the room.

Then, after another sip and a deep breath, she's no longer quite herself, not Norma Jean, not Marilyn Darvey, but someone else entirely, someone who comes into existence before mirrors, before still cameras, before strangers.

She knows she has passed men in the hallway, heard them speak to and about her as they passed, but it is not her exactly, so she does not respond. She stands stock-still behind the gold velveteen curtain as Billy Bam's music starts, a middle-tempo "Paper Moon." She begins pulsing to the rhythm; the rhythm, in fact, is inside her, revealing itself externally in the tapping foot, the quietly snapping fingers at the end of every bar. She feels she has something precious, a saving message, a gift she must deliver to these strangers. A wave of nausea comes on her. She takes a deep breath, bends stiffly at the waist. The nausea doesn't pass; it subsides to a bearable level. Marilyn Darvey peers around the curtain into the hazy room, looking for her husband. He'd be at the bar or leaning against the back wall. She doesn't see him.

Billy's sweet voice comes over the inattentive applause. He brushes the cymbals softly for background as he says, "Ladies and gentlemen, everybody likes to be able to say, 'I was there when . . .' You'll be able to say that about to-night. New gal is gonna turn quite a few heads before she's done. Talent in a real nice package. Let's hear it for Miss . . . Marilyn Darvey."

The room is noisy—drink orders, conversation. She knows her walk is ready. It's the thirty seconds standing at the mike before she sings she's not so sure about. Billy's downbeat is picked up enthusiastically by the bass player and Roscoe. Billy smiles encouragingly offstage. A voice in Marilyn's head starts to sing: " . . . won't you please come home . . ."

She zigzags toward the mike, peering from behind an elevated shoulder down at the tables close to the stage. She's something to see, but the noise level doesn't come down much. The spotlight misses her as she advances. She stands at the mike, smiling, beating time on her hip with her fingers, tapping one knee against the other; she licks her lips slowly, nervous behind a sensual pose. The music is unwinding toward her first sound. As it does, she fully loses all sense of who and where she is. She is suspended above them all as in a dream. The gift is about to be offered.

"Baby!" The word is a cooed exclamation punctuated by Billy's rim shot. Then silence. It gets almost everyone's attention.

She smiles appreciatively at Billy's musical joke. " . . . won't you pul-eeze come home . . ." There is heart and voice and rhythm in her husky, breathless crooning. There is sinuous movement in her body. This is a smoldering young woman before them, and the crowd knows it.

" . . . 'cause your momma's all alone . . . oh, I have tried in vain . . ." Conscious of Billy's advice, Marilyn is coming in milliseconds later than she usually does; the result goes beyond syncopation—it's a teasing pull between expectation and satisfaction. Billy is keeping a light rhythm with his foot on the high hat.

" . . . Never no more to call your name . . ." Billy insisted on the ungrammatical "never no more" over the simple "never more."

" . . . when you left you broke my heart . . . and . . ." Suddenly, the words are not there. A blank. The music pulls ahead of her. Marilyn Darvey puts a finger to her lips and smiles foolishly. Her body remains torrid. She's completely winning. Her voice peeps, "Oh." Then, as the melody runs ahead, some words come: " . . . the teardrops did start . . . so every hour, every day . . . you can hear me say . . . *Baby!* please come home . . ."

Roscoe's rolling left hand sends waves of bluesy sound echoing through the room. It almost drowns the bass and Billy's drum. Marilyn turns on her toes in a deliciously suggestive buck and wing. The small part of her that is apart, watching, is pleased with itself. As she dances, she looks over the crowd, isolating individuals, making eye contact, appreciating them, being appreciated, building connections.

Billy initiates a subtle change in the music, a shifting of rhythm, then of the melody. She says to the crowd, a little too cutely maybe, "Want to know exactly why I fell for my baby?"

A loudmouth at the bar bellows, "Not really." Someone else think he's funny and cackles. Randy Hagan, in protective posture, starts to make his way from behind the bar.

" 'Cause . . ." Roscoe fingers a simple, subdued intro. Billy flutters his cymbal and stops the sound with his fingers. " . . . Every-body loves a baby, that's why I'm in love with you . . ." She points coquettishly at the heckler, bending at the knees, supporting the aiming arm at the elbow with her other hand. "Pret-ty ba-by . . . pret-ty ba-by . . ."

That's when she makes out her husband, not far from the door, leaning against the wall of the coatroom. He's got a beer bottle to his lips. *He's wearing his damn uniform!* He's not the only guy in the place in uniform, but it bothers Norma.

She doesn't blow any lines or lose the rhythm, but she is suddenly not as completely wrapped in the consciousness of another person as she was before she saw him. So as not to become more distracted, she fixes on the lyrics: " . . . and I'd like to be your sister, brother, dad, and mother . . ." She remembers to give the word a coy connotation—mothering, nurturing, nursing. She looks everywhere but in the vicinity of her husband.

Something has changed. "Mother" has made unwanted connections. "Baby," which was coming up, would be even worse. " . . . mother too . . . pret-ty ba-by . . . won't you come and let me rock you in my cradle of love, and we'll cuddle all the time . . . oh, I want a loving ba-by . . ." Marilyn feels the hollow within her growing. " . . . and it might as well be you . . ." She wants it cleansed, the real baby forming inside her. Expunged. Eliminated.

"Yes, it might as well be you . . . pret-ty ba-by . . . of mine . . ."

The trio begins to bridge back to "Baby, Please Come Home." While it does, Marilyn reminds herself how important it is to hold things together. It is an act of will now to keep her persona relaxed, intriguing, entertaining.

She sees Mickie Woody's head bobbing to the music. Marilyn, too, is keeping time by dancing, listening for the changeover back to the cover song. *I'll do it myself. Alone. Dirty business. My business. Nobody's business. Nobody's . . .* "Ba-by, won't you please come home . . . your momma's all alone . . . I have tried in vain . . . never no more . . . to call your name . . ."

She has noticed the profound concentration on the face of a small gray-haired man sitting alone at a table against the wall. More specifically, she noticed his tic, an extreme sidewise pull of his tight lips. He is Milton Levy, a lawyer for Howard Hughes. Levy is there for pleasure, a jazz buff catching Art Pepper.

This girl's beauty, Levy knows, is very uncommon. Maybe not such a polished singer yet, and there's no way of knowing if she can act or even if that certain something she has will translate to the screen. Levy has been around Hollywood long enough to know that pretty alone doesn't do it. With this Marilyn Darvey, there's more; here there's a something more than uncommon. She's a rarity.

He's always amazed that not everyone can spot the rare ones. God, it jumps right out at you. Mostly, though, he perceives it by its effect—it makes him feel powerful and protective at the same time. He'll go backstage soon as she's done.

Marilyn looks over to the coatroom. The sailor is gone. This is her big finish, and she feels renewed by his absence. " . . . so every hour of the day . . . you can hear me say . . . baaaay-beeee . . . pul-leeeze . . . come . . . home. . . ." She is done and takes two steps toward the curtain. But she's not done. She tiptoes quickly to the mike and purrs, "I need your luv-ving . . . so baaaay-bee . . . pul-leeze . . . come . . ." She begins but impetuously chooses not to sing the final word. She blows a kiss to the loudmouth and saunters offstage, looking back over her shoulder, still in character, enticement still flickering on her face. Applause starts slowly and builds nicely as the Billy Bam Trio plays out. Billy's voice fills the room: "Miss Marilyn Darvey, ladies and gentlemen."

The abortion she finally decides to arrange turns out to be unnecessary. A miscarriage—the first of three in her life—takes the baby three weeks after her first Saturday appearance at the Cork and Flask.

CHAPTER FOUR

Marilyn, Johnny Hyde, and Dr. Hyman Goldfedder

LIGHTS

VOGUE: This has been the season for "Top Ten" lists. You may not pay attention to those things . . .

MONROE: Depends. "Top Ten" what?

VOGUE: In this instance, you have been named to every "Most Beautiful Women" list that matters, from our own to the *Wall Street Journal's*. What feelings do you have when the world proclaims you one of its most beautiful inhabitants?

MONROE: Except for, well, maybe, grooming, a person isn't really responsible for her looks. It's hard to take credit for what you're born with. I mean, I wouldn't criticize someone for a birth defect or anything like that. It's not their fault, you know. The same thing should go for the opposite—if you inherit features people admire, it's not to your credit as a human being. It just, well, it just is.

Now I basically believe that, but to be really honest, in my case I think there's more to it. I didn't know my father. My mother couldn't keep me, and I was raised—that's not the right word, "raised"—I was alone so much, forced back into myself so much, that I developed a tremendous imagination. My inner life became so much stronger than my life out there, it got a little scary. But by thinking beautiful thoughts I honestly believe I developed a personal glow within myself. If I'm beautiful—and that's not for me to say— it's got more to do with what's inside me than with my features. Surviving what I have, I'd feel beautiful within no matter what I looked like.

CAMERA

Johnny Hyde was simply the biggest there was. Studios called him. Even if they were committed to using another agent's talent, they called Johnny Hyde just so he wouldn't be offended. He played gin with Sam Spiegel, Harry Cohn, Billy Wilder, Sidney Skolsky. Johnny Hyde had a regular table at the Polo Lounge. He was around five feet tall.

Marilyn knew she was lucky to have Johnny Hyde. She had made her own luck, though, meeting him poolside at a party in Palm Springs and making the impression stick. She got herself reintroduced the following week when he stopped at Romanoff's for his regular Wednesday lunch. Johnny Hyde signed her the following Monday. Having Johnny Hyde was like having an option on success.

He was a mysterious man. He never told Marilyn what was on his mind when they were in bed. In fact, he was even quieter there than in the office. She never knew what he was thinking. When he told her to do something, she did it. Johnny Hyde knew things, he simply knew. Marilyn was relieved to have someone do her thinking for her. Johnny Hyde lifted the burden of decision from her, and she was certainly grateful to him for that. He also took some of her anxiety away; not all of it, but the worst of it: those irrational pangs that caused panic in the middle of the night, the impatience that almost drove her crazy between jobs.

Johnny Hyde made it perfectly clear when he took someone on that he had to control everything, reshape the talent, the personality. Marilyn welcomed that. She hadn't gotten anywhere for almost three years. After a promising start—a good screen test and a contract at Columbia—none of her expectations were met. There were walk-ons and bit parts with a line or two. She had a song in a B movie. In Love Happy *she delivered a sexy line, wiggled her derriere, and elicited a leering take from Groucho Marx. But she was still considered a starlet. Three years was too long to be a starlet.*

Marilyn thought representation by Hyde meant a new acting coach, learning how to move and talk, to dress. It meant that, but it also meant becoming raw material for the little man who decided to reshape her. It meant painful dental work, having her front teeth straightened and capped. And more.

ACTION

Marilyn leans against the plush door cushion on the passenger side of Johnny Hyde's Cadillac. That way she can look at him naturally, without seeming to be snooping. He knows she is watching but doesn't seem to mind.

Marilyn doesn't see a tiny, self-important man. She sees certainty, effectiveness. He sits so straight, his back does not touch the leather of the seat. The look is George Raft, slick and tough and tanned. For some reason, Marilyn imagines him someone else, the most successful jockey at Santa Anita, and herself his tall blond bimbo. It is just a passing, pleasing fantasy: the crowd, the horses, the money, her man out there in the middle of it, winning.

She never noticed the scar on his neck. A long, thin white line that disappears under his shirt collar, beneath the hair behind his ear. She is drawn to touch it, so she leans over and runs her fingertip from his collar upward, slowly, tracing the hard wire-thin line. She knows he might get angry, but he does not pull away. Her finger comes down along the scar.

"He did it," Hyde says.

"Who?"

"Goldfedder. An incredible graft. A burn I had there since I was a kid. Not another man in this country—country? the world, maybe—not another man could have done this kind of work. I take everyone to him."

"Everyone? What do you mean, everyone?"

Hyde doesn't answer. Marilyn doesn't ask again. There is pleasure in being Johnny Hyde's girl. It's the same thrill those society girls must have when George Raft takes one of them home. The attraction of somebody unpredictable, a little dangerous. That's where the thrill comes in.

He could hurt her at any moment. Slap her suddenly. Or, even worse, simply raise his arm above her.

Johnny did that once. Waiting for the hand to come down, Marilyn had turned away and closed her eyes. She finally heard ice cubes tumbling into a glass, so she peeked out from under her arm. He had his pants on and was pouring himself bourbon. The slap that doesn't come was scary as hell. Marilyn hated it; she was drawn to it.

Marilyn believes she could play a role like that now. She could get beyond the acting lessons and the director's explanation about motivation and breakthrough to the way she actually felt, the way she was at the moment of fear. Marilyn keeps Johnny's scar beneath her finger. It gives her confidence; she thinks she understands how to be with this man.

"John-ny." The little waif voice. Seductive too.

"What, doll?"

"I've got a bad feeling about this."

"How many times have I told you, let me have all the feelings, good and bad. The whole point is to let me do the planning, the worrying; that's my job. You're the talent. You just deal with the dialogue and all the stuff inside you. Everything outside, that's my domain." He likes the sound of the word so much, he says it again. "Domain."

"I know, but . . ."

"No 'I know, but's. That's how I said we were going to do it. That's the way it'll be as long as you stay with me." She knows he's not finished even though he falls silent at a stoplight. "I'm offering you the world on a plate. D'you have any idea how many girls out here would die for what I'm doing for you? And I'm not just doing it selfishly, either. You can become big—very big, immense—if you have someone who knows the business running interference, planning your every move, leaving you free to work the talent end. Believe me, I wouldn't be wasting my time with you if . . ." Johnny Hyde smiles and looks over at Marilyn's legs. " . . . if . . . Well, maybe I would, but that's not all that's going on. I believe in you." He looks in Marilyn's eyes for emphasis.

Marilyn believes him. Utterly. She comes across the leather seat making a low animal sound and puts the tip of her tongue under his shirt collar and brings it slowly up the scar to his earlobe, rounding the shell of his ear and plunging it finally into the waxy hollow.

"Careful. This is Bel Air. They're liable to pull me over."

"This doesn't break any law." She licks him again, longer, more enticingly.

"Careless driving."

"Pull over, then. I'll give you a driving lesson."

Usually, when Marilyn Monroe seduces Johnny Hyde, it's a dutiful exercise. But this time she feels playful, passionate.

"Can't. Got to be at the Doctor's. I know this man—he hates when you're late. We're lucky even to get the appointment." Since she doesn't know anyone Johnny Hyde has ever kowtowed to, Marilyn is impressed.

"What's he like? What's he do?"

"You'll see when we get there. His place'll knock your eyes out."

Marilyn has a funny feeling. Partly, it is as though Johnny is giving her a present, something secret. Partly, it is as though he's got some bad news he's keeping from her.

He drives silently through Culver City and up into the hills of Bel Air. The curving road takes them constantly upward, past brick walls, fences, and hedges, beyond which Marilyn can occasionally see a small part of a very large house.

Up and up, until Beverly Hills and Hollywood, in the haze below, become distant, dreamy. Hyde smiles and says, "C'mon." Marilyn's trust begins to revive.

Hyde steers his Cadillac into an entranceway in which one side of a great iron gate has been swung open. An esplanade bordered by willow trees stretches farther than she could have imagined. No house is visible. She thought she'd be going to a medical building in Gardena. All this is completely unexpected.

The last willows block the house. Then, suddenly, it isn't just a house at all but an estate—rolling lawns, gothic arches, ivied walls. "This is it?"

"When I said, 'Nothing but the best,' I meant nothing but the best."

"What's this guy's name again?"

"Goldfedder."

Marilyn whistles. "One little thing, Johnny. You didn't tell me exactly why we're here."

"Yes I did. Depilatory work." Hyde turns into a rounded path of white pebbles. "Next to nothing. Trust me, Marilyn."

Immediately after Hyde slows the car and stops, a large carved-oak door opens and an attendant dressed in white glides out. He opens Marilyn's door and says across her to the driver, "It's good to see you again, Mr. Hyde. Dr. Goldfedder is expecting you."

"How've you been, Giorgio? This is Miss Monroe. Remember the face; you'll be able to say you saw her when . . ."

"A pleasure, Signorina."

Marilyn is slightly confused; she offers her hand

weakly. Giorgio helps her out of the car. She feels a bit like an invalid and shakes off his help as soon as she gets out. Giorgio looks at Hyde with a complicitous expression that troubles Marilyn.

If the exterior of the place had been impressive, the great, round hallway overwhelms Marilyn. Its height, the magnificent chandelier that dominates, the sweeping marble staircase. The paintings, statues, tapestries. The place reminds her of something, but she is not quite sure what it is. That Ingrid Bergman movie, where they kidnap her, drug her, and try to make her think she's crazy. Marilyn can't call up the word "sanitarium," but that's the feeling she gets.

Arm in arm with Johnny, Marilyn tiptoes up the stairs—she doesn't want her heels to strike the steps; her silence helps her deny she is actually here. As they ascend behind Giorgio, Marilyn looks back to the entrance and whispers, "Jee-sus. Some doctor."

"Class of the field."

Giorgio turns and says, "Your car, sir. Do you wish me to move it to the surgery?"

At the word, Hyde feels Marilyn tighten on his arm. "No. Not if it's okay where it is."

Giorgio leaves them in a small room lined with books. Marilyn looks through the arched windows, some panes of which are leaded and make the trees beyond flow like liquid. The silence in the room feels tidal, as though it were pulling and releasing at the bottom of the sea. Through the thick stone walls she hears distant footsteps and a door close, but the sounds seem to come from miles away.

She hears Hyde riffling the pages of a magazine. "He said surgery." Marilyn is not confident this is her own voice.

"Fancy place, fancy names. It's just to remove the hair

you've got up here." Hyde rolls his hands over his jaw and the back part of his cheeks. "The camera will pick it up in tight shots. Either that or they paste up your face, and that's not the look I want for you. Natural, your look has got to be completely natural."

"So why didn't we discuss it first?"

"We can discuss it now. Ask yourself this: Have I ever had close-ups before I met Johnny Hyde? Well, with me there'll be close-ups. Stars aren't born, Marilyn, they're manufactured. And this is the man who manufactures them. You ought to be grateful."

Reflexively, she says, "Oh, I am. I just . . ." Marilyn lightly touches her jawline. She can feel a fine down running all the way to her ears. Her mother used to call it her peach fuzz. If losing it meant close-ups, she wouldn't mind a bit. It is true that in three and a half months with Johnny, more has happened to her career than in the years before.

Marilyn turns away from the window, and stepping lightly toward Johnny, comfortable in a leather chair, she says, "I swear I don't know what you see in me. I'm so lucky to have you." She stoops and kisses him on the forehead, then squeezes his face into her stomach. No one else does this to Johnny Hyde.

With his neck craned, his face smothered, Hyde says, "I see you as one of the biggest. Bigger than Harlow, bigger than Hayworth, bigger than any of them, if . . . if" He shakes his head free and looks up between pointed breasts at her downturned, intently loving face. ". . . you listen to daddy."

"Tell me again, daddy. What're you going to do for me?"

"I tell you all the time."

"Tell me again. Daddy."

"A brand-new contract with Fox. Make Zanuck want

to kill to get you. Within a year, starring with Gable and Cooper. Now get out of here with those questions."

"Will it hurt?"

"Oh, for Christ's sake, it's fuzz. I'd shave it off for you, except it'd come back."

"How can a guy get so rich taking off fuzz?"

"He doesn't usually just do fuzz. Except as a favor to me. Usually he does established stars, their faces, their bodies."

Marilyn is puzzled.

"Nips, tucks, he does. Noses. Boobs. *Capeesh?* The man is a genius. He's saved more careers than Technicolor. But he doesn't come cheap. As you can see. Where you're concerned, Marilyn, cost doesn't even register—that's how much I believe in you."

"I'm grateful. I am. But it's just the fuzz, right?"

"While you're here, naturally I'll want him to look you over, make suggestions. Rita Hayworth knocked herself out for years trying to catch a break. Goldfedder did a little thing with her eyelid, gave it a hooded look, and, bang, everyone wanted her."

"Just my fuzz, though."

"And his evaluation of your face."

Marilyn knows that if she pursues this, the layers of romance will get peeled away until the relationship, stripped raw, will become a matter of which one needs the other more. There were dozens of starlets who would change places with her in a minute, while Hyde was the only big-time agent who had given her a second look. It would come down to his saying, "My way or no way at all." She can bring it down to that level just so many times before he gets sick and tired of it.

Staring out the window, making the liquid trees blend into one another, Marilyn thinks about the debt she already owes Hyde. Doors to casting directors all over town have opened for her. Her old 20th Century–Fox screen test was dug out of storage and recirculated. He has gotten her a juicy part in John Huston's film about the mob, *The Asphalt Jungle*.

She listens for the footsteps of this doctor who is making her so nervous. Marilyn assumes he will be short, bald, with a bad complexion, thick glasses, and an accent to match. Like so many of them, an ugly appreciator of beauty.

She hears the echo of footsteps and closes her eyes. Hyde puts down his magazine. He stands. The arched door opens, a man steps into the room. Marilyn sees his distorted reflection in the leaded glass. She will not turn around until she's introduced, a combination of perversity and the desire to make a dramatic impression.

Hyde says, "Good to see you again, Doctor."

Reflected in the glass Marilyn sees the distorted image of a tall figure joining hands with a short one, a lopsided inkblot. She takes shallow breaths.

His voice has an accent, an unusual one, European but not of a particular country. "So, Mr. Hyde, who have you brought me today?"

Marilyn has transformed herself. The energy is there, the desire to please. She turns and smiles. "Hello. I'm Marilyn Monroe." She is radiant.

Dr. Goldfedder is rarely impressed by beauty. He is impressed by Marilyn's. He fastens on her face for an extended, awkward moment. Men have gazed at Marilyn since she was a child; none quite like this.

It is reciprocal. Marilyn has never seen an older man quite like this one before. The unblinking eyes, large and deep, gleam like onyx, polished to a dark sheen. Sensuous, full lips. Perfectly combed hair, half black, half gray. Long, perfectly formed face, without a wrinkle, tanned the color of natural wood. Marilyn is staring at great masculine beauty in which the perfection of parts has created an extreme grace and a perfect sense of confidence.

Johnny Hyde begins to speak, but Dr. Goldfedder raises a long finger. He circles Marilyn deliberately, gliding rather than stepping, easing closer with every turn. And studying not merely her face but her entire body, as though unwrapping layers of gauze. Marilyn twists her head until he disappears behind her, then she swivels to pick him up again, coming from behind. She is pleased, she is confused, she is slightly afraid.

Finally, Goldfedder is close enough for Marilyn to smell a curious blend of oil and cinnamon. The man is delectable. He touches her with two warm but firm fingers. "Toes," he commands. And he raises Marilyn's chin as she goes up on her toes.

"And down." She descends slowly.

Now he is inches away from her face, rolling those fingers over the fine down, but also sculpting the bones, compressing lips, softly pressing around her eyes, tracing the hairline and ears with an exploratory finger.

Ordinarily, Marilyn, who is, like most performers, a complex combination of exhibitionist and introvert, would have withdrawn at his touch, would have felt vaguely violated by such an examination. She doesn't. She feels appreciated by a connoisseur.

Goldfedder steps back again. He makes two sounds at once, a low clucking and a soft growl. He is still evaluating; rather, thinking of how to put his evaluation into words. Marilyn knows she has pleased him. She knows she is very beautiful at this moment. Occasionally, in front of the still camera, she has felt this same otherworldly radiance.

"My God. I haven't seen . . . Where did you find

her?" Although Goldfedder is speaking to Hyde, he never takes his eyes off Marilyn, never indicates he is speaking to anyone but himself. Marilyn has begun to treat the whole experience as a sensual diversion. She has forgotten being upset over Johnny's keeping her in the dark about what might happen to her here. Almost forgotten.

"Would you mind, Miss . . . ?"

"Monroe," Hyde says.

"This was an American president, Monroe. Am I not correct?"

"Marilyn's not presidential material," Hyde says. "She's star material."

"Would you mind terribly, Miss Monroe, if I take a few photographs of your face?"

"Only if it doesn't hurt."

"It would require, I assure you, nothing more than your sitting back in that chair, letting me turn on this light, and clicking my little camera."

There is, in fact, more. When Marilyn is in the chair, Goldfedder presses a button and Marilyn's feet start to come up as her head goes down, until she is perfectly horizontal. Goldfedder advances toward Marilyn holding an opaque plastic sheet with a face-sized oval cut out of the middle. Before she can flinch, he explains: "This will isolate your features. In that way, I can see them purely, without your hair. I can tell you immediately, the style is wrong for your features. Sweeping forehead like this should be celebrated, à la Dietrich, not diminished and concealed with an obscuring style."

Marilyn has long suspected as much and, without turning her head, glares at Hyde.

Goldfedder places the plastic sheet tightly around Marilyn's face and turns on a harsh blue-white light directly above. "This is difficult, I know, but try not to

blink." A camera click and the whir of Polaroid film eject-
ing is Marilyn's only clue that she is being photographed.
Instinctively, she smiles. "No, no, please. I must have the
face in complete repose. It is hard for an actress, I know."

To Hyde, Goldfedder says, as his camera clicks and
whirs, "It is a face like this that justifies my work. It is why
I do not break things off and live only for my pleasures.
Because I can never know when I will walk through the
door and see a face like this. Just when you despair that
there are no features like these anymore, that I shall never
again see a Garbo, a Bergman, a Danielle Darrieux, *voilà*, it
appears. This is why we must never despair in our work,
eh, Mr. Hyde?"

Who, Marilyn is thinking, is Danielle Darrieux? She'll
ask Johnny when they leave. Leave? She realizes not a word
has been said about removing her peach fuzz.

When Goldfedder clicks off the light, Marilyn closes
her eyes and feels herself lifted back into a sitting position.
She feels something spidery on her face and is suddenly
startled, but Goldfedder's soft hands calm her immediately.
"Please." She could not deny that voice anything. Calipers
inscribe arcs from the edge of her brow to her nostrils, then
to the corners of her mouth. "Fine."

Changing reference points every few seconds,
Goldfedder is mapping her face like a voyager, recording
distances and widths with great precision. "Just a few more
seconds." He jots down some figures. He puts aside his
measuring tools and compresses the soft flesh just under the
point of her chin lightly between thumb and forefinger. "I
can't tell you, my dear, how grateful I am to you."

"I guess if someone had to go over my face that way,
I'm glad it was you. So what do you think about taking off
my peach fuzz?"

"A minor matter. We'll have that done before you leave this evening."

At that moment Marilyn realizes there have been other considerations, that she has been brought here for other things. She looks over at Hyde, who signals her not to worry. As though applied with a brush, layers of worry begin to build. Marilyn suddenly says, "Look, something's going on here that I don't know about. So why don't we clean the air?" She meant to say "clear the air."

Dr. Goldfedder, who has been marveling over the slowly developing snapshots on his desk, looks up, mildly distraught. His annoyance is with Hyde. "You haven't been told? No wonder your confusion. I must certainly clear the air." He comes alongside Marilyn and sits down.

"Dr. Goldfedder," Hyde explains, "is the foremost facial surgeon in the world."

The word "surgeon" frightens Marilyn all over again. Goldfedder takes her hand, and she feels his calm assurance rise up her arm and begin to warm her chest. "Please. Please do not be frightened. It is normal procedure for an actress like yourself, who has the possibility of great success on the screen, to be brought to me for an appraisal."

She is again a child fearing she might have to move yet again. Someone with a kind voice is about to tell her her next home will be warm and friendly, her final shelter. She knows there is no final shelter. "It is an appraisal only. I promise. Nothing will be done without your approval. Nothing. You understand?"

A pout shapes her lips, and like the true waif, Marilyn agrees to what has been decided for her.

"I am culpable in the matter. I should have made this very clear, but I have lapsed and lost my professional objectivity momentarily. I see many beautiful women, my dear, but for many years, none quite as remarkable as you. Let me assure you, you have nothing to fear from Hyman Goldfedder."

Marilyn whispers, "I know." Her fear has been eased by his appreciation.

"Alas, my dear, after having upset you unduly, I must, nevertheless, ask yet another indelicate question. It is, let me assure you, a purely professional request. May I?" He takes her fingers in his two hands.

"May he, Johnny? I mean, after all, you're in charge here."

Hyde winces. "Don't do that. I just didn't want to upset you with worries."

Tacitly, they all agree to leave a pause. Finally, Goldfedder says, "You may think what I have told you is just part of the regular spiel. I want you to know that is not the case. I have been asked by all the major studios to evaluate girls who have made good tests, girls the camera has already embraced, so to speak. The potential for a truly great face, young woman, is another matter entirely. That is my area of expertise."

"What is?"

"Magical allure, my dear."

"That's studio language for sexy, right, Johnny?"

The room darkens as a long cloud begins to cover the sun. Hyde says, "Sex probably got something to do with it, but what the doctor is talking about is different."

"I've got allure, haven't I, Doc? Allure I haven't even used yet." Marilyn approximates a cynical Mae West, hands on hips, smirk on her face, the words slurred seductively.

"As a result, I must examine your body as well as your face. I assume you have no padding of any sort on your body."

"I don't even have underwear on." Mae West has become a bit defiant.

"So we may proceed?"

"Okay, but no pictures."

"As you wish. Would you like Mr. Hyde to leave?"

"Actually, I feel a little safer with him here. Where d'you want me?"

"Here is fine. Simply strip to the waist, if that is possible."

Marilyn has a bit of trouble locating the zipper in the back of her dress and then drawing it down. After she does, however, she pulls her sleeves off quickly and shrugs her shoulders forward. She is nude to the waist, the top of her dress hanging forward like a half-apron. She instinctively crosses her arms over her chest.

"Could you please place your arms just below your breasts, intertwined tightly as though hugging yourself? It is a way of determining cleavage, something of great concern to studios. But of course you know this."

The position has the effect of supporting and enlarging her breasts. Marilyn tilts her head, closes her eyes, and exaggeratedly says, "Cheese."

Goldfedder examines her skin for birthmarks and discolorations. There are none to speak of. "Now if you will stand here, lean all the way over, and place your palms on my desk?"

The pose, a standard stripper position that heightens the rump and elongates the pendular breasts, is, as Marilyn performs it, astonishingly sensual. Hyde stops breathing. Dr. Goldfedder kneels on the rug, satisfaction reflected in his face. He works his way around Marilyn. "Once more. Simply stand against the wall, facing into the room. Shoes off. Slowly bring your arms straight up toward the ceiling. Then again way up on your toes."

There are goose bumps on her skin.

"And the same thing facing the wall. That's perfect. Ah, thank you. Yes. Now you may get dressed."

Hyde says, "I know it's been a tough deal for you, but that's it, right, Doctor?"

"Yes, yes, we're through. Here. We can go down to the surgery and begin to take care of the facial hair." As Goldfedder sits at his desk and begins jotting again on a legal pad, Marilyn turns away and zips herself back into her dress.

Mugging broadly, Marilyn asks, "So tell me, what's the final verdict, Doc?"

"If my flattery is not too sickly sweet to bear, my dear, I should simply like to say that I have never seen a combination of face and form quite like yours. The form is perfect."

"That means the face has got to go?"

"Hardly. If pushed, however, I should recommend two things. Each of which, believe me, is very, very minor."

"And what's that?" Hyde asks before Marilyn.

"May I?" Goldfedder picks up a hand mirror and walks behind Marilyn. "The slightest amount of fatty tissue, extremely easy to remove, alongside the nose, here, just above the nostril. On your face, the difference would be subtle but profound; it is the difference between the plump, healthy farm girl visiting the city and a worldly woman who can travel with confidence in any circle. Notice." Goldfedder shows Marilyn the slightly fatty tissue. She had noticed it before, but she liked her nose. So did everyone she'd ever met until now.

With thin calipers, Goldfedder squeezes the tissue flat. Marilyn sees her nose transformed from cute to charming.

"And the other problem?" Her voice is genuinely subdued for the first time.

"The chin. A minor doubling. It could hurt you in profile. Even in full face, removal would produce a slendering effect. I would recommend both be done at the same time. We're talking about an afternoon's work. You would step into a glorious career, surely, with Mr. Hyde's guidance."

The chin struck her as less important than the nose.

"Trust me, absolutely nothing can be or will be done without your approval. We are, after all, talking about your face, your career, your life."

"You've got to know, Marilyn," Hyde says, "the man is the best there is. You know what people in the business call him?" It doesn't matter if she wants to know or not. "They call call him Dr. Perfect."

"There is no perfection. Such talk disturbs me. I merely try to complement Nature's gift of natural beauty."

"God." It is the first word Marilyn has uttered since they've left Goldfedder's surgery. Gauze covers the sides of her face; it runs under her chin and over the top of her head. "You're a real prick sometimes. You know that, Johnny?" It is difficult for her to speak.

Hyde says nothing, intent on finding the cutoff to Malibu. Marilyn will be recuperating at his beach house.

"What you did was shitty, and you know it."

"I said he'd take off that fuzz. That's all I thought he'd be interested in."

"The nose, the chin. You knew about that too."

"Marilyn, that choice is up to you."

"Some 'up to you.' Get the work done or find another agent. Right?"

Hyde drives.

"Isn't it?"

"I never said that."

"But that's the way it is, isn't it?"

Hyde doesn't answer.

"I knew it."

After another long silence, the ocean rises from behind Pacific Palisades. "Goldfedder," she says, "he really does everybody's face?"

"Everybody who can afford it. He's the best."

"How come he lives better than most of the stars?"

"Stars come and go. Goldfedder, he goes on forever."

"All of it just from a little nip here, a tuck there?"

"That's right. But he's also very big in the abortion field."

CHAPTER FIVE

Take Her Out to the Ball Game

LIGHTS

HOLLYWOOD REPORTER: When you first try to get a handle on a character you're playing, how do you enter her life? That is, what about her first interests you, draws you to her, and lets you know you can do her justice on the screen?

MONROE: Well, on the first level, it's nothing that conscious. I'm either attracted or I'm not. If I'm attracted—and God only knows why—I have a little test I call the Seven Sins test.

REPORTER: Which is?

MONROE: I ask myself which of the Seven Deadly Sins the character is guilty of.

REPORTER: I assume we're talking about the same basic sins the Church identified hundreds of years ago.

MONROE: Thousands, I think. But it still works as a good way of understanding what motivates people.

REPORTER: Even off the screen?

MONROE: *Especially* off the screen.

REPORTER: You actually believe these classic sins exist?

MONROE: I'm certain of it. When I go to a party, I'll ask people which of the seven they have. They usually joke about it at first but eventually they'll come around and tell me. Everyone seems to have a decent dose of one or another, enough at least to recognize it as a character flaw and a potential danger.

REPORTER: So how exactly does it help you to develop a character?

MONROE: If there is a recognizable sin and the character makes an effort to struggle against it, rather than just reveling in it, I'm usually drawn by the tension in that character. Of course, it's got to be a sin I have a little bit of myself.

REPORTER: Let's refresh our readers' memories about those sins.

MONROE: Mine, you mean!

REPORTER: No, the Seven Deadlies.

MONROE: You know. Jealousy. Pride. Greed. Anger. Lust. Uh, I forget the others. [Editor: Sloth and Gluttony]

REPORTER: You mention jealousy first. Any particular reason?

MONROE: You have to start with something. To be honest, though, jealousy is the one I have to fight against the hardest. Don't you?

CAMERA

It was the ceremonial Sunday Old-timers' Day in Yankee Stadium, followed by an important game against the Cleveland Indians.

In none of her previous forms had Marilyn Monroe ever gone to a baseball game. When she was a teenager and lived in Bakersfield for almost a year, she regularly used to disrupt a ball game just by walking past the playing field in shorts and a striped polo shirt. But that didn't quite count as going to a ball game.

The shiny black Cadillac couldn't be missed as it made its way across the slatted shadows under the Jerome Avenue elevated tracks. The convoy of four motorcycle police, headlights ablaze, sirens on when approaching a red light, insisted the world take note. But who were they? The mayor? The governor? Bigger, maybe.

The blonde peering from the back-seat window waved whenever someone showed any interest. She giggled. "I love the populace."

The man in the gray hat, shielding his face unnecessarily with his hand, snorted, "Yeah. God made so many of 'em because he never got the model right." Walter Winchell, Joe's buddy.

Between them, Joe DiMaggio, leaning coolly against the back seat, surveyed his old business neighborhood as the chauffeur slowed to turn onto River Avenue. First one person, then the throng, recognized Marilyn. People began to hit the hood, the windshield, the doors and windows. The situation became momentarily dangerous. They shouted, "Where's Joe?" When they saw his head in the rear window, it was too late, the car had entered a parking lot. They hollered and chased after him, breaking through the security at the parking lot gate.

Joe DiMaggio had retired after thirteen seasons with the New York Yankees (interrupted by three years of army service during World War II). He quit in 1951, after the Yankees won the ninth World Series of his tenure. He was the soul and symbol of Yankee excellence for a decade and a half. A superb baseball player, certainly, but more: in a time when the typical baseball player was a hard-drinking, womanizing, tobacco-chewing know-nothing, DiMaggio carried himself like royalty. There was an aura about him, a unique quality that was part excellence, part courage, part reserve, part gentility, and that added up to majesty. Gary Cooper and Clark Gable had it. Joe Louis had it. Garbo had it. FDR had it. Joe DiMaggio wore it like a mantle. Ernest Hemingway saw Joe as a bona fide Hemingway hero.

Marilyn knew none of this when they married. She knew of him only as a famous baseball player. When he courted her, he was serious, attentive, protective, and, best of all, decisive. He would be an old-fashioned Italian husband. She required someone like that, or thought she did.

They were married in a simple ceremony in San Francisco in January of '54 and flew to Japan for a honeymoon later that month. There they separated briefly, she going to Korea to entertain the troops of the First Marine Division; he going on a tour promoting baseball in Japan.

Now, in the midst of the baseball season, Joe, quite uncharacteristically, had agreed to appear at Old-timers' Day. Not in uniform, just a brief appearance, a wave to the crowd from the field in front of the Yankees' dugout. He insisted his presence not be publicized. Team insiders and the press knew the "Yankee Clipper" would be returning to hallowed ground for the first time since he retired. They did not know he intended to bring his new wife.

ACTION

The motorcycle police draw as close to the clubhouse entrance as possible—twelve, fifteen feet. Excited fans surround the car. They slap the roof and the windows. The driver opens his door with great difficulty and pushes his way around the front of the car to the rear door. Winchell appears. The throng doesn't recognize him. Momentary confusion. He's a diversion. Marilyn has emerged on the other side and been quickly surrounded by police. She is almost through the stadium entrance when she's recognized—there are screams, gasps, a general confusion.

Joe is next. Too late for trickery; the crowd knows he's in the car. The police and some stadium guards wade into the mob; linking arms, they make a double line between which Joe DiMaggio, red-eared with embarrassment and discomfort, pawed and entreated by frenzied fans, enters Yankee Stadium once again.

The stars, still protected by police, pass through a long hallway to a cool, cavernous part of the stadium. Marilyn was once in one of Howard Hughes's airplane hangars, which this place reminds her of. It smelled cool and musty—no sunlight ever—and made her feel small and extremely displaced. Like this one, it was a man's private world. This is Joe DiMaggio's territory, but Marilyn knows that even here, especially here, she compels attention.

She has referred to the dress she is wearing as "my answer to Bo-Peep." It's a tight white pinafore with large red polka dots. Her shoes are red patent leather with very high heels; they help define muscular calves the equal of any ballplayer's in the park. Her ruffled hem stops above the knee. Her skin is milk white, with a soft sheen. She is the picture of health for America's pastime. Of course, she is greater than the sum of her wonderful parts; she is Marilyn Monroe.

Team officials are introduced to her. The names Jim and Dan and Fred get jumbled in her head. Some players come by to shake Joe's hand and to sneak looks at his wife. Joe is friendly but uncomfortable. Marilyn gets the feeling he'd be happier if he could spit and paw the ground with his toe.

"It's best," the tall man named Jim or Fred suggests to Joe, "if your wife waits upstairs. It's the best place to get a sense of the whole pageant."

"Sure," says Joe. "Walter can stay with her. Make sure she's got whatever she needs."

Winchell bobs his chin. "Whatever you want, champ."

"I'll find you afterward, hon," Joe says, his voice

steady but fragile. Then, more forcefully and with a smile, "'Don't let any of these guys try to bull you." Chuckles all around.

"Sweetie, you know you can't bull an old cowgirl." She flexes her knees to accentuate her timing. Polite laughter.

Quietly to Winchell, Joe intones, "Watch her, Walt. No pictures." Even as he says this, a flashbulb pops. Joe turns around, annoyed. Instinctively, Marilyn had let her eyelids droop, her teeth nibble her tongue.

"Move it, pal," Winchell growls. "The lady's not on display today. No one here is." It's a judgment belied by a few more flashes and Marilyn's coy gestures.

Jim or Fred says, "No pictures are allowed upstairs. We'd better go."

Marilyn finds herself in an elevator with Winchell, Jim or Fred, and a tall, suave man—he must be the one named Dan—who seems to be the owner of the Yankees. He says, "It's virtually unheard of, a woman in the press box. We'll see if the boys'll go for it—it's their domain—but it's the best vantage point to see the field. If we can get you in, you won't be bothered."

"What is it, a men-only club?"

"Mrs. Ruth was up there a few times, I believe. Mrs. Gehrig too. But yes, generally speaking, it is an exclusively male domain. I'll introduce you to some of the senior writers. Maybe you'll discover a way to melt their hearts."

"I'm a great melter."

"Or maybe they'll owe Walter here a favor."

On entering the press box, Marilyn sees the expanse of playing field for the first time. Its green lushness causes her to catch her breath. "My. It's really beautiful," she says mostly to herself and touches her fingers to her chest. She is momentarily oblivious of the fact that dozens of baseball writers are staring at her. "I'd love a dress that color. Satin, to catch the light."

"See what we can do," says Dan obligingly. "But we've got these fellows to worry about."

Marilyn, conscious of the exclusionary press box rules, opts for a demure manner, trying to look respectful but coming off a trifle unhappy. At a certain point, however, she can't withhold her natural spirits and tosses winks and the suggestion of kisses to the boys. She's a bit like a charming troublemaker being sent to the principal's office. The younger men whistle and toss friendly welcomes; the curmudgeons mumble curses; either way, the press box at Yankee Stadium has been knocked off its axis.

Dan leads Marilyn and a trailing Winchell to a spot directly behind home plate, where, under a WORKING PRESS ONLY sign, two typewriters and more notebooks claim three or perhaps four places. This is the principal's office. At work are two middle-aged men: the dark one in a sleeveless red pullover; the rose-colored man in a zippered gray cardigan.

Dan clears his throat and says, "Miss Monroe . . ."

"Marilyn," she corrects.

". . . Marilyn. Let me introduce our press box aristocracy."

Winchell guffaws.

"Messrs. Smith and Cannon are judge and jury up here. . . ."

"Guess I'll have to throw myself on the mercy of the court. . . ." There might have been a little too much Mae West in her tone, but what the hell.

". . . Walter Wellesley Smith of the *New York Herald Tribune*—known fondly around here as 'Red'—and his counterpart at the *New York Post*, James Cannon, Esquire."

They stand, Smith awkwardly, Cannon as though meeting a long-lost friend. They're pleasantly surprised by the firmness of her handshake. Polite nods and murmurs.

As planned by the suave man, a press box usher comes forward with two folding chairs. "Dan," Cannon announces before the chairs are placed, "we'll trade you even up. We'll take the doll and give you Winchell. We might even throw in some cash." Dan doesn't know what to say. Smith's elfin eyes twinkle; he's glowing pink.

Cannon takes one chair from the attendant. "Walter," he says, "when you get that sweat stain taken out of your hatband, you'll be fit for civilized company like ours. Until then, toodle-oo, Walter."

Smith titters.

Winchell, rebuffed in front of a beautiful woman and the writers who are watching, has an awkward exit. He says to Marilyn, "That's why these guys are still writing about kids' games. They never grow up."

"They've saved your old spot near the bar, Mr. Winchell," Cannon crows.

"If you need anything, just signal," Winchell says as he takes a step away. "Marilyn," he adds possessively.

Dan says, "You people will have to forgive me temporarily. I've got guests of my own who need attention."

When Marilyn lowers herself into her seat, between Cannon and Smith, she sees the entire crowd—except for the upper decks in left and right field—for the first time. A continuous, white-shirted mass—larger than any gathering she's ever seen, even the soldiers in Korea—all drawn to the verdant surface and focused on its perfect geometry.

Cannon leans back and arches an eyebrow at Smith, who responds with the barest nod. They haven't gotten rid of Winchell just because they dislike him. Marilyn Monroe appears to be their Old-timers' Day story, a story they

weren't looking forward to with much relish, with its predictable sentimentality and old-timer clichés. She has fallen
right into their laps, literally. And it would be a lot easier
to write without Winchell between them.

"First baseball game?" Smith chirps.

"Uh huh."

"Ever?" Cannon asks.

"Ever."

"That's almost un-American."

"You won't tell McCarthy, will you?"

"Depends how cooperative you intend to be, my dear.
I have in my hand a list of names." Cannon holds a small
piece of paper close against his chest.

"I've never seen so many people in one place. How
many do you think?"

Cannon cranes forward to see the upper decks. "Full
house. I'd say sixty-five. Maybe a bit more. Depends if
they break the fire code."

Marilyn looks confused.

"My learned colleague estimates approximately sixty-
five thousand to be in attendance," Smith translates.
"They'll announce the official figure during the regular
game."

Now Marilyn is more confused.

Cannon says, "They're going to introduce the geezers
first. . . ."

"Joe's not a geezer."

"In baseball, honey, you hit thirty, you start looking
seriously at your portfolio—if you've been intelligent
enough to have one; thirty-five, time for a retirement home;
forty, you're senile. Anyway, the old-timers from the Yankees and the Indians . . ."

"*Cleveland* Indians," Smith injects.

". . . will be introduced and play a couple of memory-filled innings. Mostly they'll try not to hurt themselves."

"I didn't think Joe was going to wear his costume."

Cannon cannot believe Marilyn does not really know the proper term. "Uniform. Word is that Joe's just going to make an appearance, wave to the crowd. After the aging ritual is over, the young-timers'll play an official game. We've got no real interest in that one, right, Red?"

"Correct, James. We're much too worldly wise to get excited about a bunch of energetic young recruits fighting for a pennant."

"Can I get you something?" Cannon asks.

Marilyn has been staring at the field hypnotically, its white lines, the subtle tones of green, the dirt, the clay; she can't make sense of his simple offer. She repeats, "Something?"

"Your typical baseball repast. Hot dog. Roasted peanuts. Bottle of beer."

Marilyn indicates gastric illness with glazed eyes and a curled lip.

"Something with a head on it for you, Mr. Smith?"

"Just for the sake of ambience, James." Smith winks wickedly. This is his time alone for questioning Marilyn. Later, he will return the favor to Cannon.

Cannon exists cheerily. Smith draws closer to Marilyn but does not intrude. "Most people wonder what it's like being married to a legend."

"They ought to ask Joe." She giggles, but she's upset with herself. It should have been a joke, but it didn't come across that way; it was too quick, too glib. She tries to smooth things. "Truth is, I knew the name Joe DiMaggio for a long time. I mean, I'd heard of it, but I didn't really know what he did every day as a baseball player or how he did it. Or where. This place is really something."

"They call it 'The House That Ruth Built'—Babe

Ruth—but Joe paid the rent on it for quite a few years." He likes that phrase and reminds himself to use it. Actually, he's surprised he hasn't used it already.

A voice over the public address system ricochets off stadium facades; the echoes make the words almost incomprehensible to Marilyn. She deciphers an occasional word. ". . . to welcome . . . proud to pre . . . ever to don . . ."

"So how does Joe seem to be adjusting to life after baseball? He was such a natural on the ball field, I always thought he'd have some trouble adapting to a world without games."

"I thought you were going to ask about adjusting to married life."

Smith smiles obligingly. "So how *is* Joe adjusting to married life?"

In the bleachers, people begin to stand. They rise in other sections of the stadium too. Marilyn has noticed a woman in a black dress, carrying flowers, being escorted to a microphone on the field below the press box. Marines marching with flags approach from center field. Marilyn hears distant music, but she doesn't associate it with *The Star-Spangled Banner*. Most of the press box contingent doesn't stand until "proudly we hailed."

Red Smith is holding his bifocals over his heart. Off to the side, Marilyn sees Cannon standing at lazy attention, a foaming cup of beer in partial salute. Behind, Winchell is rigid, his face earnest, his hand cocked perfectly at his brow, his eye fixed patriotically on Old Glory drooping in center field. Almost everyone else in the press box is adoring the red, white, and blond Marilyn Monroe, who quivers with repressed giggles at the absurdity of a ritual she hasn't experienced since high school.

When they sit down, Smith says, "So how is married life?"

"Married life and Joe's adjustment to retirement go hand in hand. After a very difficult period of adjustment, he's stopped taking his bat to bed with him." Her eyes flash to emphasize the punch line.

Momentary confusion crosses Smith's face.

"Let me ask you something. When you were a kid, did the other kids use to call you 'Pinky'?"

Smith turns beet red.

"I knew it. There was a kid in school named Smith when I lived in Bakersfield. His hair was that orange blond, like yours was, I'll bet. He wanted to be called 'Red' in the worst way—you're lucky—but he had skin the color cream gets when you shmoosh strawberries in it. 'Pinky' Smith, everybody called him. I loved that name. But it doesn't work if you've got two syllables in your last name. 'Pinky' Monroe would never work. 'Pinky' DiMaggio you can forget."

"I've never been to Bakersfield," Smith says weakly.

"But I was right about the 'Pinky,' wasn't I?"

"That you were, madam. Does Joe talk much about baseball?"

"With me, never. What would be the point? I don't know diddly. With some of his male friends, I guess. I really don't know. He must talk about it to someone. You can't do something for all those years and then just never mention it again. Can you?"

Smith shrugs. "How does it feel when someone asks for his autograph and not for yours?"

"Are you going to write about it?"

"Probably not, if it bothers you too much."

"Truthfully, it hasn't happened when we've been together. Oh yes, it has. In Japan. They seem to know Joe better there than me."

"Did it upset you when it happened, even a little?"

"Not particularly. It was Japan."

The garble of the PA becomes a recognizable rhythm: "Now a man who . . . drov-it-a-da . . . drov-it-a-da . . . three-twenty-four in nineteen forty . . . drov-it-a-da . . . drov-it . . ." A balding man or a bowlegged man or a paunchy one or a balding, bowlegged, paunchy man waddles toward the white line, waving his baseball cap. Appreciative applause accompanies the short, difficult run.

Smith scribbles in his notebook.

Marilyn peeks over, but the glyphs are indecipherable. "I know it's probably dumb to ask, since I've got nothing to compare it to, but just how good was Joe?"

Smith ponders. "Baseball's not like making movies. When you come up to bat, if you're successful one time out of three, that's a remarkable level of achievement. In Hollywood, make two dogs out of three and you're probably seeking other employment. Joe's been about as successful as anyone in the game. But with Joe, it's more. He not only bats well; he does every single thing well—fields, runs, throws, thinks—and even more, he does it all with class. And so incredibly natural." That's the second time she's heard the word applied to Joe. She touches the faint scar under her chin, where Goldfedder made his little adjustment. "And he's done it all on the best stage there could possibly be—New York."

"So who would he be like in pictures? I mean if you had to make a comparison."

Smith thinks while three former Cleveland Indians are introduced. Marilyn appreciates his studiousness. "I guess I'd have to say Gable, at least as far as the general public is concerned."

Marilyn smiles with satisfaction.

Jimmy Cannon, who has been wandering the press

box making bad jokes about Smith's inability to get it up, senses it's time to return for his story. He kids his way back to his place. Smith greets him with, "You've got to watch this one, James. She asks more questions than she answers. Wanted to know who DiMag would be if he were a movie star."

"William Powell," Cannon shoots. "The way he carries himself. How smooth he is all the time, never gets thrown, unflappable. But not phony, natural like the Thin Man. Yeah, William Powell."

"I said Gable."

"Yeah, maybe Gable, I can see that, but I prefer Powell. You know, that's a good angle for a column. Who would some athlete be if he was an actor, or a singer, a politician, a writer. I like that. Thanks, Mrs. D. . . ."

"We're not using that moniker, James, even in jest."

"Oh, sor-ree. But I can see Walter and me rolling on the floor for the right to that idea."

Standing, Smith says, "James, I hereby bequeath it to you and your quicker-witted, shorter-attentioned readers. Excuse me for a minute."

Cannon slides into the vacated chair, speaking before he's seated. "So how're you gonna be known? Not as Marilyn DiMaggio."

"Not unless I'm standing over a spaghetti sauce all day with three kids pulling at my apron. Of course, I'd do it all real natural. Somehow, I don't see that."

"Only three? I figure Giuseppe would want six at least."

"Mr. Smith just told me one out of three is a great percentage for a batter." She looks delectably coy.

"Yeah, but it also depends on who's pitching and who's calling balls and strikes."

Her coyness begins to take the form of helplessness. "Mr. Cannon, I don't know the first thing about the game. Maybe you could give me some lessons."

Cannon closes his Mr. Magoo eyes. "No-o-o. I don't think anyone has to give you lessons about anything." He likes her enormously.

"Cannon. That's an Irish name, right?"

He nods. "County Kerry. They tell me it was once Concannon, but the 'Con' got blue-penciled. There are some would say I've still got more than a bit of the 'Con' in me."

"I've known some Black Irishmen, but they didn't look like you."

His eyebrows are dark and bushy. What had been a full head of wiry black hair has become two soft Brillo pads above his ears, reaching out toward one another across his pate. "Only Irish on my father's side. My mother, God rest her, was French. Near the Italian border. I got her coloring."

"That explains it."

"Explains what?"

"Why you look so much like an Irish frog."

Cannon croaks a laugh. Marilyn cannot know he hasn't done it intentionally; it's his rarely heard true laugh, not the familiar cynical chuckle. "I can see why Joe likes you." He offers her a Lucky Strike. She's tempted but refuses. He lights up. "I don't"—he shakes out the match and tosses it behind him—"I don't mean to be making a big thing of it, but it's always been a tough deal, two great stars making a go of marriage."

"That's what they all say. Maybe I'm dumb, but I don't see a problem. I really don't. Maybe if we were both in movies, it would be a problem, but we come from such different worlds. Joe is all for my career. He says he's retired absolutely; he didn't even really want to come back here today. He had to be talked into it, the dear. He sort of wanted my permission."

"And you gave it."

"We're here."

"And kids someday?"

"Someday. I know Joe wants them. I've always wanted them." Her voice has a throb in it. She wants Cannon to know she's sincere. She's afraid he detects a false note, which, in fact, he does. "But not while we're both still so prominent."

"Honey, don't you realize you'll always be prominent?"

"Maybe, but not working prominent—that's the difference."

On the field, old Yankees are being introduced and greeted with louder, more sustained applause. Marilyn is surprised at the color of their uniforms, creamy with thin black stripes. "Oh," she says, "they're so different."

"What?"

"The uniforms."

"Home team always wears white. The visitors have gray. The Yankees are known for their pinstripes. Didn't you ever see a picture of Joe in his uniform?"

She must have. Marilyn thinks but can't be sure.

"Where've you been all your life, anyway?"

"Not where they've been playing baseball."

"You think something like that will affect being married to a Joe DiMaggio?"

Did the other guy—what was his name? Pinky, Pinky Smith—ask that question? How'd she answer it? She shrugs. "Joe's moving on to other things."

"Like what?"

Marilyn wants the questions to be over. "He's at meetings all the time. Business. He has all sorts of financial opportunities."

"Financial opportunities," Cannon repeats flatly, scribbling with a thick pencil in his notebook.

"I'm sure he'll make an announcement when he decides what he intends to do." She wants it over.

"Make an announcement?" Cannon cocks an eye.

"Easier that way. He's using some of my press people."

"That doesn't seem to be . . . that isn't Joe's style."

Marilyn flashes a weary smile. "We'll be going downtown right after this. I'll be announcing a new project. Joe'll be right with me. We're going to do lots of things together."

Cannon realizes that Joe DiMaggio will probably disappear very soon after he appears on the field. Immediately, he excuses himself and leaves Marilyn to gaze at the curious ritual on the field below.

Cannon collects Smith—he'll share this scoop—and leaving by opposite ends of the press box, they make for the elevator. They will not be missed by most of their rivals, because Marilyn remains an incomparable distraction. A few writers venture over to her and try a polite question or two. Marilyn answers stylishly.

Winchell, noticing that Marilyn's been left alone, comes over. "How'd you get rid of the Gold Dust Twins?"

"Just suggested that Joe would probably be leaving in a few minutes."

"You're something." He whistles. "You know, I used to be one of the stiffs up here. Boy, am I glad I got myself out of this rut. You have any idea of what these guys make, I mean the average ones?"

Marilyn doesn't want to guess. "Walter, was Joe one of the best there ever was?"

"Not *one* of—*the* best. Ever. Was. Is. And will be."

"And if he was in movies, who would he be?"

Winchell doesn't bother to think. "Hasn't ever been one in his class."

A peculiar expression clouds Marilyn's face as she turns back to the field. She is proud of her husband. She is bothered that she must share him with so many strangers. She wishes she could wrap his past, his whole baseball history, up in her arms and carry it to some secret place.

Something about the way Joe holds his cigarette—tightly at the very nub, as though trying to pinch off its smoldering— tells Marilyn her husband is annoyed. He smiles grudgingly with his lips closed at well-wishers. The hinge of his jaw pulses with anger. Sensing his volcanic rage, everyone about gives Joe DiMaggio space in the crowded corridor.

Joe beckons Winchell closer with his cigarette. Winchell whispers into the taller man's ear. His narrowed eyes, as he talks, sweep the area. Joe says nothing but appears to be chewing with his lips closed.

Marilyn suspects that Winchell is reporting on her behavior in the press box.

There are disembodied roars from the stands above them from time to time that tremble underfoot like early quake warnings. Dan, the man who owns the team, steps off the elevator and approaches Marilyn. He offers his hand. "They tell me you made quite a hit up there."

"It was easy. They're nice guys underneath all that hard-boiled stuff."

"It's a shame you and Joe can't stay for the game. You might be our good luck charm. Needless to say, you're welcome back here anytime."

Marilyn is slightly distracted. Over Dan's shoulder she

sees Winchell nodding. Something's been decided. She's curious about what it is. "Thanks. Maybe we will." He's taken her hand in both of his.

Joe motions for the driver, who listens to instructions and then makes for the Cadillac. Finally, Joe holds Marilyn hard in his gaze for a long moment. He drops his cigarette and rubs it out with the toe of his shoe. She shrugs and mouths the words, "What? What?" His eyes tighten; a quick movement of his head is how he beckons her.

Marilyn has already learned the signs of his discontent: the tightening of his body, the cold possession of the space about him, the withdrawal of self. At first, she was sympathetic to the incredible pain his stomach ulcers caused him, but since Joe does nothing to deal with his anger, her sympathy has begun to dissipate. She knows there will be a scene in the car. Probably some hard words.

Acting appropriately cheerful and respectful of her husband's triumph, Marilyn Monroe approaches Joe DiMaggio. "It was wonderful how they liked you."

"I told Walter to take a cab. I don't want to do our laundry with everyone around."

"We send all our laundry out, honey."

A bad joke. DiMaggio stabs his wife with his eyes. His lips quiver.

Dan moves in front of DiMaggio and offers his hand. "We're really grateful you decided to come home, even for a couple of hours, Joe. The welcome mat is always . . . but you know that. And since this place always needs some prettying, don't come alone." His smile embraces Mrs. DiMaggio.

Joe escorts Marilyn to the exit. Security guards and grounds crew men and vendors wave and wish him good luck. He waves back without smiling. Most of the people who see Joe and Marilyn will feel touched by something special whenever they recreate the moment.

A great roar that Joe recognizes as appreciation of a Yankee home run greets them as the Cadillac pulls up outside. They enter the car without a word. The chauffeur closes the passenger door, gets behind the wheel, and awaits orders. "Drop me at the hotel."

Marilyn knows it's not a mistake; still, she corrects. "But we're supposed to . . ."

"I'm going to the hotel."

The chauffeur drives slowly through the crowded parking lot, his eyes framed in the rearview mirror. Not a word is uttered until the car is deep in the shadows of the Jerome Avenue el. Marilyn says, "So what did he tell you?"

Joe looks out the opposite window.

"Are you gonna pout all the way back to the hotel, or do you want to work this out?"

That she calls his rage pouting angers Joe further. He remains mute.

"Okay. We don't have to discuss a damn thing. All I want to know is what did he tell you? I'm entitled to that much at least. Joe. You know I'm entitled."

He looks down at his folded hands, and Marilyn knows that he will talk to her, but maybe not for a while.

She leaves silence and stares at the tenements that roll across her window. She thinks she has a sense of the lives that are lived behind those walls; almost immediately, she realizes how foolish she is to believe that. No one can really know anything about the secret life of anybody else. She is aware of smoke surrounding her. Joe has lit a cigarette.

She doesn't remember crossing the river and is surprised that they are already in Manhattan when Joe speaks. "It's one thing when you do it out there with your Hollywood friends, but this is . . ." Joe doesn't say what it is, but the sense is that New York is his territory.

As she asks the question, Marilyn sees the chauffeur's eyes on her in the mirror. "When I do what?"

"Being so cute with everybody all the time, so coy, so teasing. Walter told me what it was like up there."

She doesn't want to have to respond. She sighs. The eyes look away for a second or two. "It's just teasing. A little fun. People expect it from me. Everyone knows it doesn't mean a thing."

"Hell it doesn't. Flirting is flirting. You don't even have to do it—it's just become a habit with you. You wouldn't even know how to just be with people if you had to."

"It's perfectly innocent. Who does it hurt?" Dumb question. Joe snorts. The eyes are on her again.

"You can't do something like that at the ball park. You don't do it when we're at Pop's house; well, this place is an extension of my family, for Christ's sake. Everyone here knows me. Some of them have known me for almost twenty years. And my wife acts like a . . ." Joe sees the driver's eyes dart to the road; he snuffs his cigarette in the tray.

"You know like what? Like a movie star, who people expect to act in a certain way. They'd hate it if I acted the way you wanted. But I'll do it. You just tell me how you want me to act, and I'll do it." She boxes her hands as though shaping a marquee. "Come see Marilyn Monroe in her most demanding role. Directed by Joseph Paul DiMaggio." Now she becomes a reporter, thrusting an invisible microphone in Joe's face. "So tell me, Mr. DiMaggio, what were you trying for in your wife's performance?"

His lips purse. He doesn't want to answer. He says, "Just a little bit of dignity."

The eyes in the rearview mirror flash briefly. Is it approval?

Red Smith's column in Monday morning's *Trib* is headed THE MISSUS ATTENDS HUBBY'S WELCOME HOME PARTY.

The Missus came by the Bronx ballyard where her hubby used to work. The Missus wasn't particularly impressed. She thought it was a nice place to work, so green and all, but since she wasn't his Missus when he used to work here, the place just didn't mean as much to her as, say, a Hollywood studio, where she has been used to punching a time-clock. She was sure Hubby was a lot happier now.

The Missus said, "I really can't picture Joe in those funny pants." She said, "I think the gray uniforms are a lot *chic-er* (yes, she said *chic-er*). Did Joe always wear those funny stripes?"

The Missus wondered what number her hubby wore when he was working. Did he wear the same number every day? She imagined it would be a high number—45 or 53, she guessed—because she heard he was once a pretty important player. Imagine that—"pretty important"—as though we'll ever see anyone worthy of Number 5 in Yankee pinstripes again.

The Missus said she wanted to apologize for a comment she made to the press after she entertained our boys in Korea. The one where she wished Joe could only know what it felt like to be cheered by thousands of men. The Missus said she wasn't thinking clearly when she said that. Hearing the cheers in the Bronx ballyard yesterday for the Yankee old-timers and especially for her hubby, the Missus admitted she had been dead wrong.

Her hubby, Joseph Paul DiMaggio, stepped onto the field where he had worked so meticulously and fruitfully for so many years. Unlike his co-workers, he did not don his old work clothes, did not show the Missus the form we all used to admire. He preferred, he said afterward, ". . . to let the other fellows be appreciated today." Of course, it was more. "Uniforms," he once told a younger reporter, "are for playing the game. When you can no longer play it properly, you should become a spectator and appreciate those who can."

The Missus said, "I'd like to see him run out there in his costume. It'll help me picture the man everyone seems to know but me." The Missus, you see, had never been to a baseball game in her life. She still hasn't been to one.

After the old-timers—many of whom ran onto the field with hang-overs (at least above their belts)—lined up along the first and third base lines and received the applause their careers deserved, we were asked to direct our attention to the Yankee dugout.

The crowd sensed something special. Someone special. A man who had given their dreams a distinct shape, their lives a general sense of direction. If nothing else, they measured their years along with his accomplishments. As his past heroics were slowly recounted, from great to greater to greatest, anticipation grew.

Like a wind that builds in stages from breeze to gust to a roaring nor'easter, emotion grew. Like the sea building from swells to pounding, pulsing, over-arching waves, roars began to rebound in the Bronx ballyard. It shook the very superstructure of Yankee Stadium—the House that Ruth built but Joe D. maintained. Out of the chaos a chant—the spontaneous idea of a few—became an insistent plea that drowned out the public address system. *Joe D., Joe D., Joe D.* . . . Even the Missus knew that here was something, someone, special.

The Missus saw her hubby step out of his old office in a double-breasted gray business suit, raise a slender arm and turn slowly, appreciatively, to every single seat in the house. Just one graceful turn, then he disappeared. Joe D. Joltin' Joe. The Yankee Clipper. The standard against which all future workers in center field—make that all ballplayers on any field, anywhere—should be measured. Gone.

Yesterday, the Missus could not have missed the high regard in which her hubby was held by the thousands who made it to the Bronx ballyard and the millions the stadium could not possibly hold.

The Missus said, "I guess I'll have to learn a little more about baseball."

She was corrected: "About Joe DiMaggio."

Jimmy Cannon devotes almost all of his Monday afternoon *Post* column to Joe. It is in his distinctive "Nobody Asked Me, But . . ." style.

He opens with: "Nobody asked me, but . . . the reason a classic stays a classic is always the same no matter what—simplicity, skill, sense of proportion. You see it in all the classic Italian artists—Leonardo da Vinci, Michelangelo Buonarroti, Sandro Botticelli, and, most recently, Giuseppe DiMaggio."

Neither Marilyn nor Joe read those columns, but Winchell did. He wasn't surprised that Cannon and Smith had set Marilyn up. He couldn't wait to tell Joe how badly his wife had been treated by both of them.

He got a particular satisfaction from the last item in Cannon's column, which was: "Nobody asked me, but . . . did you ever notice how famous sex symbols are usually great with figures (especially their own) but hardly ever really know the score?"

CHAPTER SIX

A Dangerous, Sultry Night—With and Without Heroes

LIGHTS

ESQUIRE: Marilyn, is your life as glamorous as most people would assume?

MONROE: Absolutely.

ESQUIRE: Don't tease us. When you're working, for example, is Marilyn Monroe's existence as exciting as it's cracked up to be?

MONROE: More. Working or playing. Exciting. Glamorous. Stimulating. Fascinating. Thrilling. Pleasurable. You name it, it's all of those things and more. Nothing, absolutely nothing, ever goes wrong in my life. I couldn't be more sincere.

CAMERA

Six cars from Midtown North precinct had cut off Lexington Avenue at Fifty-first and Fifty-second streets. Blue-white flood-lights gave the street a movie-set feel. Even late on a sweltering Tuesday night, traffic was heavy: cabdrivers giving the cops a tough time. The roadblock wasn't a major inconvenience, but the street swarmed with people, so the cabbies felt obliged to perform for their out-of-town fares. The cops were performing too.

More than a thousand onlookers were already there, lined up on the east side of Lexington behind police sawhorses, for no other reason than to glimpse Marilyn. Unless you owned an air conditioner, it was just too humid, too hot, to sleep.

The director of The Seven Year Itch, *Billy Wilder, didn't like this kind of location shoot; he told all the assistants to make sure the site would be kept secret for as long as possible. Impossible. For three days a work crew had been very visible, installing high-powered blowers under the sidewalk grating on Lexington, right in front of the Chase Bank entrance. And for three days word had circulated around town that something big was up. When it turned out the "big" was Marilyn, things got almost out of hand. The one thousand spectators at eleven o'clock doubled by midnight and just about doubled again by one.*

Wilder was happy with Marilyn's performance. She would be a very different person when they worked together in Some Like It Hot.

ACTION

The crowd is festive even though the digital temperature on a building at the corner wavers between 85 and 86 degrees.

Hot dog and soda vendors have rolled their wagons up from midtown and over from Central Park. Extra police have arrived, but the crowd is fairly well behaved and the cops are an adjunct to the celebration. Periodically, a mysterious bullhorn asks for quiet and the crowd hushes, but nothing happens. Each time, the street babel builds again.

Rumors about the delays circulate. There are problems with Marilyn. She's in her trailer, refusing to come out for a variety of bizarre reasons. No, no, it's not that: Marilyn hasn't even shown up yet. They're out looking for her all over the city.

None of it is true. Marilyn has been in her trailer the whole while, waiting to be called. Wilder wants her inside because the trailer is air-conditioned. The police want her to stay out of sight in order to help control the crowd.

The actual problem is technical. The below-ground blowers, which worked fine in a tryout late this afternoon, just can't rev up to full power. The electricians have tried everything and concluded that there is so much power being used in the neighborhood the motors can't reach maximum output. The crowd hushed without urging when Marilyn's stand-in stepped over the grating and her skirt billowed up to her knees, occasionally showing a flash of thigh. Nowhere near the force they were going to need.

The skirt was supposed to billow up to the waist and threaten to carry her off. Marilyn was to struggle to keep it down and in the process show lots of dimples and panty. That kind of force just can't happen with these blowers. One of the mayor's assistants placed a call to a Con Ed big shot, who promised to send a crew right over. Everyone has been waiting for the truck.

Wilder walks over to a group of VIPs cordoned off just behind the cameras. During the delay, they've been in and out of an air-conditioned office in the bank, where cold drinks are served. Joe DiMaggio, his pal Winchell, and the mayor, Robert A. Wagner, are the ones the crowd has recognized.

Wilder has suspected from the outset the scene would eventually have to be shot on a soundstage, but the brain trust at Fox insisted on this location. They kept repeating "authenticity." Wilder kept hearing "free publicity." There was a time when he would have fought it, but after making the point that "authenticity" was absurd since the script actually called for Times Square, he acquiesced. He enjoyed seeing his New York friends, getting some European ambience and food, hitting the art galleries.

After a polite visit with the celebrities, Billy Wilder works the street. He schmoozes with the crew, with some of the cops; he approaches the edge of the crowd. He puffs on his long Cuban cigar and asks lots of questions. He says to a sound man, "For this we came three thousand miles."

"I'm originally from Jersey. So I get to see some people and eat that good home cooking. But am I getting good sound? Sure, if you call a subway running under the street every ten minutes good sound! You see what I'm saying?"

"I know, I know. And they complain whenever I go over budget." He asks a patrolman in shirtsleeves, "Do you fellows get paid overtime for something like this?"

"This is my regular shift. Some of the other guys, they're workin' a double shift. They make out."

"The crowd, it seems not so unruly."

"Good crowd, good crowd. Say, can I ask you somethin'?"

"Of course." Wilder anticipates the request.

"You know Marilyn?"

"A *bissel*."

"Any way I can get her autograph?"

"For a minute, I thought you were going to ask if I could get you into Marilyn's trailer." Wilder leers.

It takes the cop a second to understand that Wilder has made a joke. His laugh is forced.

Wilder asks an old man at the edge of the crowd, "So tell me, this mayor you've got, is he going to turn out to be a La Guardia?"

"Hah. La Guardia. Those days are dead like silent movies."

Wilder says, "Silent movies, they may not be so dead. You don't see a sound movie being made here, do you?"

"So what's the trouble? Marilyn being temperamental or something?"

Wilder doesn't deny the premise. He does, however, realize he ought to drop in on his star and begins to make his way up the street to her trailer.

Inside, Marilyn is ready, has been for more than an hour. Her voice coach, Natasha Lytess, is crocheting, which prompts Marilyn, reclining with a thin volume in her lap, to say, "You look ominous, like Madame Lafarge in *Tale of Two Cities*."

"De. *De*farge. And she was knitting. I'm crocheting."

"La. De. Knitting. Crocheting. What's the difference? You know what I mean."

Lytess raises an eyebrow dramatically. The gesture takes the place of words. Marilyn is edgy, ready to shoot; best to leave her alone.

"I was just saying, you sit there all tense, crocheting, whatever, looking like someone who's getting ready to get even with the world. So what's bugging you?"

"Me? Bugging me? Nothing. You're the one. And with an easy night. No lines. Almost like posing for still shots."

Marilyn's eyes laugh. "Yeah, but what's my motivation?"

"Showing your *tush*."

"But I have to show it and stay in character."

A knock on the door interrupts the dueling. Lytess says, "Come."

Wilder rather likes Marilyn; he detests Lytess, as he does anyone who comes between him and his actors. Lytess's fingers spin even faster. "You know," Wilder says to Marilyn as he steps in, "what the electrician told me? He's local. He says, 'Da skoit don't woik. Da blower ain't got no oomph, so da skoit don't woik.' A touch of pure New York."

"How much longer? The waiting is starting to get to me."

"Sandra just went out to try it. Her skirt fluttered and died. I'm not hopeful. I knew all along we'd have to do it in Hollywood. Let's give them another half hour and shoot something even if da skoit don't woik. What are you reading there?"

"Rilke."

"I met him." Marilyn's eyes widen. "He came to Vienna when I was a boy. He was a guest at the home of one of my father's colleagues. We were rounded up and forced to go. Of course, later I bragged about it. What's that you have?" Marilyn hands over the slim volume. "Ah, yes, *Journal of My Other Self*. It's solid. The mystical Rilke I can do without. I hope you don't let anyone see you reading this stuff."

"Why?"

"Kiss of death for a star—intellectual improvement." Lytess clears her throat and glances over at Marilyn. Wilder notices. "I saw what they did to Chaplin. The patronizing, the mockery, because he tried to improve himself. Good old American hypocrisy. If you're from no background, they tell you all the time, improve your mind. But come from nowhere, make a great success, and then try to do it, you know what they say? Well, you know."

"Who's *they?*" Marilyn asks.

"All of them. The studio heads especially. They'll get their little assistant thises and aides-de-that to spread the word. You've seen it. You're nobody's fool. Don't underestimate them, Marilyn my dear. They know a star who wants to be a human being is a dangerous commodity. Independence means they lose control, maybe control of other stars too. So they send out the word: Slap this one, knock her down. In your case, before she gets too big."

"So what are you telling her? Not to read Rilke, not to aspire?" Lytess asks in a cooing voice.

Without acknowledging, Wilder says, "Aspire, of course, aspire. Just do it quietly, privately."

"What was he like?" Marilyn asks.

"Who?"

"Rilke."

"I can't trust my memory. I was so young. I'm not sure if I recall from the photographs that were taken or what my mother told me. Or from the actual situation itself. I see it all in sepia." Wilder takes a long puff on his cigar and realizes he ought not to release the smoke in the trailer; he goes to the door and blows it into Lexington Avenue. "I remember him frail, his hair disheveled. Sickly, definitely sickly. I don't remember a thing he said, but he was the first famous author I ever met in person, so I went and read all his books. The mystical junk, I didn't understand a thing. *Letters to a Young Poet*, though, is important; I still look at it from time to time."

"That's the one I've heard about."

"I'll have a copy at your hotel in the morning before you leave."

"About wanting to learn things—it's not something that just popped into my head. It's what I always wanted. Once, when I was a girl, I was staying with my mother. She took me to a party someone at her studio threw, someone important. She didn't know whether to bring me or not. It must have been a Sunday afternoon. I remember a big lawn, a swimming pool, but nobody was swimming, I don't think. Nobody famous was there. It was just the way the people carried themselves. No one was crude, no one was awful. I saw in the library walls of books with sliding ladders that went all the way around. I connected the books to what made those people act that way. The families I'd been staying with, almost always someone drank too much or cursed or was generally awful. These people were really civilized. I can't tell you how much that impressed me."

Lytess clicks her needles and flashes a warning toward Marilyn. *Don't reveal too much.*

"The hunger to be civilized, my dear—I wish more people had it."

"That's what it was, exactly." Marilyn goes quiet and works her way thoughtfully to a realization. She is a person of different hungers. When she wanted to become a model, only that hunger occupied her consciousness. Then the hunger to be a singer. The hunger to get into movies came next. That's where Johnny Hyde came in. Then the hunger to be a star. This new thing, this trying to become a complete person, it wasn't really a hunger yet. An appetite. Maybe it would grow. "Three years ago, I took some courses at UCLA. Art history, the Renaissance. Modern poetry."

Three hard raps on the door shake the whole trailer. A voice calls, "They're getting something, Mr. Wilder."

"Something. What's something?" he says, opening the door wider.

Wilder's assistant director explains quietly, "Not quite full power on the blowers but better than before."

"You mean da skoit woiks now?"

"Just about."

"Okay, then, your presence is requested among the populace. Next time we talk, my dear, I'll tell you about the time I interviewed Sigmund Freud."

"Freud?" Marilyn squeals like a Tab Hunter fan.

During the hour while the Con Ed men worked below the subway grating, the crowd's festive attitude began to ebb. Now, with the truck pulling out, new lights flashing on, the camera, sound, and lighting crews taking their positions, creating an air of readiness, the crowd knows something, finally something important, is about to happen. An expectant hush rolls down from Fifty-second Street.

An assistant director is about to make an announcement through a bullhorn, asking for quiet. Wilder stops him. "It's too soon. They'll make a fuss with Marilyn. Let them."

The crowd near Fifty-second Street is the first to see her coming through the door of the trailer and down the steps. Their reaction sounds like something between a roar and a gasp. Whatever it is, it gets picked up by other people, who don't see her yet; it intensifies as they do.

Marilyn is transformed, not at all the unsure culture seeker worried about an uncertain future. Already the still photographers are clicking away. A couple of them are studio guys, most are from the newspapers and the wire services—this is the advance publicity the studio seeks for its star and its film. Marilyn obliges. Marilyn poses—she can't help herself—walking along the sidewalk in high-heeled exuberance; she percolates playful sexuality. Marilyn leans against a building, a foot pressed against the wall, her knee angled forward, her hands behind her back, the girl waiting; then, bending forward from the waist, showing bubbles of breast above her skintight halter.

Marilyn changes her expression slightly for each pose, resetting her eyes, mouth, cheeks, chin in different configurations, but each set makes the same statement, offers the same dreamy promise. Each is a man's irreducible desire: serve me, understand me, stimulate me, touch me, console me, help me.

The white dress is a stunner—a low-cut halter top, severely cinched at the waist, with a pleated skirt so full it gives the impression of being slit almost to the hip. It is just diaphanous enough to show the outlines of her body's turns and curls, just opaque enough to be acceptable on the midtown streets of New York. Marilyn loves exploring that playful line between licit and licentious; the dress encourages her to tiptoe along the line. She feels perfectly comfortable in it and gives the photographers more than they hoped for.

The crowd has started to chant. *Mar-il-lyn* . . . *Mar-il-lyn* . . . *Mar-il-lyn* . . . It's an eerie street song because it isn't in unison; rather, it's like a voiced wave that rolls down Lexington Avenue and rebounds against itself. Marilyn loves it.

It is coming up to 1:35. The crowd has grown huge. Marilyn and the little director have walked to a mark on the sidewalk; a cameraman has climbed the crane, the crew that will roll the number one camera on tracks along the curb is in place; the great overhead arc lights have been turned to highest intensity. Everyone senses impending action; it's not really necessary for the assistant with a bullhorn to ask for quiet, but he does: "Could we have some quiet, please, folks. We're about to shoot."

Wilder tells Marilyn, "This scene is *strudel*. Imagine it is very, very warm, even warmer than right now. You're smoldering. Looking for a bit of adventure. A small diversion. What the hell, you're young, bored, it's been hot for weeks, you've been trapped in the city. . . ."

Marilyn touches Wilder's arm. "I know, Billy."

"Here, you'll start here. We'll track you to that entrance, where the marble facing begins. You look around, stop, lean against . . ." Marilyn stops him again.

Something incredible happened to Marilyn in her last film. Almost every time she had been on camera up until then, everything had been a blur to her. Not because things were happening so fast. It was the confusion in her head, impossible to throw off, to tune out and find the calm she knew she needed, the peaceful center all her teachers and coaches talked about.

She tried breathing exercises. Yoga. Repeating a phrase to slow herself down. To no avail. She never found the control point. Then it happened, or almost happened. In a scene in *All About Eve*, while working with Bette Davis, a scene that never got into the final film. It called for Marilyn's character, an ambitious starlet, to lean over a table in a fancy restaurant and, while making it seem an accident, deliberately tip a pot of tea into Davis's lap. Then, in an effort to help her victim, Marilyn was to knock a chocolate cake on top of the mess. "Don't tell me you won't enjoy doing this to me," Davis said dryly.

"I won't, but I'll try to make it seem that way."

"You've got it wrong, honey. You've got to become that obnoxious little bitch. Or I should say, she's got to become you. At least that part of you that hates my guts for being the star of this opus. So enjoy it. Just remember what they're paying me and what they're paying you. If you do, the camera will catch it. Maybe then we can get it in a take or two. I won't have to have that *schmutz* thrown at me all day."

Bette Davis was, in fact, telling her to find her character within herself rather than by trying to invent her. By film's end, when Marilyn really did begin to understand what that meant, a sense of control came over her. It was the end of scenes going by in a blur for her. Marilyn expected her scene with Davis to be acted at half speed when she saw the rushes. They weren't; they were perfectly normal. Tonight Marilyn feels an excess of clarity, as though things are happening in slow motion and she can see to the heart of everything. She knows things about the girl she's playing she never knew before.

The girl she plays is a little younger than Marilyn, even freer, without any separation between whim and action; she is what Marilyn can be, has been, whenever that nagging sense of having to please leaves her. It leaves her now.

Marilyn stands calmly on the sidewalk, adjusting her hem. She knows precisely how this girl walks, what she needs, what she fears. A hairdresser sprays and primps a curl into place. The tracking camera is poised. Wilder has his arm in the air.

"Hey, slut."

No one is sure they've heard right. Marilyn's concentration is hardly broken.

The second time, it's louder. "Hey, slut."

Marilyn notices faces turning away. She looks into the street and sees a large man coming forward.

The man is in shirtsleeves. He wears yellow suspenders and moves in an ambling gait like Robert Mitchum's. The cops do not react; maybe they think he's part of the scene. "Got enough of you. Don't need no more sluts."

Marilyn senses danger and steps back, the calm gone. The man begins to blur. Still he comes ahead. "Fucking slut." He is halfway across the street.

From the darkness of the crowd behind the approaching man, another man, tall, thin, with glasses, his hair slightly wild, jumps the barrier and closes ground in an awkward run. "Hey, stop it," he shouts. "Get back. They're making a movie here." He approaches the lout but is pushed away effortlessly by three fingers to his chest. "Hey, what the hell are you trying to do?" And is brushed aside as easily. His glasses fall to the pavement and shatter.

Cops, first two, then two more, subdue the drunk with great effort—partially because they can't use unlimited force in front of the crowd—and wrestle him off beyond the barrier and into a distant doorway around the corner of Fifty-second Street. The drunk remains belligerent. The cops restrain and cajole.

Natasha Lytess arrives at the milling scene with a police captain the mayor has sent. She points a finger inches from the drunk's nose. "I saw it all. He shouted insults at Miss Monroe, caused all the trouble. He ought to be arrested. Miss Monroe is prepared to press charges."

"He's completely soused," a patrolman tells the captain.

"Get him out of here. Walk him down the street. Watch him, don't let him back."

The big man belches like a whale as they take him away. Arriving photographers pursue the cops and the drunk. They've got a front-page photo in the making. Marilyn's protector has picked up his glasses and melted quietly into the crowd.

Marilyn remains agitated until Lytess returns and tells her that things have been straightened out.

"So how is he?"

Lytess knows she's not asking about the drunk. "Fine, I guess."

"You guess?"

"He disappeared. He must have slipped into the crowd. Nobody saw him. I'm sure he's all right."

"Really?"

"Really. Don't be concerned."

After a reasonable delay, Wilder once again quiets the crowd. Marilyn is calm and instinctively sure again of who she has to become for the camera. Shortly before Wilder calls for quiet and the scene is struck and marked, Marilyn begins to strut blithely down the street, her body on fire again, the dress dancing with her skin, a girl on the make.

She is too young, too full of lusty health, to give way completely to the night heat. In fact, she smolders right along with it, ready for something cool and different. She takes slow, regular steps over the sidewalk, swinging her hips carelessly; her heels kick a Latin rhythm. Eyes lowered, she checks the street for action. There is none. That's utterly impossible, especially if this is supposed to be Times Square around midnight. But Hollywood has claimed this street, so it is sham reality, a condition Marilyn feels comfortable with. Eventually there will be music to make the reality convincing.

If any of these shots are going to be used after cutting—which is unlikely—sound will be laid over, so Wilder is free to cue Marilyn from behind the camera. "Slow, slower. Get ready for the train, get . . ." A subway is supposed to be roaring beneath Times Square; its rumble will cause the girl to stop, listen, and move above the grate, where a great whoosh of air will blow that pleated skirt up way above her waist and cause a memorable cooling. "Listen for it. That's right. The grate. Fine. Move over."

Five stories above the street, a window in an older office building has been thrown wide open. A cleaning woman leans out unnoticed. She observes the action below for a long moment. She shouts to the crowd, "Who's that?" Heads swivel upward. Marilyn remains undistracted; the scene continues.

"All praise to the Lord," the overhead voice declares. A long wad of ticker tape leaves her hand and floats downward in the still air like rope sinking in the ocean. The crowd looks up and begins to buzz. As the paper nears the ground, heads reach for it. It is caught, pulled apart.

The blowers rev up. Air currents lick the back of her legs. Marilyn stretches like a cat. The air gathers force. Her skirt billows out. Her face reflects pure pleasure. The cool zephyr reaches its greatest force, and the girl senses her dress might blow straight over her head. The force is not quite what it's supposed to be. Fine as the air feels, the role calls for Marilyn to become aware of her flying dress and demurely try to keep as much of it down as possible while wishing it would blow off. She does this in a way—patting floating fabric here and there—that makes modesty a sexual exercise.

Her light-colored underpants stretch around the smooth globes of her bottom. The tight V in the front is a slice of pleasure pie for any boy or old man—and every male in between—capable of dreaming of a dessert.

Wilder likes what Marilyn is doing, not for what he actually has but for what he knows he'll get under studio conditions. He hollers, "Cut. That's lovely, darling. Let's just pick it up again from where she steps over the blowers."

Without losing hold of the character, Marilyn waits about three minutes for the camera to set up and tiptoes onto the grating again. The imaginary train roars beneath her. Her skirt flies up. She teases the air, her clothing, herself.

Three more times she shoots the scene for Wilder. Each time, he's satisfied. Each time, he sees something different that he likes. When they shoot in Hollywood, he'll try to work all of it in.

After the final take, Marilyn stands over the grating, the blowers blasting away, posing for the still photographers. The publicity department's photographer, Ed Mraz, has no idea his shot will become an American icon. Or that a twenty-five-foot-high version will look down on Times Square for much of 1955.

While the photographers are still popping flashes, Wilder signals to his electrician, and the large overhead arc lights crackle and die. The carpenters begin dismantling the tracks along the curb. Other members of the crew are lowering a camera from the overhead crane, while the ground-level cameras are rolled toward the truck. *Such an expense,* Wilder thinks. *Such effort, such a waste of energy, of time. For what?*

The crowd, seeing an end to its diversion, begins to chant "Marilyn," but halfheartedly, and it dissolves into individual calls, goodbyes really. Assistant directors are telling the police that's it, they can have their street back. The police, in turn, send word up and down the sidewalks. The clock flashes 2:09. People begin to disperse. The city's heat wave will continue for another week.

Marilyn poses for stills even while the packing begins, fighting her swelling skirt yet one more time. Her expression distills the essence of female playfulness, the foretease that whets appetites for something more substantial.

Close by, workmen wait to lift the grate, to go below and remove the blowers. They stare at Marilyn, disbelieving her real-life beauty. They would like to touch her, not sexually, only to confirm that she exists. Actually, they are afraid of her. They will talk about these moments for the rest of their lives.

Finally, Lytess, hovering close by, says politely but firmly, "I think that must be all. Miss Monroe really must leave." She throws a robe over Marilyn's shoulders.

"Marilyn, how about a shot with Joe?" one suggests.

"With the mayor?" says another.

"How about the three of you?"

"Sure, if they're willing. Why not?" She giggles without a reason to giggle.

A Fox flack is sent on the run for Joe and the mayor. He returns only with His Honor, who stayed precisely for this chance to have his picture taken with Marilyn Monroe. The flack reports, "Your husband left. Said he'd see you back at the hotel."

Marilyn's face clouds over. Her beauty flickers, recedes, and returns. She asks the mayor in her innocent voice, "How do you want it, Mr. Mayor, sexy or demure?"

In the spirit of fun, but revealing the fringes of panic, Wagner says, "I'll take whatever way you're selling it." His smile is dumb-looking, and it will disturb him when he sees it on the front of the tabloids later that day.

Marilyn peels off her robe and is the girl again; this time she's found her adventure. Wagner must stoop a bit to be kissed on the cheek, and stoop even lower because Marilyn is showing some cleavage. Wolf whistles roll out of the crowd. Marilyn knows exactly what the still cameras want and gives it—the bulbs flash.

When Lytess steps in again, Wilder comes forward to shake the mayor's hand, to thank him for the city's help. "Marilyn and I are having some people over for drinks. Why don't you join us?"

Wagner checks his watch.

"Just one. It's our goodbye to New York," Wilder says.

"My pleasure."

Marilyn waves to the crowd and thanks some of the crew as she goes back to her trailer. At the last moment, she looks up to the fifth-floor window and, blowing a kiss to the cleaning lady, mouths, "Praise the Lord." The woman beams.

Waiting inside is Bernie Teplitz, one of Fox's vice-presidents. His ugly, large-toothed smile gives Marilyn a laugh, which is cut off when she notices he is holding her Rilke.

Teplitz says, "That was wonderful, Marilyn. Really wonderful. I'm your chauffeur tonight."

"Good. I'm ready." She takes her book from him.

Virtually everyone in the lobby of the St. Moritz at 2:35 A.M. is connected with Fox or the shoot on Lexington Avenue. A quiet satisfaction that the New York locations have gone relatively well, but more that they're finished, sets the tone. When Marilyn enters and moves through the lobby to the elevator, people applaud. She is vivid in her makeup, her beauty intensified. She smiles and waves with fingers. Across from the elevator, Wilder shows Marilyn the private dining room where drinks and canapés will be served. "Please come down, just to make an appearance."

"Sure. Give me a few minutes." She's about to enter the elevator when she says, "Billy." She lowers her voice: "I don't know if he'll come, but I invited Arthur Miller. The playwright."

"What other Arthur Miller is there?"

"I'm not sure he'll come. He was the one who actually tried to stop that drunk tonight."

"*That* was Arthur Miller?"

"I'm sure he doesn't want the publicity." Marilyn touches Wilder's arm. "If he comes, make him comfortable, Billy. As a matter of fact, if you could tell people *you* invited him . . ."

Wilder hushes Marilyn's lips.

Marilyn kisses Wilder's finger lovingly.

When she gets off the elevator, Marilyn suddenly realizes she has forgotten which room she's in. Sudden panic throbs in her chest. *Where? Where? The number, what? The key, where?* As the panic begins to ebb, she notices a house phone in the hallway. It rings six times before a voice says, "Hotel operator."

"This is Miss Monroe. Could you please tell me my room number?"

Marilyn hears muttering on the line. "I'm sorry, but I'm not allowed to give out that information, ma'am."

"Look, I know it's on the twelfth floor. That's where I'm calling from. I just don't know the damn room."

More muttering. "We'll send somebody up to let you in. Okay?"

It's not okay. "Fine."

Marilyn drifts around the hallway, thinking a turn to the left at the far end of the hall looks familiar. The door to room 1212 is slightly open. As she approaches, she hears Winchell's voice. She pushes the door open. Winchell is talking loudly to the bathroom door. He says, "Speak of the devil," when Marilyn walks in. He downs his drink.

With a pointed lack of conviction, Marilyn says, "Walter, don't let me keep you." She tosses her Rilke on the sofa. It falls open.

Winchell, his voice lowered to a hoarse whisper, says, "He's in a lousy mood. He didn't like your showing so much of yourself to so many people." Winchell smiles gleefully.

"Uh. Not again. I'm a movie star, for God's sake. That's my damn job. That's what I *do*. That's what I *am*. Can't he ever realize . . . ?"

"I tried to explain that, but he didn't want any of it." Marilyn suspects that Winchell has done no such thing.

"Oh, shit."

"And he got really disgusted when that drunk came out of the crowd at you."

"Which, by the way, neither one of you did anything to stop."

"Stuff like that's best handled by the cops. Could you just imagine what the papers would have done with something like that? Still, if I was you, I'd be especially nice to the big guy tonight."

"I'll take it under advisement."

In his bathroom-door voice, Winchell says, "I'll be down at the bar. See you people subsequently." He exchanges his empty glass for the gray hat on the coffee table, waves, and closes the door to suite 1212 carefully behind him.

Marilyn sits on the sofa. Her hand reaches for the Rilke. She opens it to the handwritten inscription: *To become all we can become—a Permanent Friend.*

CHAPTER SEVEN

The Method Behind the Method

LIGHTS

PHOTOPLAY: There are some doubters—there always are where you are concerned—who believe that, although it's been obscured by all the publicity you engender, you have worked very hard and become a fine actress.

MONROE: Oh really. [Laughter.] That's very nice to hear.

PHOTOPLAY: But is it true?

MONROE: Is what true? That I've worked hard to become a good actress or that almost no one has bothered to notice it?

PHOTOPLAY: Becoming a fine actress. We'd like to know how you've gone about accomplishing that.

MONROE: If it's true that I've improved, and I really believe I have, it's thanks to the help of some very good, very talented people who believe in me. But I've also had the world's best motivation for improving. Inadequacy. When you felt about yourself the way I did in Hollywood—totally inadequate about almost everything—there are only two ways you can go with it. You can use all your energy to cover it over all the time or you can tackle it head on and try to do something about it. When my contract at Fox ran out and I came to New York, it seemed like the best possible time and place to work on my craft. If I've made progress, I'm grateful. I know I've made true friends and feel appreciated for myself for the first time in my life, and that, too, helps you relax as an actress and discover different ways into a role.

CAMERA

The lights in the small theater had been off for almost five minutes, and the silence in this savvy audience had finally begun to give way to whispers. Everyone connected to the Actors Studio was here; so was almost everyone connected to the connected. This was by far the hottest ticket in town. If the master could teach an instrument like this to play theater music, he was indeed a genius. There was hope, then, for the least talented of them.

No one sat in front of Strasberg, who always watched these prepared scenes from the second row just off center. The thrust stage was wrapped by seats on each side, but no one dared take them because that would break Strasberg's concentration. The audience therefore widened into a flock behind him up into the darkness.

It was a not-so-silent flock now that the stage lights had come on, flickered, and died again. Twice Strasberg almost left his seat to remedy the problem, each time reminding himself it was inappropriate. He said in a moderate voice that carried to the last row, "Reverence in the Temple, please." And there was silence, immediately.

Marilyn had played a scene on this stage two months earlier. She was Lorna Moon in Odets's Golden Boy. *Just to get her feet wet; she wasn't great but not all that bad, either. For Strasberg the most important thing was that she actually did it, completed the scene without turning to the script, without blowing a line; she had an idea about her character and remained faithful to it throughout. On screen, it was always bits and pieces, rarely acting for more than twenty seconds at a crack, never with the opportunity to develop anything whole. Strasberg praised her a bit too much in front of the other students.*

An electrician replaced a light bulb hanging over center stage. Under a metal shade, it angled a harsh light down on three small chairs and a table. Marilyn, her hair short, unruly, its natural brown color pushing through yellow dye, wore a tight black dress, white sneakers. She was Anna Christie.

Maureen Stapleton, one of the Actors Studio stars, would play Marthy Owen. Two badly used women in different states of wear: dotty Marthy, fiftyish, alcoholic, but with an unquenchable, and perhaps unwarranted, optimism about her. Anna, a young prostitute, weary and ill, having come east looking for her father and a place to rest. She may already have lost her soul.

Physically, Marilyn did not completely correspond to O'Neill's description of Anna: "a tall, blond, fully-developed

girl of twenty, handsome after a large, Viking-daughter fashion
but now run down in health and plainly showing all the out-
ward evidences of belonging to the world's oldest profession."
Almost everyone in the room had seen Kim Stanley play this
scene a year before, magnificently. Marilyn knew she was plac-
ing herself in a very difficult situation. Many of those present
wanted to see her fail.

ACTION

Marilyn Monroe looks around Johnny-the-Priest's with an
honest expression of curiosity and familiarity. Anna's never
been here before, but places like this aren't unfamiliar. She
lists to the right, having forgotten to put down her suitcase.
She drops it and stretches like a cat.

For years, all her life perhaps, Marilyn has wanted to
create something from the material of self. For all her Hollywood years, and even before that, her longing had a relatively simple objective; she just wanted to be somebody.
She's achieved that. If she ever had doubts, the cover of *Life*
confirmed it. It is undeniable, indisputable—she *is* somebody.

Marilyn isn't ungrateful. Now she knows what she
really wanted all along—to bring up things from within
herself, shape and transform them, to be known for what
she made rather than for what she was. To make something
from nothing, at least from nothing tangible: a thought, a
feeling, an impulse. She has come to the right place
finally—New York—and the right man—Lee Strasberg.
Once, back in Hollywood, he told her, "You are one of the
most creative human beings I have ever known. You have
an emotional depth that is very rare. Our task is to channel

it, to learn how to tap the wellspring, my dear." Marilyn tried to believe him.

This is proof of her desire to believe. She is standing onstage, about to be judged harshly—an actress or not an actress. Soon she'll know.

Some of those present believe she will undo herself with her first words, maybe even before that. She'll never be able to establish Anna's formidable presence. It seems to be true: As she moves to center stage, she is undeniably Marilyn Monroe; fame has sentenced her to a lifetime as a persona. Surprisingly, though, part of her is Anna too—wearied by travel, blunted by life, haunted, in spite of everything, by a sense of who she could still be.

Marilyn does very little. She breathes deeply a couple of times, and a cough sticks in her throat. No one is sure if it's intentional. She melts into a chair, touches her forehead to the table, and comes up smiling stupidly. She looks toward Stapleton finally, then toward the bar. "Gimme a whiskey—ginger ale on the side." Her smile becomes a gross leer. "And don't be stingy, baby." Her voice vibrates but is not weak. The "baby" lacks any charm at all, is just something Anna says to men when she needs them. There is a rustle in the audience; people are shifting and reseating themselves. This won't be Kim Stanley's Anna or even Garbo's. But it won't be Marilyn Monroe making a fool of herself, either.

In the saloon, the two women size up each other, Maureen steadily, Marilyn tentatively while pretending to examine the place. Strasberg cues her with the bartender's line: "Shall I serve it in a pail?"

Anna says, "That suits me down to the ground." She wants to throw down the whiskey in a gulp but finishes it in three long sips instead. A hard look crosses her face; her eyes become watery, but the alcohol appears to soften her.

She turns to Marthy and smiles "Gee, I needed that bad, all right, all right!" She is slightly apologetic.

Strasberg has been leaning forward, elbows on his knees, hands clasped tightly. He was not sure she'd be believable until she looked over at Maureen and a muscle spasm almost closed her left eye. He leans back in his seat and runs his hand along the backs of the seats on either side.

She apparently now understands the Method. She can actually tap into feelings both she and a girl like this have lived with. He can see Johnny-the-Priest's rotgut start to work on her nervous system. She picks up the empty glass, but in the midst of the action, she seems to blank and puts it down again. From the moment he first met her in Hollywood, he was sure she could do the single, irreducible thing his method required—she could create truth from imagination. She has the concentration, the inclination, after all. Lee Strasberg is leaning back and basking.

For weeks before the performance, Marilyn was searching the details of her life, dredging up the similarities between herself and Anna Christopherson. She didn't work in a St. Paul whorehouse, but she bounced around all the Hollywood studios as a girl trying to please agents, casting directors, and producers. She didn't have to stretch her imagination very far to recall growing up virtually parentless, homeless, unloved, and uncared for. If anything, those feelings were too powerful, too much a weight.

Exactly like Anna, she wanted someone to take her in, to protect her, get her off the booze, the pills; if she could just rest up, get her strength back, not feel so damned tired all the time. To sleep through the night for once. God, only that. Hadn't both she and Anna fallen below the point where they had the capacity to love themselves? Or at least poised themselves at that point? That was the issue of the play's subtext. Marilyn decided that Anna can, somehow, still be saved, can love herself, but just barely, and that's how she has decided to play her.

Strasberg is especially pleased with the way he's cast the scene: Stapleton can be incredibly vulgar and tender; Marilyn is always vulnerable, and usually, when she tries to be vulgar, it is too self-conscious an effort. Now Marilyn is drawing from Maureen, playing off her extreme strength.

"Yuh look all in," says Marthy sympathetically. Maybe there's a drink in it for her if she pretends to care.

"No—traveling—day and a half on the train. Had to sit up all night in the dirty coach, too."

Strasberg senses for the first time a false note in Marilyn's voice and movement. She has not been on a train all night without sleep. She ought to crack her neck or roll her shoulders. Maybe just break off the line and stare. Strasberg jots "No sleepless night" on his clipboard.

Maureen saves the moment by examining the weariness in Anna's face and clucking, "Where'd yuh come from, huh?"

Anna hesitates before answering, as though she isn't sure she's been asked anything. She responds dreamily, just in case she has. "St. Paul—out in Minnesota."

Suddenly, Marthy knows this is Old Chris's daughter, shown up after years on her own. "So—yuh're—" Maureen is wonderful; she sees not only Anna, she sees herself at the moment her own life could have taken a different course. "Gawd!" Stapleton underplays the ironies by whispering the word, closing her eyes, and shaking her head wistfully.

Now that he knows Marilyn has overcome her terror and is going to be all right—in other words, that his judgment of talent is once again justified—Strasberg looks for flaws, things to be discussed afterward and worked on. The problem with her hands has been solved. He smiles as he recollects making her play a scene from *Streetcar* with her hands tied to the arms of a chair. She was your typical cockamamy Hollywood actress—all hands and facial mannerisms. An indicator of emotions.

She understood what he was after, she really did, but so many of the cliché gestures had become habit. She couldn't show surprise, for example, except with a rounded mouth, raised eyebrows, and widespread fingers. So he'd tied her up. As Anna now, she has her hands tucked away, used functionally only; she is playing with her whole body, shoulders and chin and eyes especially. She is more relaxed than he could have hoped. That was the key for her: first, relax; then she could be open to the things she can do.

He knows she is not completely relaxed. There is some tension in her upper body. Her head is too weighty, relatively immobile. He starts to jot "Tension—neck." At that moment Marilyn squeezes her neck muscles and rolls her head, trying to show that Anna needs a release from the tension of the trip, the emotion of looking for her father. Strasberg puts a thin line through his criticism.

Anna says to Marthy, "Have something on me?" It comes across more as a question than an offer.

"Sure I will. . . . Hey, Larry! Little service!"

"Why don't you come sit over here, be sociable."

"Sure thing." In their rehearsal, Maureen stood and carried her glass to Anna's table. Now, however, she stands and brings both her glass and her chair over. In other words, she enters Anna's aura on her own terms. Strasberg smiles admiringly.

The best thing happening—and Strasberg knows very few of the people present will perceive it—is that both women, thanks to Maureen's lead, are flinging themselves into the unknown. The trick in stage acting is to create the impression that the unknown future is actually unfolding before our eyes, exactly as it does in life. Never to slide predictably toward an already written conclusion. They are doing that beautifully.

Anna, with little hope, is satisfied just to have made it to New York, pleased to have a drink in her. And Marthy, whose future became her past years before, only knows she's going to have to pack her things and move off the coal barge where she's been living with this girl's father. For the moment, though, it's just two women, down and out, a chance meeting, sharing drinks on their passage to god knows where. It's totally believable.

In the darkness behind Strasberg, a consensus is forming. She's far better than they could have possibly imagined, more the actress, less the star. No, not a flawless, virtuoso performance. Her speech patterns are so offbeat, the pauses so unpredictable, they disturb many in the audience. Not awful, just different; it takes some getting used to. It also makes her seem unpolished, not a threat professionally, so they can allow themselves to like her more than they expected they would.

For Strasberg, the rhythms are of no importance, a virtue even. That's how the critics, when they eventually see her onstage, will know she is Marilyn Monroe transformed into an actress. Transformed by Lee Strasberg. And if he can do it with her, he can do it with almost anybody.

He didn't think she would disappoint him, but you never know until you see it with your own eyes, right up there where it counts. From the moment she called him, he had an unrealistic wish—to direct her on Broadway. After he had begun tutoring her, as she began to understand and integrate the Method, wish became hope and then expectation. Now it was becoming an actual plan. Not in *Anna*

Christie, though; the critics could carp and minimize her Anna. Strasberg suddenly realizes what's been in the back of his mind all along: *Rain*, Sadie Thompson in *Rain*.

He jots "Rain" and barely catches Marilyn's most important line. Anna leans away from Marthy and says, " . . . You're me forty years from now. That's you!" Marilyn squints, not so much looking at herself projected in the future as thinking very hard. She realizes she has tried to insult Marthy but has insulted herself instead. She seems unable to figure out how that could have happened.

Anna doesn't exactly understand what's happening, but she agrees to shake Marthy's hand. There is some magic when they touch, two strangers poised at a moment of discovery. Anna smiles like a hopeful girl. "I ain't looking for trouble. Let's have 'nother."

Even before she downs her drink, Anna has started spilling her guts. The police raided the house. Thirty days in jail. Until she got sick and sent to the hospital. Marilyn slowly repeats "hos-pit-al. It was nice there. I was sorry to leave it." Her face invokes those restful days, without showing any of the irony that a place where no one wants to be was paradise for Anna. "Honest!"

Maureen leaves a melancholy pause. Her face understands until a forced optimism spurs her on: "Did yuh say yuh got to meet someone here?"

"Oh, not what you mean. It's my Old Man I got to meet. Honest!" It's a different "honest" from her memories of her golden days in the hospital, a hard "honest." She says, "It's funny, too. I ain't seen him since I was a kid— don't even know what he looks like. . . ."

The hardest thing for Marilyn to grasp in Strasberg's approach is the idea of things developing by opposites. Specifically, the idea that while you are being someone else, it is possible at the very same time to retreat even deeper into yourself. She didn't see how she could remember her lines or pick up the cues, hit her marks, if she wasn't concentrating completely on her character.

Those things Strasberg brushed aside. "Automatically," he told her. "The body will automatically know how to do those things when you are truly focused. There is part of the brain reserved for that, and when you are truly relaxed, it is free to perform those actions. In truly inspired moments, though, you are not even thinking about your character. Your mind is elsewhere; it searches out its own sense memory, the one that corresponds to your character's feelings."

"At the same time I'm playing the scene?"

"At the very same time."

"Not before?"

"Then, too, but in a studied way. The true inspiration will come onstage when you are not searching deeper into your character's feelings but going the opposite way, into yourself."

"At the same time?"

"Yes, at the same time. Trust me."

Marilyn wanted to. But she didn't believe him then. Or didn't believe she could ever attain this double consciousness. Now it is happening to her. While Anna explains, "This was always the only address he give me to write him back," Marilyn is taken back lucidly to a moment almost thirty years ago. She is in her mother's bedroom in the Los Angeles apartment. Sun is streaming through open blinds. A sea breeze flutters the filmy white curtains. Marilyn remembers it as a Sunday, because Gladys is wearing a straw hat and white gloves. She recalls a flowery scent, either her mother's perfume or the smell of flowers wafting through the window. Maybe it's both.

She had asked her mother who the man in the photograph was, the thin man with such a shy smile, eyes that were worried by the camera, light brown hair combed straight back off a very broad forehead. He appeared to be leaning against the pillar in front of that very apartment building. The black-and-white photograph with sharply scalloped edges hurt her fingertips. She asked why it had been bent almost to tearing across the middle of the man's face. Her mother didn't answer. Then she said, "That man is your father. And you never have to worry about seeing him again."

Meanwhile, even though Marilyn thinks she's been far away, Anna is finding out things from Marthy about her Old Man. She has stayed deeply in her character while seeing the photo of a man her mother never mentioned again. In fact, her performance is being colored with a despair she isn't aware of. Strasberg knows something good has happened and writes the words "Double consciousness" on his pad.

Maureen is playing to Marilyn now, telling her almost lovingly what she knows about Old Chris. "Well, yuh can bet your life, kid, he's as good an old guy as ever walked on two feet."

"I'm glad to hear it. Then you think he'll stake me to that rest cure I'm after?" Anna looks down at her glass, at her helpless hands. She needs a home desperately.

"Surest thing you know." Maureen touches Marilyn's arm as though it is her daughter's, a possession misplaced long ago, now rediscovered. They've been onstage about ten minutes and established some very important things about the play—they've brought Anna on from nowhere, made her believable, given her a history, a tragic life. Strasberg has said, "Anna is the play's mystery. She is the part of our lives everyone wants to forget. The part that comes back unbidden. Not only must we deal with her, we must learn to embrace her."

It's only when Anna talks about what brought her down that Strasberg discerns a false note. "The old man of the family, his wife, and four sons—I had to slave for all of 'em. I was only a poor relation, and they treated me worse than they dare treat a hired girl. It was one of the sons—the youngest—started me—when I was sixteen. After that, I hated 'em so I'd killed 'em all if I'd stayed. So I run away—to St. Paul."

He would explain to her tomorrow how important it is that there be some sense of her own complicity along with her victimization when she does those lines. A whole dimension of character has been lost; he writes, "Take responsibility."

"It was men on the farm ordering and beating me—and giving me the wrong start." Better. Her little-girl whine works against the full truth. "And now it's men all the time. Gawd, I hate 'em all, every mother's son of 'em! Don't you?"

"Oh, I dunno. There's good ones and bad ones, kid." Marthy's smile is a stupid grin. "You've just had a run of bad luck with 'em, that's all."

Strasberg can see energy draining out of Marilyn. It is not a problem in the scene; Anna ought to be weakening. But Marilyn is not yet strong enough physically to sustain even one scene of O'Neill. He doesn't bother to write that down.

Maureen stands. "Listen! I'm goin' to beat it down to the barge—pack up me duds and blow. . . . S'long kid. I gotta beat it now. See yuh later."

Marilyn doesn't hear her cue. Or doesn't seem to hear. Maureen looks back over her shoulder as she walks off.

There's a worrisome pause. "Oh," Marilyn realizes finally. "So long." She ends the scene with a perfect sense of distracted confusion.

Strasberg stands immediately. He begins to speak before turning to the group. "Now. Was that excellent?" He leads the applause. Marilyn rushes to the darkness offstage.

A few of Strasberg's friends come down to talk to him about what they've just seen, but Lee excuses himself. "Wait, we'll talk. Now I must see the actors. I'll return."

He hears Marilyn crying even before he nears the dressing room door. Maureen is saying, "Are you kidding? That's as good as that scene's been played."

Marilyn says, "You, you were the only thing good, the only actress out there," and breaks down again.

Strasberg strikes the door with his fist and turns the knob at the same time. Marilyn's sobs have robbed her of breath; she's like a little kid who's worked herself into a state. Nothing she says is coherent. Between spasms, she takes three pills from a brown prescription bottle and has trouble swallowing them. Strasberg embraces her firmly; wherever he feels a part of her shuddering, he clamps it tight. It takes a while for him to subdue her hysteria.

Maureen coos, "C'mon, Marilyn, you were fine. Made it so easy for me. You were my Anna. A true Anna. There was truth out there tonight, babe."

When she can finally speak, Marilyn says, "I was terrible. I can't act. Hopeless. A total fraud."

Maureen starts to say, "Not at all . . ."

Strasberg raises his hand. "Total," he says. "Complete and total fraud. And believe me, in the business I've seen some frauds. You're right, you might be the biggest I've ever seen."

Marilyn tries to twist out of his grip.

He laughs. "Don't you see what you're doing, my dear Marilyn? You think if you denigrate yourself enough, no one else can do it. No one else would dare be as critical as you are with yourself. What you really want to hear is what Maureen is saying, but you act as though you don't. I've seen it plenty over the years, believe me. Marilyn darling, look at me: You don't have to do that here. You were wonderful. I'm not saying there isn't work to be done, but you don't have to doubt yourself anymore. You belong with us. Your talent warrants your being here. There was inspiration on that stage, and it was as much coming from you as from Maureen. No, you don't have to throw dirt on yourself in order to have us come to your rescue. You are a stage performer." As he speaks, he eases his hold on her. Marilyn begins to return the strength of his grip.

"Don't neither of yuh pay no mind to old, toothless Marthy," Maureen quips. She throws her arms around both of them.

"Wait," Marilyn says. "I've got something for you." From a large costume bag she pulls out a charcoal sketch of Strasberg. It's done with only a few deft lines. It's a man seated, the body coming forward, chin resting on his fist. It is Strasberg in thought.

"Oh, it's good," says Maureen, surprised. "You're real good. It's him, all right."

"Darling. I'll treasure it always." Even as he accepts the token, Strasberg is analyzing it. How pale, almost uncertain, are the gray tones. Even the lines suggesting head and face are unsure. The words printed across the bottom are barely discernible: "I must concentrate."

"For all you've given me, Lee."

"And vice versa, darling." This gift, he knows, is phase two of her please-don't-judge-me defense.

Maureen is expecting Lee's critique. He usually makes

his general observations while they're fresh. Then, when the class meets, he goes deeper and makes specific suggestions. "I want to think about the scene, Maureen. I'll talk to you next week, if you don't mind. No, I'll call you later tonight. There was nothing major. I'd just like to know what you were aiming at."

Marilyn injects, "I was just aiming to survive."

"You—hah—survive. You'll bury all of us, Marilyn, I assure you. If you could just give us a moment, Maureen dear."

Maureen smacks kisses on their cheeks, picks up her coat and purse. "I'm gonna beat it uptown. Lee, when you have a moment, we'll talk?"

"Of course, dear."

After Maureen is gone, Marilyn says, "Isn't she incredible?"

Strasberg doesn't respond. "Ever since I was a young actor, a director, I've had a dream. I saw Jeanne Eagels in *Rain*. It was '38, '39. I'd never seen anything like it in my life. Until this evening, Marilyn. I want you to think about something. I'd like to direct you in *Rain*. On Broadway. It'll blow all their minds."

Marilyn has two immediate reactions—exultation and fear. Exultant because he really thinks she is worthy. Fear because she does not.

"You are not yet ready, I know this. A scene is not an entire performance. You will need to get very strong. You must do an exercise program like a prizefighter. I want to see your body lose its softness. But there is no hurry. You have the ability—about this there is absolutely no doubting. It is only a question of commitment."

"What you are saying, Lee, frightens me. A lot."

"Why, you don't want this life?"

"I want it more than anything in the world, more than I've ever wanted anything."

"So?"

"You may be asking too much from me now."

"What, *much?* To become finally a truly responsible human being? And why not *now?* When it's obvious that you're ready. I'm here to help. You don't have to do it alone. Together, slowly. I wouldn't ask you to do something you could not do—you know that, darling. But if you don't believe . . ."

"I'd never doubt your judgment. I just need more . . ."

He knows he should just squeeze her warmly and leave; he can't restrain himself, though. "Look at the alternative. You go back to Hollywood. Of course, you will be a much better actress, but there you are only a commodity. They will take your picture, put it on a can, and sell it exactly like chicken soup. And they will make you feel insecure again, like always, because that is how they control you. But it doesn't have to be that way, darling. Here you can be responsible and control your own fate, become the actress you are destined to be. That is what I am offering you, nothing less than your freedom, to let your talent shine through."

He does not look like the devil when he says these words. There is no demonic fire in his eye, no baring of the teeth or cutting of the air with his hand. He looks, in fact, like a tiny socialist professor at City College, kindly and principled—and weary.

Marilyn doesn't look like Trilby. She wants, at that moment, to be able to hug him and say, "Okay, we'll give it a try." She can say nothing. Do nothing. The kind of risk he is asking her to take overwhelms her. Confused and frightened, she draws back and smiles. "We'll see, Lee. It's too soon."

"Don't be fearful about this thing, darling. There is no need. I can guarantee success."

The two stand in an embrace, rocking slowly, saying nothing for a long while. When Marilyn leaves a few minutes later, she promises Lee Strasberg she will try to become someone in whom he can place his trust. He takes her answer as a hopeful sign.

Three weeks after she played her Anna Christie scene at the Actors Studio, *Variety* headlines M.M.'S SEVEN YEAR RICH. The story below reveals that Marilyn has signed a new seven-year contract with Fox.

CHAPTER EIGHT

Marilyn, Miller, and Frank Lloyd Wright

LIGHTS

HARPER'S BAZAAR: Malcolm Muggeridge has said, "Miss Monroe must be a genius because the absolute telltale of true genius is the ability to make other geniuses accommodate themselves to her." Do you accept Mr. Muggeridge's opinion, and if so, to what do you attribute the attraction you seem to have for some of the world's most remarkable men?

MONROE: Malcolm is really so sweet to say that about me.

BAZAAR: Sweet. Yes. But is he correct?

MONROE: I'm just a little girl trying to make my way through this great big complicated world as best I can. If I can get some help along the way, I'm awfully grateful. I've always had a very large curiosity, and I guess my manners are bad, so I, well, I ask a lot of crazy questions of some very interesting people. They seem to like my silly questions, and I get some incredible answers.

CAMERA

The picture window overlooked the beautifully bleak, snow-spotted meadow. Arthur Miller was examining the long rise that ran to the hilltop almost half a mile away. The low sky seemed to be lightening just beyond; small patches of blue were becoming visible where there had been none earlier; the day might turn decent after all.

This was his house before their marriage. He wrote The Crucible *here.*

The fact that Frank Lloyd Wright was coming up from New York on a Sunday had an ambiguous significance, one the old man carefully preserved during his brief talk with Marilyn on the phone. Either he was making a special trip for these particular clients or it was the only day available for a visit up to Connecticut. Probably a little of both. Whatever his reason, he had made Marilyn giddy with expectation.

The Millers were drinking their coffee from mugs while flipping through Sunday's New York Times. *The architect was fifty minutes late. Arthur skimmed "The Week in Review." Marilyn had the magazine open on a low table, examining some of the expensive homes for sale. An old clock on the mantel ticked loudly and chimed every fifteen minutes.*

ACTION

"On one level, he's no different from any other architect. Meaning, he thinks we're loaded and is coming on up to see how many zeros he can get us to put on the check."

"We *are* loaded, Artie. Why do you take every opportunity to say we're not? You always act like the Depression's coming back tomorrow morning at seven-thirty."

"Stock market doesn't open till nine. Sure, we're 'well off.' But he's got to think we're *loaded*, which we assuredly are not. You just don't buy a set of plans off the man. You buy his name, you buy all his previous houses, you buy mystique, you buy his special craftsmen too—none of the local workers can be allowed to tackle a Wright design. You buy his fieldstone, cut just so; you buy his hearth, his furniture, his hangings, his glass. You buy the master builder's autograph on every blessed stone and plank and nail, if he uses nails. Believe me, he won't come cheap. Have you ever been in one of his houses?"

"All I know is that Clark said it was one of the few regrets of his life—maybe *the* regret—that he didn't have Wright design his place at Palisades."

"So let's give him Clark's number. Maybe stick Wright for our finder's fee."

Marilyn smiles, irked. "Remember when Harold asked everybody the other night at Mimi's what person you most wanted to go to dinner with and I said Nijinsky and everyone laughed because he was dead? Well, later I thought a lot about it and decided it would really be Frank Lloyd Wright. But by then everyone was already talking about something else."

Not many months earlier, Marilyn would have said something like, "I don't have to think about it. I'm already married to the man." Now it's Miller's turn to be annoyed. He says, turning a page, "So give him a call and take him out to dinner."

"You were the one who said we ought to build further out onto the meadow in the first place. I just thought it would be perfect to have his ideas."

"I did want to build out. Just continue the old line of the house about twenty, twenty-five feet. Hire some of the local men. Take the old wall down, put up a scaffold and carry the carved beam on out as far as seems reasonable. Put up a new wall of limestone, great panes of glass. Write all morning, do some down-to-earth construction and carpentry after lunch. Home improvement, dear, is a very different thing from architecture. What the working class knows as a good old-fashioned extension. Twenty, thirty grand. Believe me, he doesn't do extensions. That's an insult to the *artiste* in him. He only does or-gan-ic, and that for a bundle."

"Wah, Ahr-tee Mil-lah, ah do b'lieve yoo-ah jealous."

"The man's almost ninety."

"Eighty-nine."

More than five years I've known her, Miller thinks, and never seen this quality before. Never *this* particular quality, never diminishing herself quite like this. When she started a movie, she would be modest, girlish, woefully insecure. Mostly for effect. Okay, that's understandable, but also because she was truly overwhelmed by some of her costars. Guess she figures if you appear smaller to start with, they won't squeeze you as much. Can't feel as threatened by you, either. But this is different. Diminished not just psychologically but physically. No aura whatsoever. And when Marilyn wants aura, there's aura. When she came down for coffee this morning, already she had lessened herself.

Shoulders, hips, breasts—those famous breasts had almost disappeared. She's bound them, I swear, like a Chinese princess. The smile, the eyes, blowsy hair, cut extra short yesterday at the barbershop in town. In and out before anyone could run and get a camera or call the papers. Doesn't even care about the color. Mottled, but god, she looks great. Loves that barbershop with the old-timers making believe she's not who she is, talking weather, talking fishing. It's frightening that she can change size at will. Her own telescope, this time inverted. Tomorrow she could fill a stadium. True magic. It counts for something.

Arthur Miller toys with the idea of writing a woman who can change size. It would work visually, but unless he had an idea to connect it to, there'd be no point. He's seen aggressive personalities rein themselves in before, for effect—Joe McCarthy, Spyros Skouras, Hemingway, Hearst. Slipping on smaller personalities as though they were trying on downsized garments. And not very successfully; they only became more unreal and comical as a result, which was probably their intention. He's seen the most robust types trying to act demure unsuccessfully, Hellman, Chaplin, Olivier, Behan—but Behan was actually in the midst of dying, ready to be fitted out for his last downsized garment. None had Marilyn's true power to scale down and fill less space. No one could be vulnerable on demand like her. Frustrating as hell.

Miller has learned never to question her in this state. She'd get cold angry, smile the tight smile, pick up her coffee, and leave, perhaps for days. In this case, her motives don't need questioning; they are clear enough. An old man, larger than all his buildings piled one on top of another. History-sized, the old fraud, and she's making herself tiny to give him all the space he needs—as if there's ever really enough. He'll notice how tiny she is. He'll skirt and wander in the open spaces she's left and, eventually, envelop her. The inevitable sexual dimension. Almost ninety, for chrissakes.

How'd she choose the blouse? Never saw it before. I can just see her selecting it. Must have laid at least half a dozen on the bed. Tried on each and every one. The geometric blue and white; of course, it's architectural. Question her, even about that blouse, and there'll be an ice storm in here.

The blue is remarkable. Not quite azure but of the sky; ozone perhaps, a noncolor that gives the sky depth, mystery; intriguing for what she is not. You can't tell exactly where she leaves off and the surroundings begin, especially against the bone whiteness of these walls and ceiling. She is a force of pale light.

Miller looks outside. The day is still slate-colored. Soon, though, the sky will match Marilyn Monroe. He swallows and decides that his sour, scratchy throat will become a head cold no matter what he tries to do. There's an outside chance, though, that it's an allergy to the new wood he's been burning in the fireplace. Marilyn hates allergies. She says she knows they're not failures of the will but cannot get the idea out of her head, so she hates both the weakness *and* the uncertainty.

"What time is it?"

Arthur nods in the direction of the mantel.

"You don't like his work, do you?"

"Some of his stuff is fine. It really is. The public buildings, I like. A lot more than the houses. I just don't know how livable they are. Whether I like his stuff or not isn't important; the man is probably a genius."

Every time the world tells me who its geniuses are, I never really see it. The world is often wrong about its geniuses. And what kind of genius? For good or for evil, or just a genius for genius' sake? A genius of diversion. And who needs that?

Why do I think there's so much Ezra Pound in him? He's got the feel of someone who's pulled off the ultimate artistic sleight of hand: successful because he had the true approach; true because he's become so successful. Even when he fucks up, it's not a fuck-up at all, it's really a new vision, and they all fall in line. I guess, when you reach a certain level, when you live long enough . . .

Critics allow me nothing going in. I've got to prove it all over again every single time. And there's no way I can do that. Just lucky I had a solid base hit on my first at bat and then a home run, or they wouldn't even look at me now. He, he stays a genius no matter what he does, and the farther out he goes, the less they can judge him, the greater his genius. Jesus, she's right. I am jealous as hell. "You're right, you know."

"How?"

"I must be jealous; that's the only way to account for . . ." Miller can't think how to label his culpability. He has a sense, however, that he's apologizing prematurely.

Marilyn is gracious: "Oh, c'mon, Artie, the man is eighty-nine years old."

The sun breaks through a bit while they each sip and read and think, but the sky is still mostly steely. First Marilyn and then Miller sees a pale blue classic Mercedes coming slowly over the half-frozen tire tracks in the road. Miller smiles at the inconvenience the bumping must be causing his unwanted visitor. Marilyn rises and runs outside in her blouse, her pleated white skirt flaring more than she intends. She wants to meet the car as far down the road as she can.

I'm sure, she imagines, he'll say something memorable. Something I can start a memoir with. I've seen you on the silver screen, m' dear, but I never would have imagined that you'd be so . . . Fill in the blank; it'll be something great.

And what do I say? Nothing. Just reach out and touch him. Perfect. Mysterious. Then I'll kiss him and squeeze his arm. Old men are gristle and veins.

Words always let you down. Live by words, you pay the price. In the end, the words don't tell anybody anything. Can see it with Artie, how words promise him so much, but in the end they let him down. Even him. No wonder he wants to build something.

But to build an idea, a picture in your head, into a real thing, a skyscraper: that's just incredible. An idea you can touch, can walk inside, look around in. The connection between thinking and touching, a building, all feeling. Walk inside, doors open, close behind you, elevators go up, go down. Everything anyone needs is there, right there. No crap in his buildings. I want to live with no more crap. I want to live a long time with no crap. I want to become tight and lean, muscle and gristle and veins.

Wright rolls down the rear window as the huffing Marilyn runs alongside the car. "No, no," she urges, "don't dare stop. You'll get stuck in this goo. Don't stop for me. I, uh, prefer . . . Tell him don't stop till the house. Shameful, I know. My, my husband prefers . . . It seems . . . in-hospit . . . It really isn't."

Marilyn has run about fifty yards, and she's wheezing so hard she can barely speak. She stops as the car passes her and seeks out the frozen path. Even her thoughts come in gasps: No distance at all. Exhausted. Oh. My. Got to change. Way I'm living. Got to have new road. Paved. To go along with. New house. New body for myself.

A tawny black man, Wright's driver, is standing beside the car and staring at Marilyn as she approaches at a trot for a few steps, a fast walk for the rest. Arthur shakes Wright's hand and sweeps his other toward the approaching Marilyn.

Wright is shorter than she imagined; she's only seen head shots of him in books. His sharp chin points upward continually. A bantam rooster. Marilyn is sure, even in her terrible physical condition she could lift him off the ground. In his dark cape, floppy felt hat, burgundy satin scarf, leaning on a jeweled walking stick, Wright strikes poses in the manner of a silent-picture star.

Arthur is saying with apparent sincerity, "It's a pleasure to have you here. We have long admired . . ." He is thinking: What incredible freedom there must be in going through life as a small-sized god. When the only politics you care about are self-politics.

"Mutual admiration, sir. I assure you. Yes, admiration. That's why I've come. Now, you're going t' invite me t' stay. Not possible. Not possible. Love t', love t'. Can't possibly. Superb possibilities on this land."

"May I introduce you to my . . ."

"Always run around in yer damn skivvies middle o' winter, m' dear? Be yer death out in this damp chill. Had a sister got locked out t' house on a day just like this. Took cold. Died. Pneumonia."

"I was curious what your first words would be. And you tell a barefaced lie. Shame. The biographies say you're an only child." Marilyn is trying not to use her persona voice and rhythms, but much of them come through.

"I am, indeed I am. But that was, of course, after my beloved sister passed away." His small, rheumy eyes flare. He pins her with a gaze as he has been doing successfully with beautiful women most of his adult life. He extends a hand. Marilyn thinks he wants to shake, but he bows and kisses her hand lingeringly. Marilyn can only laugh and shrug. She throws her arms around Wright's long neck and kisses his cheek loudly. Camouflaged white stubble scrapes her lips; he smells like a rare book.

"Since your time is so precious, Mr. Wright," Miller suggests, "perhaps we can go inside, have a drink. We can talk about what we had in mind for the house."

"No need to. There happens t' be, fortunately for me on such a blustery day, only one possible site for a house on this terrain. And 'tis there." Wright points his stick across the meadow to the bluff beyond. He is not looking where his stick points but into Marilyn's eyes. She giggles. Miller wipes his runny nose on the back of his hand.

Miller knows people with money really want to buy certainty. Want to be told, "Do it this way! Trust me because everyone knows that I know." It is the triumph of the old man's life to have attained such certainty.

I can learn from him. I can learn old-man strategies. Building monuments to himself to the very end. Maybe even beyond the end. Incredible. Most old men only know gloomy things with no certainty in them. This is an old man who hasn't doubted since Teddy Roosevelt stormed San Juan Hill.

"Unmistakable," Wright said, still pointing. "Coming up that road of yours, anyone can see 'tis t' only site for my house. Only place I can design for. T' meadow will flow into it from behind. 'T will command the valley. Fit for playwright and player. Must be there."

Says Miller, smiling broadly, "That's not ours. Where you're pointing, that's not our land."

"Buy it, then, if you want my house. Only site that interests me, I'm afraid. Only possible one. No, no, not debatable."

"It's for sale, Artie. I inquired in town. It can be had."

Miller thinks they must have set this up in advance,

playing out a scene. This isn't even Frank Lloyd Wright; he's an old actor she's hired to . . .

"I'll fetch my pad. And you, m' dear, throw something on. Remember m' poor sister."

Marilyn runs inside. Miller doesn't recall her ever moving so athletically before and is distracted by all he still does not understand about this woman. Miller knows there is always the option of saying no in the end, but with Marilyn you exercise that option at great cost. Something dies every time, and this could be a crucial death. "So, your trip up, it went smoothly?"

"Smoothly, given t' way we choose to live in this insane country. In stifling compartments, clustering about a bloated, toxic, heart-city. If t' routes to it were true arteries, t' heart would have quit years ago; nothing passes through them as it should."

"No one really wants to have it that way."

"Disagree, sir. There is always choice and nothing but choice. Now, don't try to draw me into your famous political quicksand, sir. Charity, education, social legislation—all t' liberal answers t' all human problems everywhere and for all time. Cast on tablets. Live this way, brethren, live this way."

Miller wonders what the hell Wright is talking about, when Marilyn reappears. She stumbles into a pair of boots while slipping into one of Miller's oversized pea jackets. Miller is dressed about the same way.

Wright strides quickly ahead, his hat brim flapping. Miller doesn't know what pace to move at, so he lags back slightly with Marilyn, who is thrilled by the idea of chasing Frank Lloyd Wright across a muddy field.

Marilyn's thoughts run before her. Just look at him. Eighty-nine and rooster tough. Like the materials he uses. Fieldstone. Slate. Granite. Wrought iron. Hard woods.

Cantilevered. Thrusting out. Old man defying gravity. The fun of it. Kiss, lick the slate of him.

When I used to screw boys, I'd say, real dramatic, "No matter how long you live, Dale, you will always remember this—me. When you get real old, you'll be able to remember my doing this for you, my face looking up at you like this, always, forever. If we meet as real old people on an airplane someday, say, we'll talk about our lives, but you'll remember doing this with me, and you'll be young again while you remember." I'll live in a boy like Dale. I'll live in the movies the same way.

Wright must be a man with a memory of an unforgettable moment with an unforgettable girl. I could have been that girl. He'll see her again in me. I want, all I want is a little of his life, his past.

"Hope the old guy doesn't take a chill, like his sister."

"Don't say things like that. I love this day, Artie."

"If he ups and dies on us, the press'll descend like a plague of locusts. Tracing our footsteps out here. 'That's where Wright stepped. Monroe ran up here; you can see her boots. Look, Miller turned back here to get help, left Monroe alone with the old man.' "

"Don't, Arthur. Please."

Wright stops at two hundred yards and begins making swift, heavy pencil lines on his drawing pad. Marilyn, heaving, approaches coyly and peeks. He admonishes with a biblical eyebrow. Sterner than Olivier. She smiles openmouthed and steps back.

Miller gazes up at a lopsided V of Canadian geese heading toward New York. "Spring comes to the northeast," he says, and points.

Marilyn returns to Miller: "I always know the moments I'll never forget. Right while I'm living through them, I mean. This is the best one ever. Him against that sky. Look at him, Artie. I mean, my god. The vision of the house is already there in his head, and he transfers it right to the paper. And it will be wood and stone. And the vision comes from absolutely nowhere. That's genius. You have to write about a man like this, Artie."

"Ibsen did already."

"You should. I shoooould." Marilyn spins gaily, flapping her jacket open and closed with her fists, thrust deep in the pockets. She slips down in the mud. Wright doesn't notice and walks even closer to the house that does not yet exist. Miller picks Marilyn up without enthusiasm.

Wright's mind selects from a storehouse of ideas. Atrium, half below grade, half above. Hanging plants, vines, Japanese garden. Revolutionary War stone walls all about, some cut, some flat, others rounded by river wear. Make a home for her and for all her previous incarnations. Street girl from Liverpool. Comes t' America, nothing t' keep her in England, no longer pure. So what, America's the place. Doxy t' a Boston tavernkeeper. T' officers on both sides. Thrives on adventure. Lands on her feet every time. All the surface woods have to be local, fruit woods— cherry, apple, some walnut still around. Roof line continues t' meadow, upward, outward, like a weather vane pointed perpetually west, like America. Atrium divides. Two lives. His an' hers. Her side, her life. He should have to ask permission to enter.

She's the appreciator. The perpetual student. Not really worth more than two years of a man's life, but ah, what years they'd be. Clara was a bit of her. My lord. Clara. Velvet gowns, bustles, tiaras. The thrill of watching her disrobe. The long, unforgettable thrill of it. Chicago Clara, turn-of-the-century Clara. Head thrown back, so proud of herself, telling the ceiling no matter how long I lived, no matter how many women there were, I would remember her, these moments. This one has that same spirit. Men marry them. Clara four times. Why, I'll never know. Would suck you under in six months.

"I'll show you the rendering when we get back. I'll answer any sensible questions. Then I will leave. If you agree, you must tell me by this time tomorrow. Seems mysterious, I know, but I no longer have time, time even to explain myself."

Marilyn says, "We understand."

But Miller doesn't understand. He says, "Your reputation gives you certain privileges, and you certainly don't mind exercising them."

"True. I don't have the time or the inclination for drivel, and that's what most of the talk about building is. So why shouldn't I take advantage of my reputation? Wouldn't you?" Take hubby's arm, Clara dear. Soothe him. It's sure to have just the opposite effect.

"I honestly don't believe I would."

"Merely a difference of style, then, not of substance."

The three sit at a long table in front of a newly activated, crackling fire. Marilyn and Miller look at the remarkable sketches. Every time Miller asks a design question, Wright answers it with another quick, accurate, three-dimensional drawing. Wright can already see the house built and lived in, so he can put any piece of it to paper at will.

Miller is comforted slightly that the old man is not a complete fraud. Marilyn feels the thrill of proximity to genius and conveys it to Wright with devouring eyes. Her fingers touch the soft flesh of his inner wrist as it rests on the table. His pulse is exactly there. A blue vein beneath pale white skin soft as fresh dough. He smells completely different now, like the basement of the rooming house in Santa Monica. With the boys, playing hide-and-seek.

Damp wood, damp cement. Cool. Dale hiding in the bicycle room, she was sure. Finding him, saying nothing. Doing nothing actually when it happened. I could hide in this old man. "I want it very much, this house."

Wright puts his telephone number at the bottom of the page that has his overview. He underlines the number. "I hope your husband will agree."

Miller says, "And what would something like this run us?"

"Without the land, of course, it would run, all my fees included, one point two five."

Miller is confused. He needs precise tens of thousands to understand. "What does that mean?"

"One and one-quarter million, more or less."

"Million."

"Million, sir."

"Oh, Artie, isn't it exciting?"

"It is even more exciting than you think, because we do not have one and a quarter million dollars. And we will not have one and a quarter million dollars for the foresee . . ."

Wright stands in midsentence and moves toward the door. He knows from experience that extremely acrimonious discussions often follow his professional visits. They are as much a part of the building process as tongue-and-groove construction. He has not cleaned his shoes and trails caked mud across the old, wide-boarded floor. Miller watches, displeased. Disruption has walked through his front door and now leaves a clean-up job behind.

"You'll call t'morrow if y' wish t' proceed." Wright is certain Marilyn Monroe will call.

Arthur Miller decides it's better to be direct now: "We just couldn't possibly afford that kind of money, even though we appreciate . . ."

Wright takes a deep breath and, for some reason, deigns to give a pitch. "Not merely a house, an investment, sir. Thirty, forty years from now, it will have appreciated twentyfold. Like a Cézanne. Your children will be left with a valuable work of art to live in or to sell, as they wish."

"Let my husband stew in here awhile. I'll walk you to your car, *maestro*." Marilyn giggles. "I've always wanted to say that word in real life, and with you it fits."

Fifteen minutes later, Arthur Miller and Marilyn Monroe sit with feet up on the low table. The fire is crackling, devouring new wood. Wright's drawings have been spread sequentially and studied in silence. Both have whiskies cradled in their laps. At different times, each stares out on the distant meadow. Marilyn sees Wright's house there. Miller sees virgin meadows.

"Before you say anything," he begins, "let me just tell you I once met the Kaufmanns. In Pittsburgh. Three years ago. You know who they are, the Kaufmanns?" No response. "They're the poor souls who commissioned him to build the house in western Pennsylvania, the one that's built over a falling stream. It won awards and awards. It's quite beautiful. The only trouble is, it was unlivable, at least according to old man Kaufmann, who tried to live in it for a while. The walls never dried. Ceilings cracked. It vibrated, for god's sake."

"I won't argue."

"I know. You prefer the grandiose pout."

"Words."

"You're going to call him. Whether or not I agree, you're going to call him. And I become the bad father who says no."

"So let's just agree, then. It's so much easier that way. I like it when things are easy. That's when I show my appreciation, Artie."

"Don't do that."

"I don't *do* that. I *am* that. And I've never wanted very much out of life. But I'm ready to dare now. Something new and big, and that means I'm feeling strong. Don't you see how amazing it is of me to dare to want something like a new house?"

"Come on, you know that's not what's really involved. Why not at least be honest about it?"

"Don't let's get into a big intellectual debate. I couldn't stand that. You'll win and I'll feel stupid. A person, you know, can be right even though she loses an argument."

"Logic's all we've got going for us in a situation like this. We're talking about a million and a half dollars, for god's sake."

"You are jealous of him, aren't you?"

"A little."

"Arthur, he is eighty-nine years old."

"Yes, and you've already started to seduce him."

"I just want him to build me a house."

"You know, you said that with the same tone, the same feeling, as 'I just want to have his baby.' " Miller realizes that the word once out can never be recalled. "Say the secret woid . . ." And begin to lose everything.

Marilyn smashes her cocktail glass in the fireplace. She slams the door to her room and throws herself on the bed. She wants to cry but cannot. This infuriates her. Eventually she settles into alternating moods of extreme anger and self-pity.

Then she recalls something that doesn't seem to make any sense. One time, waiting with Billy Wilder for the crew to set up a shot, he mentioned how upset he was with Zanuck. Wilder, just for the fun of it, was calling her Millie that day. She loved when he did that; it made her feel like a waitress in a diner, an honest, hardworking one.

Zanuck was driving Wilder crazy. It wasn't the movie; it was their chess game. Wilder could never beat Zanuck. Never. Marilyn told Wilder it was no big deal. "It *is* a big deal," he said. "He says I can't beat him because I don't see the end of things until after the middle. He tells me that by then it's too late. That the end is always right there in the beginning. Can that really be true?"

Marilyn glimpses a truth—the end is in the beginning.

By dinnertime the following day, Marilyn and Miller still have not spoken to each other.

Finally, Arthur says, "You called him?"

"Yes. He wasn't in."

"Will that count against the deadline?"

"He's in the hospital."

"Oh."

Arthur Miller sneezes. Marilyn Monroe does not say, "Bless you." It is the beginning of a nagging cold.

CHAPTER NINE

Marilyn, Simone Signoret, and Harlow's Mexican

LIGHTS

PLAYBOY: Some very beautiful women, a great many models, especially, have admitted they're tremendously insecure about their looks, a fact that astounds most of us because they are obviously gorgeous. They've said they don't like to look in the mirror because they notice every slight imperfection of feature and distort them into terrible flaws. What sort of relationship do you have with your mirror?

MONROE: We're old, old friends. So we can tell each other anything. Since I've never believed I was beautiful, my mirror never has to lie to me. What it does, it really lets me look past my features into myself, into my emotions. If my acting has improved over the years, it's because I play scenes hundreds of times into the mirror.

[Lee] Strasberg once told me anyone can star in her own mirror, at least for a few takes. I've probably played some of my best scenes into mirrors; it's just a shame there wasn't a cameraman behind some of them.

CAMERA

Bungalow 21 of the Beverly Hills Hotel wasn't a bungalow at all. It was a convenience apartment on the second floor of a suburban house along a shaded mimosa walk far behind the hotel. It had a living room, small kitchen, large bedroom, and bath. It was quiet back there. And safe. Almost all the guests were stars either working on films or about to start shooting. Very important people.

Marilyn had checked into Bungalow 21 three years earlier with Arthur to begin shooting Let's Make Love *for George Cukor. Miller thought the project a good idea and was with Marilyn for support, but he had been called back to New York, where a revival of* The Crucible *was having problems in rehearsal. Yves Montand, her leading man, and Simone Signoret, Montand's wife, were in Bungalow 20, whose overhead deck joined Bungalow 21's. Proximity had made for juicy studio gossip, box office stuff linking Marilyn romantically with her costar.*

It was a Saturday morning, and Marilyn, not shooting today, had invited Simone over for coffee and to have her hair lightened. Marilyn had called her the night before and said, "I want you to meet this woman. She's a wizard—or a witch, I don't know which. Great with blondes. She used to do Harlow's hair. What stories she tells."

She did Marilyn's hair whenever Marilyn was on a picture. The woman refused to stay in Los Angeles; she had to be flown up from San Diego every weekend. Marilyn insisted on having no one else color her.

ACTION

The tiny woman who is rinsing plastic bottles in the sink is wrinkled and berry brown. Her eyes and eyebrows are jet black, front teeth gapped the width of an invisible tooth. The long strands of her wire-straight hair, parted widely down the center and pulled tight behind into a bun, glow like a golden helmet.

"She was the first to call me the Mexican. I didn't like it, not a bit, but since it was Harlow, it caught on. I'm not a Mexican, though."

The other women are sitting at the kitchen table— once art deco, now chrome cheap. Each lounges in a terry-cloth robe—Simone's is pink, Marilyn's creamy white. Large blue towels muffle their necks. Their heads are covered with shimmering thick foam. Marilyn's head looks like a greaty frothy canary. Simone's mousse is the color of a polished copper pot.

Marilyn is barefoot. Simone wears pink slippers. They're sipping coffee from oversized mugs imprinted with the 20th Century–Fox logo.

"I'm not even close to being a Mexican," the woman explains while rinsing the sink. Then she takes an oven timer out of a black doctor's bag. "Almost forgot. That'd be a disaster, wouldn't it? Start a movie, hair one color, finish it another. Seen that once. Alice Faye in *Tin Pan Alley*. Whole damn movie she's as blond as a lemon, except for her musical numbers, which they shot at the end, where she's just about a redhead. Colors different as the two of you, even more. Studio tried to sue the company that processed the film, but we all knew. You're ten minutes more," she says to Signoret while winding the timer, "because you just want highlights. The platinum takes exactly eight and a half after that."

The timer starts to tick loudly. It cadences her words. "I'm brown like a Mexican, but it's all the sun. I wasn't so brown when I was with her. I have those sharp-looking eyes like a Mexican, I guess you could say. And I still roll my *rrrrs* a little and maybe clip some of my words too. My mother was born in Chile. But Chile ain't Mexico, not by a long shot."

Marilyn is studying this woman as never before, noticing the quick, abrupt movements, dreaming of playing her someday.

"My father, he was Belgian. I ask you, does that sound anything like a Mexican to you?" It isn't rhetorical; she waits for an answer.

Marilyn eyes Simone and says, "Uh uh." Simone, working hard on her colloquial American, says, "Not in a pig's sty."

"It's not like I don't know why Jean called me that. I know. Because when I first did her, she asked me where I was from. I said Chula Vista. That's right near San Diego, everyone knows that. Not Jean. You know what she says?" Again the expectation.

"I can't possibly imagine," says Simone, lighting a Kent and inhaling deeply.

"Jean said, 'That's Mexico, ain't it?' I told her it wasn't, and she says, 'Down there, it's all Mexico to me.' She could be that way, so bitchy. God, I loved that girl. Ever see her movies?"

"See her movies? Are you mad? In Paris when I was twelve, thirteen, *Dinner at Eight*. And *La Belle de Saigon* and *Imprudente Jeunesse*—I don't know how you call them in English—and, oh yes, *Bombshell*. Aunt Sophie, my god, how she adored her Harlow, whispering so much to me everyone around was shushing us." Now Signoret transforms herself into her aunt: " *'Regarde*, Sisi, see how she is so careless with her body. See how she is not only that body but much more. The body is just what she wears. See, see how she admires herself but not the men who want her so desperately. For them she cares nothing until they despair.' 'Shhhh,' the man behind us said very strongly. Aunt Sophie paid him no attention. 'She is so daring, Sisi, she does not say her lines like any of the others, even the Barrymores do not have her understanding. *Regarde.'*

" *'Shhhh, madame.'*

" *'Silence, monsieur cochon.'*

"That is when he dared to tap Sophie on the shoulder with his newspaper. A very grave mistake. She pulled it suddenly from him and beat his head, while shouting in a whisper, 'I am explaining the secrets of Harlow to my niece, you fool.' So you see, my friend, I was raised with the secrets of Harlow."

Marilyn envies Simone that story, that aunt: She's forgotten she has an "aunt" and a story of love to match it.

Simone draws deeply on her cigarette and says, "Ah, American cigarettes, I love them. Long and sweet, like your men, I think. My Sophie, she could tell fortunes. From coffee grounds. She warned that Harlow would die young. And tragically. She also knew always I would become an actress."

"My own mother," the hair dyer said, "she could read people's hair. No, don't laugh." Neither was inclined to. "Almost no one's hair grows straight out. It grows in whorls. She told me she could read the deepest character traits in the bends and turnings near the scalp. When I went to bed, she would put my head in her lap and run her fingers through my hair. I remember her always telling me, 'You will be valuable to someone very important and very good.' "

Marilyn doesn't remember when her mood changed, but she realizes she has grown sullen and distant from the other two. She pulls her knees up out of her robe and wraps her arms around them.

"The reference in your mother's prophecy, you think it relates to Harlow?"

Harlow's Mexican frowns at Simone. "I don't really know. My mother never read Jean's hair, but I told her exactly where the clusters were, where it grew out against the grain and where it turned back on itself. I told her exactly how it felt under my fingers, where it was rough and where it was very fine. 'Problems will come for her soon,' she told me. And my god, didn't they come! Of course, you didn't have to have the gift to predict that about Jean. From the first day I came to her on the set, I could see something was wrong. She had to break for a pee every five minutes. Really, I'm not exaggerating: at least every five minutes. A kidney infection, she said. Whatever it was, it's part of what killed her eventually."

"In Europe, they said many bad things. Even it was the platinum dye in her hair."

That, Harlow's Mexican shows with a glare and a scowl, does not deserve an answer.

"They also said it was injections she took to make larger her breasts."

The glare is no different.

"Could it not have been a sexual disease out of control? That's what many of the girls at my school whispered, but it was a Catholic school, and we stupid girls found such possibilities thrilling."

"They all interviewed me. All the sob sisters. Hedda Hopper, Louella Parsons, Sheilah Graham. They all swore they'd never print what I told them, said they just wanted to know for themselves. Sure, sure, I'd believe that. Jean was certainly no angel, but she loved her body too much to be that dumb. The syphilis story got spread around by her enemies at the studio. I won't say who, but she had plenty, because they hated how good she got in pictures and how popular." She walks over to Marilyn, dabs at the flattening foam with a towel, and rolls some strands of golden wet hair between her dark fingers, examining color and texture like a tobacco auctioneer. "You want it evened all over like last week?"

"We're still shooting the nightclub scenes. Until Thursday. So don't make me Alice Faye."

She dabs some of the mousse off Marilyn's hair with a cotton swab. "How's it going?"

"They say fine. They always say that. I have no idea. I just do what they tell me."

"All Jean ever wanted, even after she made it big, was to belong to herself again. She belonged to so many different people. To her dumb-bunny mother, her good-for-nothing stepfather. To Mr. Mayer and all those other studio big shots. To the gossip writers, to every man in America who could still get it up. To those who couldn't too."

"Not the fans?" Marilyn asks casually.

"No, not really. She had to be aware, sure, and to make those tours promoting her pictures, but no, she sure didn't belong to them. They were just out there, like the ocean is just out there. The real shame is that just before the end, the right man wanted her."

"Gable?" they guess in two languages.

"Mr. William Powell. My god, he loved her, and he'd have been so good for her. If she could have stayed with him and come to believe in herself, America would have seen a star it'd never be able to forget. Because like I said before, even though she loved her own body, she never belonged to herself."

The distinction is too subtle for Simone's English comprehension. Marilyn, however, understands perfectly and feels a pang that makes her want to cry.

"You know what she did once, not too long before the end? Right in her kitchen, waiting for her hair to take color, just like you this morning, she said to me, 'This is all I am.' I couldn't believe it. She reaches into her satin nightgown and puts her hand over her boob, pulls down the strap, and she lifts it right out. They weren't real large, you know, her boobs, not by modern standards, anyhow. Thirty-three, C cup. Not like either one of you two ladies." Harlow's Mexican is virtually without breasts.

Both the tintees become self-conscious at the same moment. Signoret rolls her shoulders forward. Marilyn tugs her robe across her chest.

Simone says, "In my country, if you are a serious actress, it is a great deficit to have large breasts, even with producers. After I became thirteen, I did whatever I could not to appear too large. Onstage, I used to wrap myself up like a mummy. Unless I was playing a peasant; then it was necessary to be of the earth, a big, full-sized passionate woman. I played peasant women forever."

Marilyn listens to Simone, but she is fascinated by what the tinter has just described. "Was that," she asks softly, "the only time she ever did something like that?" A strange question; she doesn't know why she asked it.

"No. Plenty of times she reached into her robe or even her dress and touched herself, but this was different. She took it out of her gown and just sort of held it up. It really scared me, because she threw her head back after a while and her expression made her look exactly like she was touching someone else's body. Then she got up and went over to the mirror, real close, and stared at it, examined it, even held the nipple high up in the air between two fingers. There was a disgusted look on her face. It looked like it was hurting her. She started talking to it. She wasn't drinking, I swear. But I can honestly tell you that she started talking to her own breast."

Simone Signoret drew deeply on her cigarette and swallowed the smoke. Marilyn had a dreamy, dull-eyed, yet frightened look that came naturally to her off camera.

"I tell you, I'd seen Jean do lots of crazy things, but this wasn't funny. I got real worried for her. I started talking about the studio, about Wallace Beery, about Thalberg and Shearer, just to get her back, to get her mind off what she was doing to herself in front of me. She didn't even hear me talking, it seemed. Just stared right at that mirror and said to her own boob, 'You think you're so damned wonderful'—only she didn't just say 'damned'—'you think I wouldn't be anything without you.' And she started to laugh in a quiet, real scary way."

Marilyn closed her eyes and tried to imagine the moment.

"She worked the nipple with her fingers like it was a puppet or something. And she talked and answered herself, like Edgar Bergen or someone, trying to keep her lips from moving too much. 'Of course I'm wonderful, all the world knows it. How many tits can talk?' It was supposed to be funny, but let me tell you, I didn't think it was funny.

"Then Jean moved her lips and talked like herself. 'What about me? Don't I count for anything in this deal? I can talk too. I can walk around,' and she turned in a circle.

'I can drive, dance, sign autographs, go on tours, screw like crazy. I can even make money.'

"Then the other voice says, 'Hold it right there. I'm the one who makes the money.'

" 'No you don't. You're just a part of me. I own you. You just hang off me like a . . .' She couldn't think like what, but it didn't matter.

"Then she made it curse back at her. 'It's me and my silent partner made you, dearie. And you better not forget it, just stay grateful. Even the Mexican knows I'm just telling you what everyone knows. Ain't that right, Mexican?' I said, 'Don't get me involved in this.' I just wanted it over. But Jean laughed crazy again and continued to have her boob talking. 'You know what Mayer calls you? The healthy whore, that's what. Well, we're what make you look so healthy. You better treat us right or we'll go on a sit-down strike, right, partner?' And so she pulls out the other one too. It wasn't funny, and it was going on too long. 'Now put us away, we need our beauty rest,' she says finally.

"You know what scares me when I think about the whole deal now? It happened only about a week before they stopped production on *Saratoga*. Mr. Mayer was going to take her off the film, anyway. You know, she never finished it, and three, maybe four months after what I saw that day, she was dead. They can say whatever they want about what killed her. Something was going seriously wrong upstairs. A brain tumor is what I believe now."

Simone isn't exactly sure what she has just heard. The gist, yes, but the details, no, not quite. What had this Edgar Bergen to do with the Mexican talking with her teeth clenched? Wasn't he the choreographer at M-G-M? It didn't matter; something very important had just passed. She would discuss it with Marilyn later; maybe it would become clear. Simone lights another cigarette slowly.

Whenever Marilyn is told something very personal these days, she assumes it has immediate significance to her own life, certainly to her work. When she heard Sinatra was having problems with his voice, her throat was sore for two days and she finally went to the same specialist. Acquaintances who had marital or serious health problems just about paralyzed her, for a while, anyway. So now she was sure she'd heard something about herself. She had touched her own breast unconsciously while the Mexican told the story.

"People didn't know that for so many of her greatest roles, Harlow wore a wig, even though, believe me, her real-life hair was finer and shinier than any wig. Wigs saved the studio money and gave her the same look in all the shots. For Mr. Mayer it was always the money that mattered. Still, Jean made sure I was always the one who did her hair and that I got paid, wig or no wig. Near the end, I was there mostly because she felt completely safe with me around. She could trust me. Tell me anything. I took it as a bad sign, though, when she started wearing wigs when she went on tour. The crowds always used to want to see her run her fingers through her hair. She couldn't do that with a wig."

The timer bell rings suddenly and frightens Marilyn, who is imagining Jean Harlow a captive of Louis Mayer, of platinum wigs, of her own talking breasts.

The tinter resets the timer for Marilyn's hair and brings Simone over to the sink for a rinse. Simone balances her cigarette on the edge of the yellow countertop and says something Marilyn cannot understand as the Mexican ducks her coppered head under the spray nozzle. While the

Mexican squirts a clear solution from an unmarked plastic bottle on the hair and works it in vigorously, Marilyn rises, walks barefoot into her bedroom, and closes the door. A headache is fingering its way up the back of her neck. Arthur is not there to talk and massage the tension away.

Marilyn opens wide the louvered doors of her closet. When she adjusts them properly, full-length mirrors behind each door display Marilyn to herself at left and right quarter angles. There she stands, whole and in parts. She examines each angled image, the Monroe on her right more critically; it is the side the assistant cameraman on *The Asphalt Jungle* told her was the weak one. "Sweetie, if you're going anywhere in this business, give the camera your left side every chance you get. There's no comparison. I'm only telling you this because I like you, and no one in this town's gonna give you the time of day."

As she studies her "bad" side, Marilyn realizes that she has believed him all these years. Some complete schmuck of a cameraman, and she just accepted his judgment. Her right side is softer; the eyelid droops a little more. It is the side she was in love with when she was a girl, gazing continually into mirrors. She sees in that right side much more of the girl she used to be. Why couldn't she ever trust what she really knew? She shrugs.

After all the good talks with Miller, with Strasberg, about self-belief, self-discovery, about realization and fulfillment, she could not just dismiss a schmuck's judgment. The right side was chubbier; that's what he must have meant. Even when she got heavy, she could get away with it on her left side if she cocked her head and made her left cheekbone prominent. Even right now. See. It is obvious. The left Monroe is the switch that turns them on.

Marilyn tilts her head and draws her cheeks into a

pout. She swings her right hand over the sticky foam that covers her head; the sleeve of her white robe is stained yellow. She opens her mouth and runs her wide tongue very slowly over her upper lip. She has not yet brushed her teeth. Her stomach growls; she hasn't eaten in fourteen hours. It doesn't matter; neither does the chatter echoing from the other room. She is beginning to lose herself in her mirrors.

Marilyn starts singing "My Heart Belongs to Daddy." She had rehearsed it for a week. And recorded it in just three takes. They'd already shot some of her lip sync. Cukor said he loved it, and she believed him. Now she rehears the jazzy, almost bebop intro, which she was certain she'd never be able to do before she actually did it. She begins to sway her knees and roll her bottom. She sings a breathy first line. "While tearing off . . . a game of golf . . ." She unwraps her blue neck towel as though it were a feather boa and tosses it on the bed.

She likes what she feels and what she sees. She sings the line again, with broader movements and a freer interpretation. "While . . . tearing off . . . a game . . . of golf . . ." She begins to feel a warmth of delight; she is playing, she is sensual, she is happy.

Marilyn jumps ahead: "But when I do, I don't follow through . . ." She pulls the belt of her robe, and it falls open on cue. Many more parts of Marilyn are moving rhythmically now. Her headache is still there, but she doesn't bother to notice it. Swaying and rolling and sliding, she is slipping into the character of Amanda Dell. She keeps the beat. " 'Cause my heart belongs to dad-dee. Yes. My heart belongs to dad-dee, and it simply wouldn't be fair . . ."

Dancing in place in Bungalow 21, Marilyn is dissolving in play. She bends, back straight, knees and thighs tight together, toward the thickly carpeted floor. A lowered shoulder and the flick of two fingers lift the robe off the shoulder and well down the arm. Still singing, she notices her arm; it is, you'd have to say, fleshy; she loves it that way.

"Da-da-da, da-da-da, dad-dee. So I want to warn you, lad-dee, though I think you're perfectly swell . . ." The other shoulder doesn't need as much urging, and the robe is off and sliding down while Marilyn wriggles upward. She isn't so much looking at herself now as enjoying all her moving parts. She's alive and Jean Harlow is not. Harlow made a movie with Gable, so it couldn't have been that long ago. Harlow died at twenty-six. The thought makes her shiver.

But she dances and sings. Marilyn pleases herself. She'll ask Cukor if they could reshoot the song; this time she has it perfect. Her skin is flawless. The rounded flesh gives her a feeling of health, almost too much health. Not a line in her face now that she's smiling. Even in the pout, where her chin wrinkles, the lips purse, and the eyes narrow, she is nothing but delectable. Still singing and dancing without lifting her wide feet, Marilyn, cross-armed, cups her hands beneath her black slip and over her soft-nippled breasts. She dares to do this because Jean Harlow had dared this and more.

"That my heart belongs to dad-dee . . . and my dad-dee . . ." Again she dips low, knees almost to the carpet, and flips the straps of her slip off her shoulders with fluttering fingers and a shrug. Now the breasts are exposed, altering themselves as she dances, lengthening, streamlining, rounding with various movements. Her nipples are coloring, hardening. *Who controls who?* Now she is frightened, but she does not stop singing or dancing. Marilyn's eyes start to glaze over. They close. *Oh god.* Is she thrilling or being thrilled? It doesn't matter. She is approaching the border of someplace threatening. She welcomes it. ". . . dee, he treats it so . . ."

As long as Marilyn can remember, she had a sixth sense that told her when eyes were on her. Strasberg told her all the great stars had that sense. Dozens of times in her life, when she believed she was alone, she has gotten a peculiar feeling, a chill high up on her neck, that told her she was not alone, was being watched. On the porch in the house at Bakersfield, she knew, she just knew someone else was there. No idea it was those boys up in a tree, but she knew it was someone. And that same warning feeling helped her find the peephole in her dressing room on the Fox soundstage. When she shouted, she heard whoever it was running away.

The frisson is there now. Marilyn closes her eyes to give whoever it is a chance to go away unseen. She keeps them closed a long while, tightens them. If she is unseeing, maybe she will be unseen. Still closed-eyed, she straightens and pulls up her slip. Only when she reaches down for her robe does she open her eyes.

The woman who is not a Mexican stands beside the half-open door and says dumbly, "I need to have you at the sink before the timer goes."

"I'll be there."

"It's got to be now."

"I'll *be* there."

When she comes out of her bedroom, barefoot, silent, almost composed, Marilyn imagines that Simone, flipping through a *Life* magazine, knows. Otherwise, why is she averting her eyes?

Harlow's Mexican already has a nozzle in her hand, the tepid water spraying in the sink. She beckons Marilyn with a crude gesture to hurry. The timer bell rings and echoes. Marilyn freezes. Simone tilts her head.

Her true hair is not golden. Her true name is neither Marilyn nor Monroe. Her true face never had to search out expressions for itself. Her breasts were meant to feed babies—twins, she once hoped—but that is not their purpose any longer. Her true body has slipped away from her. Stronger than all the things she knows are true about herself is her destiny—to be true to other people's expectations, to their dreams. That's what must have frightened Jean Harlow.

Simone looks up from her magazine. Marilyn senses something present in the room, as when "Aunt" Ana Lower would hush an already hushed room and whisper, "Something powerful is passing."

"Quick, sweetie, or I can't be responsible. I won't be able to control the color." It is almost a whine. Harlow's Mexican begins rinsing even before Marilyn's head is fully in the sink. Just as she is ducking under the nozzle, Marilyn notices the limousine parked alongside the next bungalow. She glimpses a man's legs crossed behind the open rear door and other men nearby looking around alertly. The tinter tries to force Marilyn's head lower. She resists. A voice beyond the spray says, "Please. I can't be responsible."

Marilyn stays up for one last look at Howard Hughes waiting discreetly—and visibly—in the driveway of Jean Peters's bungalow. A strong hand forces Marilyn's face an inch from the drain.

A chemical smell comes off the warm liquid, and Marilyn feels nimble fingers working at roots all over her scalp, especially at the back of her head. She feels the headache begin to retreat. She moans weakly. The nozzle rests in the sink now, its stream hitting her cheek, while a new, cool liquid is worked into her hair. It tingles, and she does not want the sensation to stop. Fingers caress and massage her scalp; they probe and soothe. A new aroma—medicinal wildflowers—calls up the sense impression of innocence, a new beginning. Marilyn feels faint, and her body slides down and away from the sink just a bit. *Why not faint? Why not?* The voice, more distant than ever, says, "You okay?"

Marilyn has heard that car on the gravel, doors slamming, seen those men lighting up cigarettes in the dark, for two weeks now. *Why does he wait in his car? It's weird.*

While she is being turbaned in an oversized towel, Marilyn mumbles. "They call him a mystery man. Well, he sure doesn't hold any mystery for me. If he wasn't rich, he'd be the perfect creep. To my mind, a creep's a creep whether he flies around the world in his own plane or hangs out at drive-ins trying to get in the waitresses' pants." She neglects to mention that Howard Hughes arranged her first screen test.

Because she has been rubbing the towel vigorously while Marilyn was speaking, Harlow's Mexican says, "What'd you say, sweetie?"

"I was just wondering why Howard Hughes would spend so much time sitting in his car."

"Because he is a rich American businessman," says Simone, not bothering to look up from *Life*, and feeling across the table for her cigarettes. "He wants to seem the good puritan, a perfect gentleman, while he is, in fact, a very hot rabbit."

"Then he's a hypocrite."

"Yves and I have talked when we have seen him out there. Yves believes he does his business affairs from his limousine; it has a radio-telephone. All very compartmentalized. Time set aside for business. Time set aside for *l'amour*. Strictly separate. He knows very well we all see him out there. He wishes to be seen. It is a notch for his gun."

"He's been out there for weeks," Marilyn observes.

"So it is a deep notch. The only true purpose of sex," Simone says, stretching in a bored way that makes her seem better informed than anyone else on the subject, "should be pleasure. It is not to get your name in history books, not to dominate or manipulate. . . ."

Without turning from her task of patting Marilyn's hair, Harlow's Mexican says: "Harlow had him when she first came to Hollywood." They stare at her. "Yes. She told me about it. She said, 'It was a very, very *little* affair.' " The Mexican flashes her gapped smile and holds her hands half an inch apart. "He signed her to her first contract."

That would have put a cap on the morning if Harlow's Mexican hadn't also screamed. The sound was actually halfway between a gasp and a word. The intended word was *Fire*.

Marilyn is on her feet, spinning round; her towel comes off her head in a whirl. Simone runs around the table, batting at the air, yelling, *"Où, où, où!"* All three smell smoke. For some reason, Marilyn believes the danger is on the floor and hops from one foot to the other, shouting, "Where, where, what?"

"Où, où, où!"

"What, where, what?"

Harlow's Mexican does not speak; she slaps a wet towel at the countertop near the sink. Sparks fly. She throws a pot of water at the countertop. Plastic bottles tumble and roll on the floor; a fork flies across the room.

Simone had left a cigarette on the countertop. It burned the Formica and beyond. Ruined.

Marilyn is the first to laugh—she acted so stupidly so

suddenly, it was wonderful. Her laughter rises from her stomach, exactly like "Aunt" Ana's, deep and loose and cleansing. Simone's supporting giggles come from her head and turn into snorts and then laughing coughs that leave her heaving and red-faced. Harlow's Mexican smiles sadly. She will have to clean up the mess. But her benefactor has sent out the laugh signal, so she tries some laughter. She doesn't laugh long, because there is the hair dryer to be rolled out of the closet and Marilyn to be got under quickly.

Later, with the room neated up and the dryer put away, Marilyn and Simone smoke long cigarettes. Their hair looks unworkably new.

"I have to prepare something for Yves. What time is it?"

"Don't worry. If he's been at the studio, they'll have fed him plenty."

"No, not to cook. I don't cook in America; that was part of the deal. Martinis. He likes them made just so, and chilled in the *frigo*. You'll come over?"

"I'm not getting out of this robe all day. He's coming over here tonight. We're going to shoot lines tomorrow. You come too."

Harlow's Mexican has put the last of her preparations in her black doctor's satchel. She is stalling, waiting for Marilyn to notice it is time to write her a check. She hates this part of it. She goes over to Simone and pulls a high-lighted curl away from the middle of her forehead. Before sticking her hand mirrors back in the case, she fluffs Marilyn's hair and shows her the rear again. She lifts the gold and lets it fall lightly. They both make contented sounds.

"You know what you ladies need?"

Marilyn really wants to be alone and almost says, "Some privacy." She takes a breath and says, "No, what?"

"You need a pet. A little lapdog. Jean loved hers so. Made all the difference in her life."

That night, after Yves has been in Bungalow 21 for three hours, Simone finally puts aside a French script she has not been able to concentrate on very well. She slips into her robe and pours the last of the martini. She remembers very clearly now that her aunt was absolutely certain that Harlow had committed suicide. "Twice," Simone says in French, imitating Aunt Sophie, "with pills. Once, with a strong overdose that would have killed a bear, but it did not. They got her to the hospital just in time. And then two days later in the hospital, she did it again, successfully. The studio has submerged the whole affair."

More comes back. Sophie said that toward the end, Harlow would dress plainly and go to the worst sorts of places, bars on the waterfront, and sell herself to men. And not even sell herself; give herself. And she would let them abuse her. So much did she hate herself. In such a condition, finally, she slipped lower than abuse. And it was time to end everything, the hating, the abuse, everything.

Simone decides to bring the last martini to Yves and to tell Marilyn her aunt's version of Harlow's death.

She leaves the door of her bungalow ajar and crosses the deck to number 21. At the door, she makes a loose fist but does not tap. It is not Marilyn she sees through the small glass; rather, Marilyn's angled reflection from a full-length mirror in the bedroom.

The shimmering hair is in a black net. The nude body, round and pink like a Renoir, is flawless. Simone holds her breath. In one hand, Marilyn proffers an elongated breast; the other hand has disappeared between her legs. She is on her toes, her rump high in the air. She is tittering like a girl.

The reflected Marilyn is offering herself in a playful

dance to someone unseen, someone on the bed. The next moment, Marilyn's reflection dances off the mirror and into the room.

It could be anyone, Simone tells herself. Miller has finally come back. Howard Hughes. Anyone.

CHAPTER TEN

The Road to Jakarta

LIGHTS

COSMOPOLITAN: Are you aware of the fact that President Sukarno of Indonesia has called you the most desirable woman in the world and has referred to you as "my obsession"? He has even gone so far as to tell a Japanese journalist that it is his abiding fantasy to seduce you before he dies. How does knowing something like that make you feel? Especially on those occasions when you are forced to meet one another?

MONROE: Oh, gosh. Let me think. I've only met President Sukarno once in my entire life, and I've got to say he was a perfect gentleman. He told me he always admired me from afar and I believed him—there was a large mahogany table between us. Maybe it was teak.

189

President Sukarno is a world figure and considered a very great man in his country. He is a Muslim and has four or five wives, I think. I'd never want to do anything to make him be unfaithful to all those ladies.

CAMERA

The occasion was the royal command film performance of The Prince and the Showgirl *at the Empire Theatre, Leicester Square. Stars, British and American, had been invited to the gala and been requested to line up behind the royal box to greet Her Highness, Elizabeth Regina II.*

The queue of accomplished invitees was arranged alphabetically. Marilyn found herself between Victor Mature and Anthony Quayle. She wished she was Marilyn Gifford—the name of the man said to be her father—so she'd be standing between John Gielgud and John Huston.

Photographers had preceded the queen along the reception line, stationing themselves for what promised to be their best shot, a film queen curtsying before a real queen. It turned out to be an extraordinary shot. Marilyn, in a daringly low-cut brocaded gown that held her breasts as on a serving tray, her hair swept back and upward to become its own tiara, descended slowly with perfectly straight back, a graceful gesture right out of the film. Elizabeth Windsor waited until the performance was over, nodded, and smiled; she uttered nine words, which Marilyn heard and understood individually, but not collectively. Nevertheless, she knew enough to say, "Thank you, marm."

She had accepted Sukarno's invitation for a late, after-the-queen's-command soiree. The Indonesian consular officer who called said, "The president is having over a great many world

*luminaries and would be extremely grateful for your atten-
dance."*

*Marilyn said, "Then I'll be happy to loom right along
with the rest of the crowd."*

*There would be, he said, a limousine waiting for her at the
theater. It will have an Indonesian flag on the antenna. "How
could anyone miss that?" she said. In fact, she almost did miss
it. The movie and the reception had run more than an hour
late. When she finally left the crowded lobby, surrounded by a
ring of bobbies, she was met by a tiny brown man in a fez—the
Indonesian consul general—surrounded by a smaller ring of bobbies. Both groups of bobbies joined forces and, with great difficulty, escorted the celebrities through the clutching crowd. The
consul general's fez was knocked askew; Marilyn was poked
above the eye by a ballpoint pen and her hair came undone. The
following morning, the* Daily Mail *had the photo on its front
page under the incorrect banner:* M.M. AND SUKI BATTERED AFTER
QUEEN'S BASH.

ACTION

Marilyn's soul has always responded to the exotic. The
colors and textures, even the smell—the entire ambience, in
fact—of the embassy take her breath away. This *is* Indonesia. The mysterious East. Nowhere has she ever seen
woodwork so deeply lustrous, especially the teaks, bur-
nished like red copper. The ivory carvings, delicate and
complex beyond imagining. Tapestries in ruby and gold,
mysterious in subject, inimitable in craft. A huge temple
gong is embossed with demon faces; silken cloth with batik
designs edge the ceilings everywhere she looks. Marilyn

cannot believe she has stepped off a London street into this Oriental palace.

Nehru-jacketed servants in white, with thin gold piping on every seam of their suits, appear and disappear so swiftly they make the already giddy Marilyn even giddier. One helps her remove the short matching jacket to her gown, so delicately she hardly realizes it's been done. As she turns in a circle to scan the entire room, the consul general disappears, replaced by an exquisitely dark and angular Indonesian woman in a long lavender silk dress, carrying a tall drink on a silver tray. Marilyn cannot believe it is possible to move in such a dress, but the woman leads her gracefully up stairs carpeted in different shades of wine; only her ankles seem to move.

Gamelan music played on instruments Marilyn has never heard before comes from a filigreed balcony. On the second floor, large carved doors swing open silently into a book-lined room that is filled with even greater treasures. The room is not dark, merely subdued.

Marilyn is surprised because the first face she sees amidst everything foreign and strange is so familiar she has trouble recognizing it. Bob Hope says, "I've run all my material past the Prez twice, waiting for you to show up. I was just about to dig up my old vaudeville stuff. I know it's tough to get a cab in London, but it can't be this bad." Then, tipping his head toward his host and speaking out of the side of his mouth, so Sukarno can still hear, "This guy's not exactly what you'd call a laugh a minute." At which Sukarno laughs heartily.

Both men come forward to greet Marilyn. Hope defers to the elder Sukarno with a grand gesture. Sukarno has an alert face with monkeyish features; he reminds Marilyn of someone. Who? It will come to her.

But his wise, simian eyes are unlike any she's ever

seen; they dart over her, take in her bare shoulders, but do not dare offend with an overt examination. So in control of his emotions is this calculating man, there is no external indication that he has been struck weak-kneed with desire—as he knew he would be. Even Marilyn, with the world's best antennae for such things, does not sense his overwhelming lust.

Sukarno intends to kiss her hand. She offers it demurely with just a touch of embarrassment, again as she has in dozens of takes in *The Prince and the Showgirl*. Her other hand rests on her bare right shoulder, and that shoulder is cocked almost to her ear. Coy yet innocent at the same time is what Olivier wanted and what Marilyn finally managed to give him. She doesn't know why she is offering her hand to the president of Indonesia in this manner—she has other poses. Maybe it is the comic tone Hope has set. Sukarno does not take his eyes off her face as he touches his dry lips to the pale freckles on the back of her hand.

Hope, in a stage whisper: "Better count your rings, dearie." Sukarno laughs automatically while shaking his head at Hope's practiced irrepressibility.

When it's his turn, Hope wraps his arms around Marilyn as though they've been friends for years—she's met him only twice before, briefly—pats her bare back and plants a loud smack on her cheek. Marilyn can smell the blend of gin and mouthwash. She can tell from the indelicacy of his touch that he is in no way a sensual man; she knows the opposite is true of Sukarno. Hope's kiss lingers; then he breaks it off with an exaggerated pop of suction, turns to his host, and says, "Grrrouggghhh."

Sukarno does not laugh. He does not wish to offend the beauteous one. Seeing the tension that shows in his face, which is revealed as ennui, Marilyn realizes whom she has mistaken him for. Peter Lorre. She stifles a giggle as

Sukarno, ever attentive, says, "Yes? There is something?"

She's tempted to tell him the something, but it would be rude. She simply laughs to herself and says, "It just seems like I ought to be Dorothy Lamour in a scene like this. I'll order a black wig from wardrobe."

"We're off on the Road to Jakarta," Hope sings, sitting back on the couch. "They'll have a shooting script by the end of the week. In this scene, Marilyn stumbles into an Asian opium den and has got to sing and dance her way out. Okay, kid, let's see what you've got."

Sitting on the couch alongside the comedian, she says, "I'll wait until I see the script. I've got to know my motivation." Her knees are inches away from Sukarno's, who sits directly in front of her in a chair with a long stiff back.

"Motivation? Motivation? It's a *Road* picture, for Christ's sake. Lamour never needed any motivation, long as the checks kept coming."

There is a momentary lull because neither Marilyn nor the host responds to Dorothy Lamour's lack of motivation. Marilyn cannot remember how the tall drink got in her hand or how the mysterious woman she remembered offering it disappeared. The room is warm and smells like tangerines. The Oriental music is distant but clear.

Hope cannot abide the silence and tells a generic leading-lady joke into which he plugs Dorothy Lamour because hers was the last name mentioned. "Yessir, Dorothy sure is a wonderful gal." He sips his gin. ". . . erful gal. She'd have finished paying for those acting lessons too, only the springs in her mattress gave out."

Sukarno, absorbed in watching Marilyn's reaction, does not laugh. The clouding of Marilyn's brow tells him she thinks Hope's joke is cruel rather than funny. They've said similar and worse things about her. Sukarno dips his fez toward Hope, indicating he has heard.

Achmed Sukarno has imagined himself—fantasized is the truer word—alone with this woman, this astonishing woman, this ultimate woman, for many, many years. In his fantasy, he is alone with her behind the great walls of the Merdeka Palace. This embassy, although situated near Hyde Park Gate, is in all other respects Indonesia; there is a sense in which the fantasy woman really is in Jakarta, alone with him in the palace. Hope? Before Marilyn arrived, Sukarno had asked Hope to excuse himself at an appropriate moment during the evening. A monkey-eyed wink. Hope had winked back. Quite a guy, the Prez.

In his sexual fantasy, Achmed Sukarno is not required to say anything to Marilyn Monroe. She is simply there to accommodate him. He desires her, and the depth and duration of that desire, along with the fact that he is the president of a great nation, would cause her to want to disrobe in a most delicious manner. As she did in *Niagara*, but there, alone with him in the Merdeka Palace, she need not stop.

Once he had a great seer from the island of Sumatra brought to him in Jakarta to divine if his fantasy had any chance of becoming a reality during his lifetime. The seer read the half-entrails of a goat on the palace floor and determined that it would indeed occur if, and only if, the president wore a jade amulet in the shape of Sumatra around his neck for the rest of his life and promised to improve the roads around the seer's village. Sukarno promised. He feels the amulet warm against the hollow of his chest.

He has lived out his sexual fantasies with many beautiful women. Indonesian women. They were always told in advance what the president preferred. They were always thrilled they had been chosen and came to their task proud and prepared to render the state all the service they were capable of supplying. In his great Marilyn fantasy, however, it is he who approaches the idolized one; he who will do anything to satisfy; he who plays the role of supplicant and worshiper. The reversal, the humility, excites him.

He has envisioned it all. His brown body climbing her like a monkey slipping over a great, rounded greenheart tree, his head disappearing into its crevices, into places where the branches fold back upon themselves. It is those cosmic breasts he craves beyond anything, to bury his dark flesh in their delicious pink plumpness, losing himself in the sensuality of that flesh, its taste, its texture, its odor. If that could only happen one time, he would be satisfied until he drew no more breath.

In his fantasy, it all simply happens as he wills it. Here, in the reality of his London embassy, on the very brink of success, he must induce the act. He decides he must speak in a remarkable and seductive way. "In my country, Miss Monroe, you are considered the embodiment, no, rather the absolute distillation of the Caucasian woman. . . ."

"In my country too, Mr. Prez. Grrrouggghhh."

"In fact, there are religious purists in Indonesia who see you, therefore, as a danger to the state, who would have you banned. That is, have your films restricted and permit no photographs of you in magazines. They make no distinction between the illusions you create as an actress and the totally different person you actually are."

Marilyn loves the melodic manner of his speech. She is not particularly listening to what he says.

"If you bare your shoulders in a film, if you open your moist lips and slide your tongue over them, if, as they have heard, you have posed without garments . . ." As Sukarno reaches this point in the objectionable particulars, he imagines the calendar photos of the girl, Norma Jean Dough-

erty, that he has in his palace and feels himself going woozy
with desire; his mouth is suddenly very dry, his brow
moist, a pang below his stomach is most difficult to control.
He takes a long, shallow breath and falls silent.

Marilyn knows male glands and hormones are assert-
ing themselves, knows this brown man is struggling to
master a swiftly mounting desire. This intrigues her. For
the first time, she tries to imagine his sinewy body, its
range of tawny colors, its old man's stiffness. If it is to be,
she thinks, tonight and only tonight, nothing of duration.
Sheer diplomacy. A secret I'll love living with. Whenever
I'll see him on the news, hear about him on the radio, I'll
smile. An image of Dietrich as Mata Hari pops into her
head.

Sukarno sees the suggestion of a smile on her face and
imagines she finds him laughable. Reality is always so much
more untidy than fantasy. He rushes ahead: "These religious extremists in my country, they are not to be laughed
away. They have political power. I have had to maneuver
them, placate them whenever possible. Your films have
been, let me assure you, a serious point of contention. Fortunately for many of the people, they are very popular,
your films. I have seen every one, shown privately in the
Presidential Palace."

Her host expects to be thanked for his efforts on her
behalf, and Marilyn flutters her lids and blows him a kiss.
The kiss is a masterpiece—comic but slow enough to be
sensual also. She has leaned forward as well, and Hope's
cheek twitches as he watches the cloth of her bodice strain-
ing to hold in the floating breasts.

Sukarno wants to touch her so badly, his efforts at
restraint force a silent sigh from his lips. He looks at Hope
sharply, a sign, he believes, for the comedian to begin to
extricate himself, but Hope is intensely focused on an em-

broidered rose on Marilyn's bodice that is being stretched to bursting by Marilyn's right breast.

To get Hope's attention, Sukarno says, "Mr. Hope is partially responsible for your predicament in Indonesia, Miss Monroe."

"Oh, no, no, Mr. Prez. You can't pin that one on me. I'm innocent." Hope does his "innocent" take. "I've just been sitting here quietly admiring the flowers."

"I am referring, Mr. Hope, to the fact that you were responsible for bringing to my country at the end of the war some of the most beautiful Caucasian women in the world."

"You're not referring, I trust, to that little white slavery ring I've been accused of running. There was nothing to that. Rumors. I was cleared."

"U.S. troops, Miss Monroe, were going home from the Pacific theater, and Jakarta was one of the central staging areas for the withdrawal. Mr. Hope arrived to entertain many thousands of the troops. He had in his distinguished entourage many beautiful Hollywood stars. Indonesian men had never seen the like. Women with such golden hair and pink skin. Miss Joan Caulfield. Miss Joan Leslie. Miss Betty Hutton."

"And Kathryn Grayson and Laraine Day. All in all, quite a little harem. Wasn't Veronica Lake in that group?" Hope asks.

"Miss Veronica Lake, most assuredly." Sukarno repeats her name, slowly, admiringly. "It is hard for Westerners to imagine the excitement a woman such as Miss Lake can hold for the Oriental male. There is a widely recognized mystique the Oriental woman holds for the European man. I would not be surprised, Mr. Hope, broadly traveled as you are, if you haven't acknowledged privately the enormous attraction a beauteous Oriental woman may have exerted upon you."

Hope does not deliver the punch line. He just clears his throat. Marilyn leans over and taps him naughtily a little above his knee. Oh, how Sukarno wishes he were touched by her there.

Sukarno continues: "I believe the attraction of the blond, blue-eyed Occidental woman upon a full-blooded Oriental man has an even greater force and depth of passion. Of course, I can't prove this in every individual case. It is simply something I have come to believe."

Marilyn says, without trying to be especially provocative, "You appear to be speaking from personal experience."

"There is always, of course, the possibility that one can generalize wrongly on the basis of personal experience, madam. But there is no fear of that in my case. I know absolutely whereof I speak. It is precisely that powerful attraction that drives the religious purists to attempt to stamp out your films in my country. I believe even they are afraid they will succumb to your Western charms."

Marilyn enjoys the slow and subtle pace with which the seduction is developing. A combination of true curiosity and coyness prompts her to wonder aloud, "Are you willing to tell us, Mr. President, who your particular American dream girl was?"

Sukarno had, of course, heard the term before, but had not, until he heard it from her lips, realized how perfectly it described these women. They did indeed have the power to induce dreams. And the dreams, unless fulfilled, persisted night after night, year after year. He dared to think, since he was asked the question by the dream girl of dream girls, that his dream of her was close to being realized. "It was that very same Miss Veronica Lake."

"Oh, great," says Hope. "If the Feds ever find out about this, it's Leavenworth for me. They'll take away all my medals except the ones for good conduct."

"She was—how can I begin to describe how she seemed to a young man newly launched on the path that would take him to prominence in his country?—she was nothing less than an angel alighted in Jakarta." His expression frightens Marilyn a bit. The eyes especially have the slightest hint of madness behind them. This excites her too.

Perhaps it is only the lighting, because Sukarno has tipped his head back in recollection and picked up the red tints from the lampshade on his desk. "Of all the dream girls who were present then, Miss Lake struck me because of the manner in which her golden hair covered half her face."

"That was her shtick, the peekaboo hairdo, Mr. Prez."

"At any rate, because of the way she wore her hair, she struck me, in a sense, as a woman bridging two cultures. The covered face, the modesty so attractive in our Muslim women, and the quite immodest sexuality that is virtually the calling card of a Hollywood film star." Sukarno stops abruptly and looks down at his fingers. There is a thoughtful silence even Hope does not want to disturb, but he does get Marilyn's attention and rolls his eyes.

"At the reception, I was selected to dance with her. I knew many of the Western dances. Previously, I had danced with some of the ambassadors' wives and daughters but never with a woman of this ilk. My knees weakened as I approached her table, yet I did not wish any of my colleagues to see me falter. I repeated to myself what I intended to say to her: 'Miss Lake, may I have the honor of this dance.' " Marilyn is becoming increasingly attracted to him. Sukarno, however, is so absorbed in his recollection he does not realize it.

"The orchestra of American servicemen began to play 'Moonlight Serenade.' I approached her table and waited until her companion made her aware of me, my hovering, quaking presence. I began, 'Miss May . . . I would Lake

. . .' Realizing I had utterly misstated my request, I was about to bow and withdraw. Before I could even be plunged into embarrassment, Miss Lake was on her feet, with her hand extended. Her words are etched in memory— 'Anything you say, Cutey Pie.' *Cutey Pie.* My heavens, that was a woman. She led me to the dance floor.

"When I placed my arms in the normal dance position, she would have none of it. She planted herself closer than any woman I have ever known. Her small, sinewy body pressed completely against my own. I could feel through my clothing her muscle fiber, her bones, the soft flesh of her stomach, everything. Miss Lake was petite and matched me part for part; her blue eyes were on a level with mine. Knees, hips, chests. When I stepped with my leg, her thighs entwined it. I could not help the change that began to occur in me."

"Yeah, Veronica was always that way—great in sizing up a guy."

Marilyn is touched by the story of Achmed Sukarno's dance with Veronica Lake.

"There was a series of slow dances," Sukarno, smiling broadly, recalls. "I was trying to keep my body from Miss Lake's to give myself some respite, but that proved impossible, for she wished quite the opposite. So I surrendered to her desire and did not struggle against the urge any longer. My member on that particular occasion, at least, had a very strong will of its own."

No, no, Marilyn senses, something is not right here. She is not a prude, but the detail about his "member," especially with another man present, is a little creepy. Of course, she also recognizes the possibility that culture might account for differences in what is considered appropriate conversation. This was, after all, a respected world leader, at least that's what it said in the papers. Maybe this is what gets talked about on that level. Maybe this is what is considered humorous. Maybe she's just missed the point.

"We danced thus. She pressed against me, my member fully extended, disturbed beyond my desiring. She smiled like a woman with a great secret and whispered in my ear, 'Keep up the good work, Cutey Pie.' In that wonderfully soft voice I recalled from her films. I cannot tell you how close I was to fainting, not so much with desire—although there was a great deal of that mounting too—but with a profound confusion of emotions. I wanted to hold Miss Lake in an unreasonable way. Finally, she whispered, 'Now I know what they say about the natives is really true,' and she danced me off the floor toward the lobby. She took me in a taxi to her hotel. We sported the entire night. It was truly a matter of West meets East in every way conceivable, and neither hemisphere was disappointed. When it was done, because our lives rolled on tracks that would never again touch, it was done forever."

Nothing else could explain it, Marilyn decides: not class differences, not the extremes of culture, not divergent standards of propriety. This was just a little man bragging about his dick. If it was intended to turn her on—and she believes that was the point—it sure as hell had the opposite effect. All she has to do now is figure out how to leave.

"Let me show you both my sole souvenir of that chance-yet-fated meeting with Miss Lake." My god, Marilyn thinks, he's not going to show me . . . Sukarno rises deliberately and moves into the darkness of the room.

Marilyn leans inches from Hope's ear and whispers harshly, "You've got to get me out of here."

"That won't be easy. Before you arrived, Fu Manchu told me to cut out when he gives the signal. He wants you all to his inscrutable."

"Bob, I'm not kidding. Don't you dare leave me alone with him. Get me *out* of here."

"What's it worth to you? A couple of slow dances in Jakarta?"

She winces.

"You're gonna owe me one," he whispers.

"Anything," she agrees, "—within reason."

Sukarno returns was a faded publicity glossy of Veronica Lake. She's in a white two-piece bathing suit, sitting on a huge polka-dot beach ball. Her hands are supporting her on the ball, forcing her chest out; her head is thrown back in profile; long blond hair trails behind her. "See what she has written, Miss Monroe. You are among the few who will know its true significance." It reads: "To Suki, who knows how to make a short time go a long, *long* way. Love, Vicky." Sukarno places a stained fingernail below the underlined "*long*."

Before he sits down again, clutching his souvenir to his chest, Sukarno says, "But I have already kept Mr. Hope far too long from his rendezvous. Before you arrived, Miss Monroe, Mr. Hope had informed me he must be at the Hilton no later than midnight. I see he has already surpassed that time by a considerable amount and is too polite to apprise me. Those who await you will be already deeply concerned."

"Oh, no, no, I've got my reputation to think of. If I'm not at least one hour late, they won't think of me as a star. Besides, it's a bunch of honchos from M-G-M, fat, bald, and flatulent, who blow cigar smoke in your face, among other things, all the time."

Sukarno's eyes narrow. "I will call my driver." He stretches for the buzzer on the desk.

Marilyn says, with a worried aspect that can't be ignored, "I take it you haven't heard what's happened to Veronica."

Sukarno stops. "Not a misfortune, I sincerely hope."

"Tell him, Bob. About the hair."

"The hair. Oh, of course, the hair. Well, all her hair was, well, destroyed. Yes, burned off in an accident under the dryers at Warners. Everybody in the business heard about it, but I guess it takes a little longer for word to get to Jakarta. She couldn't work for two years, waiting for her hair to grow back. The only way she got back in pictures at all was to sign a release saying the studio was not responsible."

Sukarno appears deeply concerned but says nothing.

"Her hair, it never came in right. It never covered her face. When you saw her entire face, the old magic just wasn't there. That's when she started hitting the bottle pretty hard, and who can blame her."

"I never knew of this. She could have written to me. I would have aided her."

"Guess she had too much pride."

"Bob, don't spare the President. Tell him about how she died."

"Died? Do I have to? It's so depressing. And I'm sure he doesn't want all the gory details."

"I can assure you, Mr. Hope, I wish to know everything that pertains to Miss Lake. Even her demise. Spare me nothing in the name of sympathy."

"Things were so hard for her," Marilyn prompts, "that she fell into a deep, dark depression. She disappeared for long periods. When people saw her, they said she looked just terrible."

"Yeah. We all tried to help her, but she'd have none of our charity. Too proud, too depressed. Who knows what gets into the minds of these poor wretches. Her agent dropped her. No studio would take her calls. Then she just disappeared off the face of the earth."

"But before that, Bob, before they found her in the hotel room, all those disgusting one-nighters with lowlifes down by the waterfront. Bob," she whispers, "the social disease. The President wants to be spared nothing."

"I . . . I can't." Real tears form in Bob Hope's eyes, brim over, and begin to run down his cheeks. If he leaves it at this, he will be a convincing crier. But he cannot. He starts to sob. Marilyn wishes he hadn't. "You," he coughs, "you tell him."

"The end was hard. No money. She moved into worse and worse neighborhoods. Finally, she had to resort to, you know, the world's oldest profession. Drank too much, got beat up by some of her clients too. She developed the diseases that such a life brings."

Sukarno's face is absolutely immobile, his mouth slightly agape. His hands hang limp below his chair seat. His small body seems to have gotten smaller.

With Hope sobbing accompaniment, Marilyn bravely finishes the tale: "They found pills beside her bed. No note. The coroner was kind; he called the death 'accidental.' " Marilyn has to make a quick decision and cannot resist the temptation. "The autopsy revealed that her syphilis was, surprisingly, not a recent development but a particularly virulent form she'd had most of her life."

Sukarno's lips purse and ease and purse again, the only facial movement.

"C'mon, Bob, we'd better leave the President to his grief." Marilyn stands and grabs up the still-sobbing Hope by his shoulder pad. Using Hope as a shield, Marilyn sidesteps toward the door.

"She was," Hope weeps, "a great little gal, great little gal. Don't think the evening hasn't been interesting, Mr.

Prez. From my point of view, I can't remember ever having a . . ." They are at the door. Marilyn reaches behind her back for the knob. After fumbling a bit, à la Dorothy Lamour, she feels the spring yield and the door open. Sukarno remains stock-still.

Now if they can only make it down the staircase, out the door, and off the embassy grounds. They start down the stairs arm in arm. At the bottom, servants and guards wait attentively. Hope is faking charming conversation— "Dit-doo-datta-and-dit-doo-datta"—while chuckling from time to time. His nonchalance is as unreal as his sobbing was. Marilyn is smiling with half-closed lids, trying to become the Dorothy Lamour character and, therefore, not a corporeal being who could be obstructed. Five steps from the bottom, they pick up the pace. In the foyer, they are approaching a trot and glide past servants holding their wraps. The Indonesians look startled.

They are almost in a run. Marilyn's high heels clack irregularly. Hope is at the front entrance first and pushes hard against a heavy door that opens inward. "Pull it, for god's sake, pull it." Surely Lamour's line. Hope pulls, and it opens.

They dash past the guards standing at each side of the open iron gate. One salutes as they disappear into the darkness of Curzon Street. The air is frigid, and still they do not stop. At the distant corner there are bright lights. *People, civilized human beings, safety*, Marilyn thinks. Hope thinks, *Taxis*.

They continue to run toward the neon, slower and slower. Marilyn wobbles on her heels; Hope wheezes furiously. A taxi turns into Curzon from Piccadilly, and the two, standing in the middle of the road, force it to stop.

"Get us out of here fast, chief, and there's an extra tenner in it for you," Hope tells the elderly cabbie, who has seen plenty of Americans drunk in these streets in recent years. The woman, though, is a better-looking bird than he's used to.

The driver is cruising, looking in his mirror for a clue as to where they want to go. Finally, Hope says to Marilyn, "I really am staying at the Hilton. How's about your coming up for a drink, just to warm the cockles, as they say."

Lamour would have said, "Gee, I'd love to, Bob, and I sure am grateful for your getting me out of that mess back there. But Aunt Mary expected me home hours ago, and she'll be worried to death, the poor dear." Marilyn says, "Gee, I'd love to, Bob, but all I want right now is a nice warm bubble bath." Hope starts to speak. Marilyn puts a finger to his lips. "Alone, Bob. Alone."

"So what'll be yer pleasure?" the cabbie asks.

"If you mean where are we going? We'll be dropping the lady off first. And there's no 'pleasure' in that."

Late the following afternoon, Marilyn's maid brings her a box from the Indonesian embassy. The wrong size for flowers. It is her jacket, the short-waisted brocaded top to her dress. The note says: "You disappeared so abruptly you neglected to retrieve this. A part of me was certain you would call back for it today, but such wishful thinking is not necessary. I am certain destiny has further plans for we two. Suki."

Marilyn takes a sheet of hotel paper from her desk and writes: "Thanks for the jacket. The ensemble was *really* expensive. If destiny has any plans for us, I hope it coincides with a time when my rash has begun to respond to medication. Yours truly, M.M."

CHAPTER ELEVEN

An Ace in the Hole?

LIGHTS

MADEMOISELLE: How important is luck in a career?

MONROE: It's everything. Not only in a career, in every single phase of life. It's all there is.

MADEMOISELLE: Some actresses say that talent is the most important thing and that getting the chance to show their talent is where luck comes in. Some performers get their chance early, some later, but if you've got real talent, the world will eventually take notice. You don't seem to agree.

MONROE: Of course not. Because whether you have talent or not is all a matter of luck in the first place. Why you and not somebody else? So is whether or not you'll even have a chance to develop it—if you were lucky enough to have some to begin with. Luck touches every single thing about us.

MADEMOISELLE: Then you don't believe in the idea that we can make our own luck.

MONROE: That's just a myth perpetuated by the lucky ones. It makes them feel they did more than they really did. It makes them feel as though they earned their success.

MADEMOISELLE: But didn't they?

MONROE: Does someone really *earn* being lucky?

CAMERA

John Huston realized early he might have a disaster on his hands. Huston first suspected as much when he worked with Miller on turning Miller's short story into a screenplay. Miller was professional in every way: disciplined, enthusiastic, full of ideas about how to turn the very short and spare, three-character, all-male piece into a full-blown film. The main script problem was Roslyn Taber, an educated eastern divorcée: she was not a presence in the story, merely someone alluded to often by two of the cowboys as someone strange and different and desirable.

She had to be brought alive and integrated into the scenario, brought by believable degrees to the scene of the central action, where a small herd of wild mustangs are trapped to be hauled off to a factory where they'll be slaughtered for pet food. Roslyn tries to save them. It was a powerful scene and a powerful symbol, a strong climax to a thoughtful script. Marilyn would play Roslyn.

There wasn't a doubt that Miller could make the script adaptations. What troubled Huston was Miller's constant sense of desperation about his wife. Huston felt that Miller was writing to hold on to his marriage; it was as though he searched for the power to choose words that could cast a spell and bring back someone who had departed years before.

Since desperation also happened to be a main theme of the film, Huston believed he could control and shape the real events in such a way as to get the performance of her life out of Marilyn as well as a brilliantly powerful script from her husband.

Huston had directed her in The Asphalt Jungle, *the movie that first got her noticed, in 1950. She trusted him implicitly then; he had tried to reawaken that trust.*

And Huston had allies. Gable had signed to play Gay Langland, Roslyn's steady, the fellow who organizes the mustang roundup. Montgomery Clift was Perce Howland, the young bull rider who chases rodeo prizes for his unsteady living and sees no particular purpose to anything else he does.

It was an extraordinary cast. Gable and Clift were as solid and reliable as two stars could be; Huston would set the tone, and the three would keep Marilyn in bounds and carry her to a brilliant performance. That was Huston's plan.

She arrived in Reno two days late, telling anyone who would listen, including the wife of the governor of Nevada, who was on hand to greet her with flowers, "Other women have periods. I have historical eras."

On the set, which was mostly a desert location miles south of Reno, she was usually ready hours after the shooting schedule. No one wanted to figure the days that had been lost because of her lateness. She was drinking heavily—vodka straight—with some of the crew well into the night. When she did shoot, she always knew her lines and took direction well.

Gable was miffed by her lateness. Huston tried to convince him that Marilyn was in serious trouble—a borderline hysteric—but was giving a remarkable performance, at least some of the time. Gable would mumble something about getting her to behave like a damn professional, but he bore her selfish helplessness silently for the most part.

Clift stayed to himself more than anyone else. He carried a thick book always and shot his scenes without Marilyn when they were scheduled, but he also accommodated Marilyn's whims. Miller delivered his rewrites to Huston daily, but most of the time he stayed off the set. He kept his distance, believing the words he wrote for his wife, the ideas, the finished film, would have the power to heal Marilyn. Huston tried mightily to hold things together with, at various times and combinations, strength, humor, intelligence, and his fear-invoking demeanor. After examining the rushes daily, he was never quite sure of what he had; he knew that whatever it was, it was something unconventional.

The torrential rains that disrupted electrical power in the area for three days—except for some Reno hotels and casinos— came at a very good time for Huston. There was less than a week of shooting left; tempers were frayed, nerves shattered. Gable had become almost sullen. He looked very weary. Clift had withdrawn to the point where he rarely talked to anyone. It was a good time to relax and regroup for a final assault on The Misfits. *Huston wanted his cast and crew to come together in the face of the common natural hardships they were all being asked to face.*

Huston seized the opportunity of still another day without reliable electric power to invite Marilyn, Miller, Gable, Clift, and Al Garson, the second cameraman and an old friend, to his

suite on the seventh floor of the Mapes Hotel for a night of seri-
ous poker. Each of them—except for Garson—begged off, but
Huston insisted. Only Miller withstood his insistence, claiming
the need to rework some of the final rewrites.

Huston's guests—all wearing casual western clothing—
stood around a green felt poker table in his suite. Even though
the room was well lighted, a dozen tall candles burned.

ACTION

"Just a precaution," Huston, nodding at the candles, says
in his most cordial voice. "Electricity's been off and on all
day. Just want to be sure I'd be able to catch a cheater in
case the lights go out." He draws on an unusually long
panatela.

Gable wonders aloud, "And who the hell is going to be
watching you?"

"I suggest you assign someone the task."

"I'll sit on his left," Marilyn offers. "I think I can
handle that much of him."

"Fine. I'll take the right." Gable sits down.

It is obvious to everyone where Huston intends to sit.
A green eyeshade, red sleeve garters, and two sealed decks
of playing cards are arranged next to an unopened bottle of
Scotch almost as old as Marilyn.

Al Garson approaches the table, rubbing his hands and
licking his lips in anticipation. He has a reputation as a
gambler, and specifically as an excellent poker player. Clift
hangs back a bit, as Perce Howland might until he had a
drink in him.

"House rules," Huston announces in his director's

voice. "Rule one. Straight poker only. Dealer's choice. No gimmick games." He is looking at Marilyn.

She flutters her lashes. "Do you consider Grab Bag a gimmick?"

"What precisely is this Grab Bag?"

"Deuces and nines are wild. Eights, you get an extra card. Oh, and one-eyed picture cards are wild too, provided you already have a deuce showing. But it's played like straight poker."

Huston doesn't deem the game worthy of a response. "Rule two. Ante ten bucks. Three raises, no more. Twenty-dollar limit, except for the last hand—pot limit. White chips are five, reds ten, blues are twenty. You'll observe the house has carefully counted out five hundred for each of you, so you're all deeply in my debt even before we begin. We'll settle up after the last hand. Need I remind you that the house has its means of collecting?" Huston pulls his ear forward and bends his nose.

"Rule three. Each player must imbibe. Anyone can play poker sober. The real test of character is how one plays with a potent glass in his hand. *Her* hand." He bows to Marilyn.

Clift, the lightest drinker in the room on this night, says, "Why don't I just write you a check for five hundred now, go back to my room, and save myself a terrible humiliation."

"All you might want in the way of libation is on the sideboard. Help yourselves." They're all seated now. "Rule four. Only one subject is forbidden. *Verboten. Interdit.* And that, as you've already anticipated, I'm sure, is our noble project." No one, in fact, has anticipated the forbidden subject. "I have a superstition about discussing a film that's almost in the can." He didn't really; he simply thought it was a good psychological ploy, what with just one final push remaining. "So if we're all amenable, I suggest we choose our poison and go about the pleasant task of tearing each other's hearts out."

The mood is exactly as Huston wishes it—not yet relaxed but with the possibility of getting there.

"If there's nobody else for vodka," Marilyn announces, "I hate to open a bottle just for myself. I can do Scotch like everyone."

"Scotch's fine with me," says Gable. "I just want to be able to answer the phone coherently. In case. Kay's expecting anytime now. It's early, but it's possible. Spoke to her earlier. Some discomfort but generally okay. I told her I'd be here, John, in case there's some news."

"Bet you want a boy. Mature men seem to want boys." Marilyn has become Roslyn just for the hell of it. She's teasing Gable gently.

"I've got six of 'em. All boys. All ages," says Garson. "Anyone's short, I'll be glad to make a deal. Everything's negotiable."

Gable is earnest: "First of all, I just want a healthy kid—and Kay to come out of it all right—but sure, at this time of my life I'd like a son to carry on the name, the family tradition. I don't see a darn thing wrong with wanting that."

"That's what I said the first time it happened, and the second," Garson added. "But now, enough already."

Huston mumbles something about a film he shot in Africa—he does not want to seem to be place-dropping—"where male children were highly prized. The belief was that the more virile the father, the more likely he was to produce a son. They circumcise and nail the foreskins to trees in front of their kraals. The man with the greatest number of foreskins on his tree became the tribe's warrior, their general, in essence."

"I'm not looking to become commander in chief," says Gable.

Garson centers his pupils in his eyeballs, creating an expression of quivering comic stupor: "Jeez, I never shoulda quit. I coulda been king of the jungle."

"Hardly, Alvin. There were scores of foreskins on those trees. The tribe practiced polygamy. The most incredible thing was that the greatest warrior, when we were there, was a scrawny chap who had the unique capacity to impregnate all his wives with male offspring."

"I'm not surprised," says Marilyn. "It's always the small, silent ones you've got to watch out for." She hooks Clift's arm and gives him a soft kiss. His ears redden.

"No, no," continues Huston. "Precisely because he accepted the symbolic power of those foreskins, he really believed he was the greatest warrior amongst them. He was a fierce little rooster. And I'll be darned if all the other warriors, great powerful men, some of them, didn't believe it too. I'm not saying they just went along with it; they absolutely *believed*."

"All of which goes to show what exactly?" Clift is genuinely curious.

Garson can't miss the opportunity: "That it's not the size of the man that counts. It's the sperm count in the man."

Huston says, "Well, among other things, any system, no matter how irrational or arbitrary, will probably work as long as people believe in it. And that there can be no doubt a mighty warrior, such as you, Clark, should produce a male child."

Glasses are raised and clinked. Marilyn is glad the subject of children has finally been dropped. But the point Huston made about the power of belief interests her. "So if, say, we're working on a project we all believe in, that means it'll come across in the end?"

"Rule number four," Gable warns.

Marilyn looks into his weathered face and sees more than weariness; she sees a touch of sorrow. He's been pre-occupied these last two weeks, not at all the Gable everyone knew. Even though his character, Gay Langland, is some-one very like himself, Gable's not had much conviction. It's the baby, she thought. Now she thinks maybe it's some-thing more. She wishes impulsively she had been better to him on the set, more thoughtful. She's kept him waiting too much. She wants to explain she hasn't been herself lately, either. It had gotten so that she couldn't look at her hus-band. Can't sleep. Can't concentrate. Can't . . . do any-thing right.

"Since I just broke rule four anyway, here's something I want to give you, Gay." Marilyn gets up, walks behind Huston, and jumps into Gable's lap. She gives him a long, tender kiss on the lips. Spilled Scotch soils the table. "And I hope to hell you have twin boys; no, triplets. That's all I wanted to say."

Garson, imitating Gable perfectly, lifts his glass and says, "As far as triplets, Scarlett, frankly, I don't give a damn."

Gable brushes Garson aside. "Frankly, I give a great big damn, Rosie." That's what he's been calling Marilyn on the set. Gable holds his hug a long time while looking helplessly at the other men. His smile twists his mustache sidewise.

"I must remind you, friends, this is supposed to be a night of competitive poker, not a cast party." Huston snaps his sleeve garters, adjusts his eyeshade, and starts to mix the cards.

"Speaking of cast parties, I worked . . ." Garson, trying to light his cigar, puffs violently. ". . . on Linda Darnell's first picture. She was . . ." Puff, puff, puff. ". . . absolutely awful. At the party, Paul Henreid, Lee Tracy, Forrest Tucker, Alfredo Cortez, everyone, got up and gave a little toast about how good it was to work on the picture, and everyone managed to work in a little something about how talented Linda was and how they all looked forward to working with her again. Then Shirley Booth stood up and said, 'Well, it really was fun, but I guess I'm the only one here who doesn't want to fuck Linda.' "

The story gets nasal laughs.

"I loved that woman." Garson puffs.

"Worked with Shirley in my third film," says Huston as he deals. "She was a stage actress and wasn't savvy about the camera, but I learned more from her about leaving holes than from anyone since."

Clift says, "Leaving holes?"

"When not to talk," Garson explains. "Leaving holes."

Everyone has thrown in a red chip except Marilyn. "I can put in two whites, can't I? Just for the aesthetics." She holds them over the pot and lets them fall sharply. The cards whirl across the felt.

"Draw poker, jacks or better to open," the dealer asserts.

"Wheeee, isn't this fun? Just one thing I'm not sure of. Is five cards all the same . . . I mean the same color . . . ?"

"Suit."

". . . the same suit. Is that better than three of a kind and a pair all together?"

Garson intercedes: "A full house. A full house beats a flush. And if I didn't know better, I might fall for the Little Miss Gullible act, but I've seen you pluck the fillings right out of the teeth of the guys who worked on *Some Like It Hot*."

"That was ages ago. A girl forgets the finer points if she doesn't play regular."

"Just play cautiously at first, Rosie," Gable advises with mock seriousness. "Till it comes back to you."

"Wonderful idea," she says vacantly while staring at her cards.

Clift lights two cigarettes and gives one to Marilyn. "Philip Morris," she says. "They're strong." She accepts.

Gable says, "Doctor says I shouldn't, but I've been a real good boy." He reaches for the pack. Everyone at the table is smoking.

Gable's two pair beats Huston's kings and Garson's queens for a nice-sized first pot. Clift and Marilyn dropped out after Garson's opening bet.

Given rule number four, there isn't much of mutual interest to talk about. Garson tells some more show business stories out of the side of his mouth while working his cigar. Clift is almost silent. Marilyn complains about the cards she's been getting. Gable checks his watch frequently. Garson's cigar keeps going out. Only Huston, who is absorbed in the game and the human dynamics around the table—he's also winning—is content.

"Maybe I'd better phone, just to see what's up."

"Clark, you can only do mischief," Huston advises. "These things are better left to the women. They've been giving birth ever since Eve. Right, Marilyn?"

Marilyn looks around the room quizzically. "As the only human being present who could never have a piece of human tissue nailed to a tree, I must say that if I were Kay, I'd love a phone call. Every hour on the hour, if possible." She covers Huston's wrist with her pale fingers and pats him consolingly. "Sorry, boss."

"I'd better call. Just deal me out for a while."

"Phone's in the bedroom. More private."

Gable, in his distinctive rolling gait, moves toward the bedroom. "No one touch my chips." An afterthought: "Or my drink."

"Tell Kay how much I care." Marilyn hears her voice coming from a great distance. She's getting high. "And don't tell her anything about that African craziness."

Clift adds, "Give her our best."

Huston indicates it might be better to wait until Gable returns before the game continues. Garson, whose turn it is to deal, flips four aces off the top of the deck, picks them up with another card, mixes the deck thoroughly, and takes the same four aces off the top. He does this three or four times, each time making more intense googly eyes when the aces reappear. Finally, he offers the cards to Marilyn to cut. She cuts and cuts again. The aces tumble off the top.

"Why," Clift wonders aloud, "are we playing poker with this man?"

"Because," Huston assures, "Alvin would never do anything improper during the game. I know every trick he has."

Now Garson, as though to show the magic spell has been broken, coughs up the ten and seven of hearts, the six of clubs, and the nine of spades. He looks as innocent and lovable as Harpo Marx, while producing a happy horn sound inside his throat.

"I swear, except for Monty here, I feel that I'm the captive of . . ." Marilyn doesn't quite know whom she is the captive of, but rather than hurt Huston's feelings, she settles for ". . . zanies."

Clift makes his eyes wild. And threatening. "Why do you say *except* for Monty? I could be the most dangerous of all."

There has always been a peculiar, otherworldly quality about Clift that Marilyn loves. His reactions onscreen are never predictable but always true. More than anything else, his voice gives him a foreign quality she finds alien but attractive. It's as though he doesn't have earthly parents but appeared suddenly as himself, without a history, without background or experience. Someone Marilyn wants very much to protect.

Huston is using very little of the alien Clift in *The Misfits*. He wants Monty to play against those tendencies as much as he reasonably can, to be the wet-behind-the-ears cowpuncher who barely realizes his life of drifting, drinking, and winning an occasional rodeo contest will leave him broken down and alone.

Working against his essence as hard as he may, Clift cannot quite reach into himself to become "your typical rodeo shit-kicker"—as Huston described the character. Huston is trying for more by asking Monty to do less. No one is sure if it is working. Without complaint, Clift has persisted.

Marilyn says to Monty, "You're not from the West Coast. There's an accent I can't place. Something unusual, sounds almost foreign. From where?"

"I've got to congratulate you on being so perceptive. It is foreign. Omaha, Nebraska. My father was a bank president there. Things don't get any more foreign than that, now, do they?"

She shakes her head. "Still, it's got to come from somewhere. The unusual quality."

"Maybe it's just because I'm an actor. We've been known to make believe a lot."

She's not convinced. "No. There's something."

"I'm a twin. Does that help? I came second. Always the gentleman. I let my sister see the moon first." That spooky quality Marilyn was talking about is there now.

Huston's eyes have narrowed: he has never inquired into Clift's background. Garson is shuffling the cards expertly. He's hoping someone will notice.

Clift, checking his watch, says, "I wonder if you'd mind if I flipped on the debate. It's the last one."

Huston is clearly not enthusiastic.

"It wasn't one of the rules," Clift reminds. He gets up and turns on a TV console against the far wall. Faintly at first, then more boldly, a black-and-white Richard Nixon begins to emerge. His brow is moist; his eyebrows want to descend, but he pulls against them; his head quivers with the passionate whisper of his words: "No one believes in a stronger defense than I do, having been vice-president under one of the most notable generals in the history of this great Republic, which has remained great precisely because . . ."

The camera cuts to a reaction shot of the opponent. John Kennedy's face is attentive, thoughtful; the eyes twinkle.

"That hair," Marilyn says. "Can we afford a president who looks like he's going to his first holy communion?"

The moderator says, "Thirty seconds to rebut, Senator."

"We're not speaking here about whether or not Americ-er was victorious in World War II. We know the entire free world owes its freedom to the men and families who made incredible sacrifices. . . ."

"Smart cookie," says Garson, still shuffling nervously. "Reminding everyone he served."

"And of the brother who was killed, too," mumbles Clift.

". . . Or even in Kore-er, where success came at a great cost. We are speaking about being prepared, not about reacting. And that is not a matter of presidential rhetoric.

That is a matter of hard numbers. Numbers of bombers, numbers of fighter groups. Numbers of missiles and of warplanes. Numbers of warships and of guns and tanks and of men in the field. And when I look at the numbers, they do not add up to a country that is prepared to enter the 1960s as the world's best hope for peace and stability through strength. I wonder if the vice-president could . . ."

Marilyn says, "He might look like an altar boy, but he sure sounds like an Irish kid spoiling for a fight."

"What he's saying makes sense," Garson says. "The best way to have peace is not to let anyone think they can start anything. Besides, just look at this guy." Nixon fills the screen. "Would you buy a used missile from a face like that?"

Huston wishes he had wisdom enough to have anticipated a fifth rule, or had the television removed from the room. He smiles when he sees Gable emerge. "Ah, now we can get back to business. Everything's all right, I trust."

"Fine. Fine. Glad I called." His voice has a slight gargle to it. He sees Nixon's face and shudders. "I need a drink. We all will if he . . ."

"Turn that thing off as you go by," Huston requests.

Clift says, "I'm interested."

Marilyn supports Clift. "A little background distraction is good for poker. It'll help me when I try my supersmooth, never-seen-anything-like-it-before, once-in-a-lifetime, walk-away-with-their-pants bluff."

"Try a bluff in this game, lady, and the pants'll be on the other ankle," warns Garson, beginning to deal.

"She's all right," says Gable about his wife, responding to nothing that's been said. "I guess it's a little tough for her, alone. Her mom's there, all the best medical attention you can have." He picks up his cards. "Let's see. I'll take three."

Clift is turned sideways, more attentive to the vice-president's lips than to his cards.

"Monty?"

"Pass."

"How many cards?"

"Oh, I guess I'll take . . ." An ace tumbles to the table as Clift examines his cards. He picks it up, smiling apologetically. "One."

Clift bets twenty dollars. Garson, with a pair of queens, calls, just to keep things honest. Huston, with jacks, drops. Monty wins with two pair. Marilyn applauds.

"So what do you think you'll call him?"

Downing what's left of his Scotch, Gable says, his words melting into one another: "Haven't picked out a boy's name. Don't want to put the hex on. If it's a girl, I like Elizabeth. Aristocratic-sounding. A boy's going to be a lot tougher."

"Why not Prince?" There's a pause, then Garson explains: "The King . . . Prince—get it?"

"Or Clark junior," Marilyn offers, gathering up the discards.

"Stay away from juniors at all costs," Huston insists. "They're the mark of Cain. I was almost Walter junior. Thank god my mother had some sense, or I'd still be the old man's kid to the entire world."

"What about Milhous?" Clift is smiling sneakily.

"Speaking of nailing a dick to a tree," says Garson.

The game continues without real enthusiasm—the hands are generally unexciting; except for Marilyn, the winning is fairly well spread around the table. The banter Huston anticipated is sporadic and subdued. The booze has thickened tongues, not loosened them; the heavy smoke is a separating veil.

Huston refills glasses. Cards are dealt automatically.

Voices say the minimum: "Three cards." "Raise ten." "Call." "I'm out."

Marilyn has become as silent as Clift. Her expression is distant, almost insensible.

"S'matter, Rosie? Your luck'll change."

"S'not that." She seems on the verge of tears. "It's that I just realized something."

"What?"

"Can't say. Rule four."

"We'll suspend rule four."

She looks at Huston for permission. He doesn't stop her.

"I figured out why he called it *The Misfits*. It ain't just those poor souls in the movie who are the misfits. It's all of us. It's everybody in the whole world who can't find a niche, a real home. Look at us. We're half looped and playing poker in the middle of the night in a room filled with candles. You're having a baby you won't even be there to see born. I got a marriage . . ." There was no point in finishing what everyone knew was already finished. Her eyes fill with moisture; two large tears form on her lower lashes and swell. The men watch silently as they fall to her cheeks and mark lavender trails to her chin. No one speaks.

John Fitzgerald Kennedy's voice, full of reasoned hope and contagious confidence, is the counterpoint to Marilyn's despair and the helpless silence of the poker players. Maybe we do not have to be misfits; maybe there's an alternative.

Suddenly, Kennedy's voice breaks. At precisely the same moment the lights in the room flicker and fall to half-light. Kennedy's pale, diagonal image bounces across the screen. Then he is reduced to a diminishing dot. The lights go out.

The candlelight gives the room the charm of a comfortable mausoleum.

"Might as well be misfits in this world," says Huston. "There is no certainty, no real security anywhere I've ever been. Uncertainty, that's the name of the game, always has been, always will be."

"But Clark's baby?"

Huston shrugs off the burden of her question. "The real misfits, they're the ones who have no saving illusions. We create illusions; we know what power they have. And that's why we've got such a darned good movie. Or just about got one." He reaches for Marilyn's hand, takes it to his lips, and kisses it with great delicacy and feeling. He closes his eyes.

Garson, who has not understood much of what has transpired since he lost to Clift's two pair, says, "Call it a night?"

"A night?" barks Huston. "Is Richard Misfit Nixon, there, calling it a night just because his opponent's smarter, better-looking, got more money, is ahead in the polls, and the lights just went out on him? Course not."

"Rule number four," Garson says with a warning finger. "Can't say *Misfit*."

"Where've you been man? We've suspended rule four. Now here's what I propose. We play once around the table. One deal apiece. It goes around to Marilyn. But please humor me, folks: let's make it real poker."

"Sure, *mon capitaine*," says Marilyn, saluting and smiling her friendliest smile.

The cards do not cooperate. One player in each hand is dealt commanding cards, the others nothing at all. The virtue of this, at least as far as Clift, Gable, and Marilyn are concerned, is that the time passes quickly.

The deal comes around to Marilyn. Huston says, "Okay, last hand."

Garson says, "Fine by me."

Gable nods and Clift waggles a finger. Marilyn dumb-blondes a response: "Goody. Now I can try my famous bluff. The dealer would like to change her luck by changing the game a little. Five-card stud. Hole card down, next four straight up. Let's ante fifty—what the hell." Her smile charms compliance out of the others.

Chips clatter in the middle of the table. "Bit steep," Garson says as he throws his in.

"Last hand, Al," Marilyn teases.

Marilyn slowly deals out the hole cards to each player. For a moment the lights come on at half strength and the room seems darker. On the TV a momentary shot of the debate audience applauding. Then the lights and the TV flicker and die.

The betting is modest until Huston shows a pair of fives. He bets them heavily. Marilyn throws in most of her remaining chips. Clift drops out. Garson stays. Gable says, "I'll look at one more."

The next round gives Garson a pair of sevens on board. The betting becomes intriguing. Garson bets thirty dollars on his sevens. Gable drops out. Huston must stay for the final card—he needs another five or a second pair to beat Garson.

Marilyn raises Garson fifty dollars, and suddenly Garson and Huston notice the ace of hearts sitting prominently among her face cards. There are no other aces showing anywhere. They each call Marilyn's raise.

The last card changes nothing on board. Garson, wary, bets ten. Huston, beaten by Garson, folds his cards. Marilyn injects a tone of seriousness under her silly voice: "Refresh my memory." She touches Huston's hand. "When you were reciting the rules, there was something about being able to bet the pot on the last hand. Rule two, or something?"

"So stated."

"How much is in there, then?" Her voice has become more businesslike by degrees.

Huston counts. "I get six hundred and ten dollars."

"Fine. Then I'll see your ten dollars. Al—that'll bring the pot to six hundred and twenty—and I'll raise you the whole six hundred and twenty. I don't have the chips, but I'll be glad to buy some more."

Huston is thrilled. This is poker. He says, "The house advances you the credit."

Garson's in a bind. He's the only one at the table to whom that sort of money still means something. He doesn't want to complain that the rule was originally made for a game that was supposed to run until midnight. If he tries to invoke a technicality now, he'll look chintzy.

She probably has the other ace, and that beats his sevens. Still, the gambler in him knows you can't ever let someone steal a pot when you've got him beat on board. Al Garson ponders in the candle-filled quiet. No other aces played; chances are she has one.

The room is more than silent. Marilyn steals a look at the clock without realizing that it has stopped. Twenty to eleven. "Aunt" Ana Lower used to tell her, "Princess, when there is a great stillness in the room, and it is either twenty minutes before or twenty minutes after the hour—that means an angel is passing."

The candlelit stillness in Huston's suite is really a type of paralysis. It grips them all; they are locked in it. None more than Al Garson. He does not want to have to break out of it with a decision.

It is not he, really, but his fingers that decide not to decide. They turn his cards over and toss them toward the middle of the table. "You've got the aces. It's yours."

Only then is everyone free to move.

Marilyn leans far over the table, her breasts forming swaying spheres as she sweeps the noisy chips toward her.

"You had the bullets, didn't you?" Garson asks.

Marilyn slips her hole card into the mélange of unused cards. She goes dumb again: "I was under the impression that the name of the game was poker, Mr. Garson, and in poker you pay to see what another player has."

"I know you had the aces. You had to have 'em."

Marilyn clucks her tongue and flutters her lashes.

Marilyn was scheduled to shoot three short scenes with Gable in the morning, after power had been restored. She was in her trailer getting made up while flat on her back until almost eleven. Ill, an assistant director reported. Gable waited two hours before Huston had to cancel. They shot the scenes successfully when the light softened that afternoon.

The Misfits never was the movie Huston thought he could finesse out of Marilyn and Gable and Clift and Miller. Or the movie it should have been. Every time he looked at it, he saw how Marilyn was tearing emotions out of herself at great personal expense—hitting the mark sometimes, missing others, but weakening and diminishing herself in the process. Never bluffing.

The Misfits was a jinx picture. On the day John F. Kennedy was inaugurated, Al Garson was shot by his ex-wife. He hadn't paid child support for over a year. He never fully recovered use of the left side of his body.

Kay Gable gave birth to a son, a boy the King never saw. Gable died of a heart attack nine days after the poker game.

Montgomery Clift, who had been in an automobile crash that almost took his life and left him disfigured a few years before *The Misfits*, died at the age of forty-five in 1966.

Marilyn's marriage, a body long grown cold, was interred in an expeditious Mexican divorce soon after shooting ended. She never completed another film.

John Huston, the oldest person at the candlelight poker game, left Nevada with a long creative period ahead of him.

CHAPTER TWELVE

Dream Girl, Dream Cycle, Dr. Waxx

LIGHTS

PARIS MATCH: As the world's number one "Dream Girl," doesn't it feel strange to be the object of someone else's dream?

MONROE: It's really crazy. As long as you're the person who is dreaming, you still exist. I mean, you might get completely caught up in your own fantasies, but you are still the one who's creating them, so you must be real anyway. When you're the dream, my god, everything gets all mixed up. You don't even belong to yourself any more. You belong to someone else, you're their creation.

231

MATCH: Are you saying the two things—your dream and the dreams of your fans—get confused?

MONROE: That's the least of it. Sometimes I actually swing back and forth between my dreams and the dreams of people I don't even know.

MATCH: If you don't know these people, why should you take it upon yourself to fulfill their dreams?

MONROE: It's too . . . it's too complicated to explain. It's my job. It's what I do. But I know that what I've been dreaming lately is a great big mish-mash of emotions. Really confusing stuff.

MATCH: Are you aware of the latest dream theory? It is the only true advance on the subject since Freud and Jung. It says, in essence, we get the dreams we really want or, more to the point, the dreams we deserve.

MONROE: Oh. What a horrible thought!

CAMERA

Marilyn didn't have friends. She had people she needed; they, in turn, had someone who needed them, although the mutual need was not a steady one but wavered in ways no one quite understood or could predict. Marilyn convinced herself often that because so many elements of friendship were there, these people were her friends. Mostly because she wanted that to be the case. They were maids and secretaries and drivers and actors and writers and cameramen and agents and directors and crew mem-

bers; but no matter what sympathetic sentiments were aroused in them, those sentiments could never be sustained. Simple friendship was impossible because she had become Marilyn Monroe.

Marilyn counted Mickie Woody her best friend in the late '40s. But except for the trip to Fontana when Mickie was pregnant, Norma Jean held herself emotionally aloof, planning a very different life from the one waiting for Mickie. After Marilyn got her first speaking part, in Dangerous Years, *Mickie offered to move in with her. Marilyn held Mickie off for a long time before she herself moved in with Johnny Hyde.*

It wasn't only fame and position that created the imbalance that prevented friendships from developing naturally. It was also how screwed up Marilyn had become. After Marilyn died, Monty Clift said, "I never knew anyone who had so many different parts hiding inside her, and they all ended up working against each other." Which was his way of saying there was always something Marilyn did that made you dislike her when she felt you were getting too close. Winchell, by the way, had concurred in his fashion, saying, "She's an unstable bitch, but the talented ones usually are."

Because the roles of friend, employee, client, confidant, and co-worker had gotten so confused, Marilyn's Hollywood analyst, Dr. Adrian Whiteman, became her best, most consistent friend. He had the purest of motives for caring about her. She was his patient, and her well-being was his concern and responsibility. He also happened to be sincere in wanting her to be happy. For Whiteman, the complexity of her conflicted, passionate personality was an attraction. He knew there was no cure, only a lifetime of adjustments, but that really wasn't so bad, given what life does to so many.

Dr. Whiteman was particularly concerned about the increase in recent months of her tendency toward lateness. It had always been bad, but it had become insupportable, prompting

Fox to threaten legal action. The letter from the studio's lawyers cited this clause from her contract: ". . . said employer has the right to seek redress in the case of wanton acts of disruption or such other attempts to subvert the authority of said employer that may result in the loss of production time and increased cost to said employer. . . ."

While shooting the studio scenes for The Misfits, *she was late ten days in a row, never by less than forty-five minutes and twice by over two hours. "Said employer" lost a bundle. About a year after the film, and while she was in New York trying to get well, Dr. Whiteman made an appointment for her to see Dr. Jakob Waxx, a respected Gestalt therapist, in an attempt to help Marilyn begin to understand the nature and source of the problem. Sharing certain types of behavior problems with another analyst was a desperate strategy that sometimes worked for him.*

ACTION

Whirling slowly, like a human Busby Berkeley centerpiece, she sees herself and the dark tropical trees surrounding her, their steamy fronds curving down to the water's reflecting surface. She turns slowly, made slightly dizzy by the movement; the turning is a lulling comfort.

She is both above the black water and rising up from it, a healthful, lusty platinum blond Venus emerging, more postcard kitsch than mythic dream. Sequined into a skin-tight silver gown that tapers into the water, she is a common fantasy of a mermaid rising.

Unsure hands on muscular arms stretch from the water, gracefully at first. Then they gradually begin to grope as the soft swaying and turning of her ample body becomes a playful defense.

Still she turns in and above the floating lagoon. The hands, more aggressive now, take insistent, nasty shapes; they grasp and clutch at her. She dodges them successfully for a while. Then one grabs at her rump and tears away a strip of sequins. The dark crack of her posterior puckers through the hole in her gown. Another grasping hand clutches the point of the shoulder and rips off a strap. She holds her bare arm with her opposite hand like a wound. There are more wounds now—the back, her hip, her flank, part of a breast.

The turning has not speeded up but has become irregular, as though a clutch in some mechanism were slipping. Her vision blurs then clears then blurs again. The hands are stripping her piecemeal, and while she is occupied in fending them off, she is aware of nothing else. It is a game, becoming increasingly dangerous, but a game nevertheless.

When much of her dress is gone, the sequin strips float like dead fish on the surface of the black pool, and fear begins to come as a chill rising from the warm water. She starts to turn slightly faster, and that, too, is ominous. The movement is not smooth. She does not—must not—lose her balance and fall into that water, that deathly water. She is a wobbling top. Paradoxically, the more unstable she is, the faster she turns. In a moment she will be thrown off center and tossed out in a curving arc into the pool. She knows she must stay erect to be safe: let the fingers take the final few patches, but stand tall.

Hands reach for the cloth covering her crotch and parts of her thighs. She can't resist and tries to swat them away. A mistake. The movement throws her off balance, and she begins to lurch and reel in widening circles out over the water, the top about to tumble.

Her fear is sudden and severe, an immense pressure on her chest, a clutching fist at her throat, panic in her heart. She cannot breathe. Panic multiplies itself; it is everywhere. There is no air. She is thrown, twisting, into the air. Breathless, she hovers momentarily, like a diver, over the black lagoon. Below her, everything is blurring, blurred. Death would be a relief now. She begins to fall. Tumbling. Twisting. Falling. And suddenly something in her knows. A dream. Again. After all, a dream. It isn't happening; rather, it is happening again. The dream. In a moment she'll be awake. And if not awake, at least in a safer dream place.

She doesn't know quite when the falling stopped or how, but she is in her bed. The small second-floor apartment in Burbank. She moved there when she got the part in *Ladies of the Chorus*, or was it just after the release of *Dangerous Years*? She couldn't be sure. It doesn't matter; she is there and safe. She has stopped falling but hasn't woken up completely. Or has she?

The sound came to her from a great distance and from only a few feet away. From afar, it is a car's motor turning over and not catching, then silence and another try. Nearby, it is a window being raised then halted then raised again. Then there is only a single sound—the window. The large blot of shadow on the softly billowing white curtains moves rhythmically from midwindow to the sill, climbing her curtains and the half-lowered shade and falling again softly. It is, she believes, the shadow of the mimosa tree on the lawn projected against the side of the building by the harsh street light.

Sleeping lightly, she senses the movement. It is a restful, pulsing rhythm, like the slow bobbing of a boat moored

on a quiet lagoon. Then there is a movement, not so predictable or gentle. Does she see it or merely sense it, or
perhaps dream it?

The shadow raises the sash a few inches, waits, and
raises it further. The window is almost completely open
when hands reach in and push the curtains apart. The
head, the torso, are compact and well-proportioned. He is
poised for a moment, half in, half out, examining what he
can see of the room, peering intensely at the bed.

She feels someone's presence but doesn't want to confirm her fear. It is not yet a true fear, just the onset of
fright. Fear will come if she opens her eyes and sees what
she senses.

She hears a breath. No doubt, a breath. A body dis-
places the air inside her window; that, too, is something
that can be heard. The debate over whether or not to look
is irrelevant. He is in the room.

She opens her eyes. He is in front of the window in a
half crouch, a position as much animal as human. She is not
terrified until something glints—a gold tooth, a flash of eye,
a blade, what!

He comes toward her slowly. He may be smiling.
That is the final straw. She screams herself awake and again
awake.

"I'll bet," Marilyn says a bit boastfully, "you haven't
heard one quite like that, eh, Doc?"

Jakob Waxx has been tapping the tip of his pen ab-
sently on his steno pad all the while as Marilyn recounts her
recurrent dream. He is looking at the page to see if the
random marks have made a discernible pattern. Waxx looks
like Sigmund Freud, the result of small resemblances and a
great deal of effort, especially the nurturing of a Vandyke.
Some patients are immediately reassured by his historical
appearance. Others think it an obvious pretension and turn

away. Dr. Waxx does not want for customers. Marilyn likes the similarity; she thinks he's cute and among her intimates will call him "my own Freud."

He pulls on his cigar. It has almost gone out. "You may know the classic Freudian interpretation of nakedness dreams. The fear of being unmasked publicly. The more realistic second part is related . . ." Marilyn is distracted because Waxx has pried the dying cigar out of its holder and is scraping at the mouthpiece with a penknife. Replacing the stub in its holder and relighting it, Waxx says, while staring at the flame, "I should charge you at a double rate for a dream within a dream."

"Sorry." It is her little-girl apology.

Waxx sneers. "You realize we may not ever come to the truths of the dream. Singular. Dream. This, which you have told me, is not two dreams. This is a single dream in two parts, one abstract, one direct, folded, as it were, back upon itself."

Marilyn's eyes darken. They ask, *What causes this dream all the time?*

"It could well be indicative of a double-rooted problem. As with a mandrake. Each root buried deeply. Neither unrelated to the other, but not too much the same, either."

Like the dream, Marilyn's brow folds on itself.

"By which I mean to suggest that a protective dream organism has anticipated being revealed. Complexity appears to be its survival mechanism."

Marilyn understands all the words but not the idea.

Realizing her confusion, Dr. Waxx explains: "Your nightmare is protecting itself, but which is the camouflaged segment, so to speak—the mythic lagoon or the prowler in the bedroom? What is the older? Which actually came first?"

"I swear to God I don't know."

Untrue. Marilyn does not tell Dr. Waxx that when she was living in the apartment in Burbank, she ran out in the street screaming late one night. It was 2:45 A.M., and she was wearing a transparent nightgown with lacy black panties under it and a filmy black bra. She wore high-heeled shoes. Her shrieks, coming in staccato whoops like those of a freshly wounded animal, brought bedroom lights on immediately. Windows were raised. Men shouted, "Who's out there? What's going on?" Women shrieked in sympathy.

Marilyn was on her knees, shivering and squawking, when the first man arrived, a kindly old vaudevillian she knew from the Fox commissary. When he touched her shoulder, her screams renewed themselves. It wasn't until three familiar women surrounded her that she began to calm down. The police had been sent for—rape, or an attempt at it, was supposed. But where? Out on the street? Dressed like this? Why?

The police patrol car came fairly quickly: an older officer, whose sideburns were snowy white, and his young, raw-faced partner. Marilyn seemed afraid of them but more frightened of the younger. She kept searching in the crowd and beyond it for something, perhaps a familiar face. Virginia Wergeles was a familiar face; she had done the makeup for Marilyn's first screen test, and they still occasionally drove to the studio together. She helped the police get Marilyn on her feet and put a blanket over her shoulders. Marilyn looked about continually, partly in fear, partly in expectation.

When Marilyn was sufficiently calmed, the police brought her into Virginia Wergeles's ground-floor apartment. Wergeles prepared some tea. The police asked Marilyn to tell them what had happened. A breathless, broken story followed.

She'd been asleep, dreaming perhaps. She heard sounds at the window, wasn't sure if they were real or in her dream. She awoke. A man, the shadow of a man, hovered in the window.

Wergeles, in the kitchen, listened. Her bedroom was directly below Marilyn's. She had heard nothing, no scrambling down the stairs, no screaming until Marilyn was on the sidewalk well in front of the building.

He came, he definitely came, into her room, Marilyn said. No, he didn't touch her, but he was definitely in the room. You can sense when you're not alone, she said. The younger policeman went upstairs to check out the bedroom and talk to some of the neighbors. The older scribbled some notes, trying to establish the time, the general size, race, and specific appearance of the intruder. Virginia Wergeles refilled the tea. She was asked if she'd heard anything. She said she was a very sound sleeper. That wasn't exactly the truth.

When the police had finished their inquiry, the sky had lightened but dawn was still an hour away. The police advised Marilyn to keep her window locked. Virginia invited Marilyn to stay with her. Marilyn said she was okay now and thanked her for everything. She walked out of the apartment and up the stairs like a creature who was so brittle pieces of her could fall off at any moment.

Neighbors talked about the incident intensely for a day or two and, of course, whenever Marilyn passed by and reminded them of the strange occurrence. Or nonoccurrence, because most of them believed, after a few weeks without any other incident, it was all probably a publicity stunt, and not a very well thought out one since no reporters rushed to the scene and there was never a photograph taken of the distraught and scantily clad potential victim.

Marilyn knows the answer to Dr. Waxx's question

about which part of the double-rooted dream—the dark lagoon or the shadowy intruder—came first. She has dreamed variations of the hands plucking off her clothing since puberty; the intruder at her window began a few weeks before she actually ran screaming onto the street in Burbank. She is unwilling to tell Waxx the truth. It would give him a crack, a rift into which he could insert his prying intelligence, and she does not yet trust him. He senses, by the weight of its absence, there is something important his patient is not telling him.

"Most likely, the segments of the dream developed in the order they appear. But this is not an assumption on which to build an understanding. If you desire understanding of this dream, you should," he says, trying to suppress accusation, "devote serious private thought to a determination of which part rests upon the other."

Marilyn nods thoughtfully.

"Let me ask, then, what are the immediate effects of the dream?"

Marilyn does not quite understand. Jakob Waxx shows some impatience. "How do you awake? Is it with immediate recall of the dream, as though it has occurred not to you but to somebody very like you? Or are you, yourself, frightened awake by the intruder each time? Do the screams in the dream diminish until you awake? Are you fearful after you awake, or are you purged of the fear? The details of how the dream affects you is of great significance."

Marilyn still looks puzzled. She moves a finger toward her lips. Dr. Waxx has already noticed the terrible condition of her nails. "I don't honestly remember all the details."

"I suspect you do."

"Hey. Whose dreams are we talking about, anyway?" Marilyn forces a laugh. "Actually, it's become something so familiar. I know I don't wake up screaming, or anything like that. It's just there, you know, like all the unpleasant things you get used to."

Dr. Waxx has yet to write a single word on his steno pad. He doodles a shapely jar in the middle of the page and leaves some silence. "So. Tell me, do you have this dream even when you have medicated yourself in order to sleep?"

Marilyn tenses in response and realizes instantly that Waxx hasn't missed her reaction. She despises what he's done and thinks of leaving. She sighs. She smiles coyly. She shrugs.

Dr. Waxx tosses his pad on his desk. "I am not a young man, Miss Monroe. I have aided a few people in my time; not as many as I would have liked or believed I could help, but a few. I pride myself on having few delusions about what I or my patients are as people. I am not confident that you and I are destined to be successful. I simply don't have the inclination or the time at my age to play at therapy." He takes an audible, punctuating breath.

"And you, for your part, are no longer a child. You are coming into the fullness of your life, or the potential thereof. You, also, have not the time to waste playing at therapy. If we cannot cut to the heart of things directly, really what is the point? Diversion? I think not. This is not to the advantage of either of us." He attempts to push himself out of the deep chair, but he is too rooted and falls back. The leather squeals, and Waxx becomes momentarily disoriented, breathless.

Emotion has welled up in Marilyn, triggered by the old man's stern words and the pathetic gesture. What touches her is not his momentary weakness but his strength so suddenly betrayed. Until that moment, he has been the no-nonsense father she never had.

After a brief silence, Dr. Waxx becomes potent again.

"That you medicate yourself severely is obvious to me. I cannot be wasting time with coyness, with evasive responses. I ask a question about the ingestion of drugs for a reason. If you are not able to respond in a manner appropriate for an adult who wishes to make sense out of the events of her life, there can be no, as I've said before, no purpose in our attempt."

With greater effort and a gasp, he pushes himself out of his deep chair. He takes up his pad and on the second stab finds his breast pocket with his pen. "So here is what I propose. I will leave the room for a few moments, after which I will return. If you wish to leave, take this opportunity." He nods toward the door to the outer office and liberty. Marilyn is still, her lower lip slack. "If you choose to be here when I return, I shall assume we can begin to explore the things that incapacitate you, not merely to joust with one another."

He exits through a door to an inner office. After a moment, Marilyn can hear his voice on the telephone.

Waxx remains out of the room for almost five minutes. When he returns, Marilyn is gone. He takes his seat again and writes in his notebook: *Personality not so much mysterious or unfathomable as extremely complex. Everything turns back upon itself. All the forces—positive and negative—are counterpoised and counterfaced. Perhaps counterfeit too. No easy way through the maze. As she has said, there is a fear of being unmasked, but first you must also unmask the masker.*

Dr. Waxx does not believe he has seen the last of Marilyn Monroe.

Marilyn called Dr. Waxx's office twice during the following three weeks. The first time, she wanted the doctor to call her when he was free. He did not. The second time, she made an appointment to see him for a session.

But Marilyn did not come. She did not cancel or send word. Still Dr. Waxx believed matters were not finished between them.

Months passed. Marilyn startled most observers with her performance at Madison Square Garden for President Kennedy's forty-fifth birthday.

She had been scheduled for much earlier in the evening. Twice, in fact, Peter Lawford, the emcee, had been told Marilyn was in the wings. Each time he started to cue the band for her entrance music—"Too Darned Hot" with a heavy backbeat—frantic waves from the wings caused him to stop in midsentence and fumble his way through a distracted joke and an introduction for someone else. Lawford wasn't sure if Marilyn was even in the building, and when he went offstage he got contradictory answers to his queries.

Sitting in the front row, a cigar in his mouth, his feet up on a footstool, John Fitzgerald Kennedy was enjoying all the speeches, the mild ribbing, the gifts of song and story. The private Kennedy giving the public a peek, a great sport. Marilyn was to be the evening's revelation; she was proving to be its biggest mystery as well.

When Lawford gets word that she's there and then that she's ready, it's close to the end of the show. The house darkens, and a spotlight hits the edge of the curtain. Lawford leaves a tantalizing silence before he finally says, "And now, ladies and gentlemen, Mr. President . . . the *late* Marilyn Monroe."

The music's beat pulses in the semidarkness. Every eye is on the spotlight, but Marilyn has entered from the other wing and taken three or four uncertain steps before the searching spot finally picks her up. She wobbles as she walks, partly because her long, skintight gown is not designed for movement. It is a sheer, tapered version of the dress she wears in her black lagoon dream. She moves very slowly, back on her heels, one foot directly in front of the other, toward the microphone. The band stops when she arrives on her mark. She caresses the microphone with one hand while holding it steady with the other. She surveys the darkness of the vast arena and fastens finally on the beaming President.

"Hap . . . py birth . . . day . . ." It is a moment or two before anyone can quite figure out that she is actually singing. She is leaving marvelous holes. The pauses are as much singing as the words; the words are whispered so coyly they're whimpers and sighs and murmurs. If Billy Bam were still alive, he'd have punctuated the droll timing with appropriately droll rim shots. But Marilyn sings without accompaniment.

As she sings, she fondles the mike and rolls her shoulders and hips evocatively. The temperature in Madison Square Garden is rising. "Happy birthday . . . Mr. President . . . hap-py birth-day . . . to-o-o-o . . . yo-o-o-u." The band comes in on the final note.

Marilyn Monroe blows John F. Kennedy a slow, sexy kiss.

Afterward JFK tells the press, "I can now retire from politics after having had, ah, 'Happy Birthday' sung to me in such a sweet, wholesome way."

Unquestionably, Marilyn has been the hit of the evening. Her outrageous performance, however, was offered so clearly within the confines of her screen persona that only a prude could have objected. That same persona veiled the fact that Marilyn was drunk.

In the audience, Dr. Waxx, a generous contributor to liberal causes, saw a woman in grave trouble.

Less than a week after that appearance, Marilyn again calls his office for an appointment. Waxx has instructed his secretary to give Marilyn the last appointment of whichever day suits her schedule. She chooses the 4 P.M. session the following Wednesday.

She arrives at the office at ten minutes to five. Waxx's secretary leads her into his working office. He is in shirtsleeves and suspenders, writing at a large, cluttered desk.

She apologizes. "It took an hour, really, an hour, just to get crosstown. I'm sorry if . . . I'll go away if you'd rather. . . ."

He glances up at her. She looks terrible. Paunchy and pasty. Her eyes are torpid, hair lusterless. He has reason to worry about her.

"No, no. Please sit down. I have only to jot these few lines. It is what happens when you can no longer trust to memory; you must commit everything to paper." He does not tell her he has seen her performance at Kennedy's birthday party. He wants to see how patiently she will wait.

She selects a demure posture, knees together, fingers folded in her lap. He writes, leaving a silence that stretches for three minutes. She remains patient and poised. Finally, he claps his hands together and says, "So. We are ready to attack?"

"I think so. I hope so."

"I hope so also."

Marilyn's face sets itself in thoughtful repose; it is far more reflective than Waxx could have imagined. She says, her voice hoarse from recent disuse and abuse, "I don't know, Doctor. Maybe I take the pills and some drinks at night so I won't have dreams. Maybe, when I've got a good buzz on, I won't remember the dreams. I know—*dream*. There *are* times when they give me some kind of sleep. But it isn't real sleep. There's no rest in it. Nothing calming or easy. No recharging or storing back up, I guess you'd say.

It's more like just stopping for a while but knowing you'll have to get up and go on. But at least it all stops for a few hours. Without some of the stuff I take, there's no stopping. The dreams are like being chased by a madman or something, and you can't let yourself be caught. Your heart's going to explode, but you can't stop. And you're already so exhausted."

Her voice is that of a woman much older, without the protective mannerisms and rhythms of Marilyn Monroe. She has begun weeping silently as she speaks. Mascara stains her cheeks.

Dr. Waxx is expressionless as he jots phrases. He believes there is truth in her words, probably a good deal of it. The problem, he knows, will be to open a path for truth that does not become subverted in the maze of other paths—true, half true, and untrue—that have both shaped and undermined this woman.

"And what specific medications have you taken? This is important to know toxicologically."

"Nembutal, Seconal, Valium, of course. Those I remember. There were others. They'll come to me. Oh yes: Thorazine, Dexedrine, and some Demerol."

"And at the present time, which?"

"Nembutal."

"And how long have you taken this medication?"

She looks at the ceiling and draws breath. "Hah. No telling. If you mean in a major way, I'd say about five years, six, maybe."

"Do you relate your chronic lateness to your lack of healthy sleep?"

"Being late today, you mean?"

"No. Today, as we both know, it was the traffic." Dr. Waxx is generous in his forgiveness. "I refer to the lateness at the studio about which Dr. Whiteman has informed me."

"Usually, yes. If I do sleep—I call it sleep, but it really isn't—when I wake up, I'm tireder than if I stayed up all night. I'm like a zombie. I can't afford to let anybody see me that way. It takes me an hour to move, two to allow myself to be seen. I'm like a corpse."

"Do you take something to help you along?"

"Sometimes. Not usually."

"When you do, what is it and in what dosage?"

"Oh, doxepin or doxeprin, something like that. Three or four pills, usually. Sometimes more."

"You don't know the dosage." He tries not to make it sound like an accusation.

"Not exactly."

He writes hurriedly. "Do you ever recall being late intentionally? Or not particularly making the effort to be on time? Perhaps the first time you did so consciously?"

There was such a morning. Marilyn hasn't thought about it for years, longer ago than she realizes. She knew at the time and for quite a while thereafter that what she had done was astonishing, even by her own unconventional standards. But until Waxx asked the question, she had tucked it away in absent memory.

Marilyn has a difficult and delicate choice. She can tell Waxx that entire story, just let it roll out unchecked; or she could reshape it, let it come out in pieces eventually. It is essentially a matter of how much she believes she needs this man's help. Then, all at once, choice is not choice at all; she is telling Jakob Waxx about something she has never told anyone before. "I don't exactly remember the movie. It must have been *There's No Business Like Show Business*, because I had my license back and was driving one of the black Cadillacs. I guess I'd gotten in the habit of being a little late, but that wasn't because I couldn't get myself together."

"Because you were the star?"

"I don't know 'star.' I did know I was important."

"So you were just fashionably late."

"I guess so. Anyway, I was driving to the studio from the house on North Palm, and I swear to you, Dr. Waxx, I'd love to be able to tell you what was on my mind at the time, but I can't really remember. I believe I was reasonably happy; I mean, nothing was really bothering me, at least not consciously."

Waxx knots his hands and places his thumbs against his chin; the gesture conveys the depth of his interest. His eyes tighten.

Marilyn has begun to feel protected. "I was stopped at a traffic light. I can see the exact corner. Just off Ventura. A gas station and a hot dog stand. A Marlboro ad on a billboard. I was thinking about being late, wondering what they would do without me. We were supposed to be shooting three pages without cutting, but I had only a couple of lines and some reaction close-ups later on. For some stupid reason, I got this idea in my head to pull off the road and fall asleep in the car. To make believe I was asleep. I wasn't tired or anything."

Marilyn pauses, anticipating a question; when there is none, she continues. "No, I wasn't really tired. It was just an urge. I wanted to see what would happen. To see who would come to my rescue."

"You say 'rescue,' but you weren't in danger."

"Who knows; maybe somebody would think I was. At any rate, I saw a grassy place just past a bus stop where I could pull off to the side. I didn't know whether to shut off the motor or not. Eventually, I did shut it; I didn't want to be asphyxiated. I let myself fall across the passenger seat, closed my eyes, and waited. I heard cars rolling by. The sun was on my face; it was pale green, almost lemon, when

I squinted. I said my lines for that day over and over in my head, or maybe I whispered them. I promised myself I wouldn't move no matter what until somebody came."

"What was the upshot?"

"The what?"

"What happened finally?"

"A mailman. He came by. He must have looked in and seen me. He said something to me, but I didn't hear him at first. I was in a state by then, like I was dreaming what was happening to me. I'd been saying my lines over and over; it put me in a sort of trance. He asked me if I was all right. I told him I was tired, that I'd just pulled over to get some sleep. He said something I still remember; he said, 'Lots of people who are dead would be alive if they'd be a little less haughty and knew to take a nap.' It was funny, the word he used. 'Haughty.' "

Waxx would like to tell Marilyn a great deal at once. He knows he must check the urge. What was involved with the car incident, he believes, was a questioning of her worth—she wanted to know who would miss her when she didn't show up, who loved her. What is particularly troubling to Waxx is the elaborate manner by which she acted out her mock death.

"This was, you say, how many years ago?"

"Seven or eight at least."

"This was the only time you have done something like this? In a car, I mean to say?"

"Only time."

"Robert Frost believed the most gratifying feeling human beings can experience is to be brought to the very brink of danger and then to be saved. It is especially satisfying when you have seen the Specter." Their eyes unite. He repeats slowly: "Yes, the Specter. The feeling gives us everything our lives need, especially the saving. And now maybe you'd like a cup of tea?"

" 'A glass tea'? I'd love one."

Over tea he will tell her what she already knows about her lateness, at least before it got completely out of hand, that it is her way of punishing others by withholding herself. Like everything else Monroe, it turned back on itself: she became the victim of her victimizing.

Marilyn does not show up for her next appointment. She eventually does call the office to apologize and set another time. Which she once again misses. Dr. Waxx does not close off the possibility of her return. For various reasons. Because he likes her a great deal. Because the complexities of her personality pique his curiosity. Most important, because the story of the feigned sleep in the car is worrisome and, he believes, again puts Marilyn at risk.

Hers is what Dr. Waxx has described in his writings as a "circular personality." He once compared dealing with it to a Chinese puzzle: the more you try to pull your patient out of it, the tighter it binds. Release always remains the objective, but finesse and indirection are the only workable approaches.

Marilyn begins most mornings intending to call Dr. Waxx's office but does not. Since she talked to him, her lateness has been under reasonable control, at least when it wasn't drug and sleep related. She believes things are getting better.

She is staying the weekend in East Hampton with discreet friends of the President, who have arranged to be elsewhere when he will fly in on Sunday evening. Marilyn is tense but less so now that she is the one who must wait on someone else's whim.

Marilyn hasn't driven a car in more than a year and loves the freedom of the Mercedes she has taken this morning, rolling along the beach road and dividing her attention between the tranquil ocean and the highway ahead. She is thinking in images, each of which calls up the next with a random logic. The eyes of Dr. Waxx. The monkeyish face of Billy Bam. Montand's ironic laugh. Skouras's heavy, misaligned eyebrows. Johnny Hyde's scar. Gable's mustache. Clift's delicate eyes. DiMaggio's impassive stare. A life in men's faces.

There is a very long traffic light at the intersection of Bay Road and Montauk Highway. The morning sun breaks through the overcast. Marilyn's short hair is bound tight in a red bandanna. She had fun last night, learning new card games with her hosts. She slept tranquilly for a few hours. The sun strikes the silvered hood of the car; she squints at the traffic light and reaches into the glove compartment for dark glasses. Suddenly, as she puts on the glasses and surely without her wishing it, a wave of sadness rushes over her. The light changes; she doesn't notice. A car honks, then all the cars behind her work their way past.

Her sadness distills itself into a single thought: *No one knows I'm here.* The irony, of course, is that she has sought anonymity so often in her life. The Mercedes sits before the green light. *Right this minute, no one knows I'm here.*

The light turns red again, and when she finally notices, she believes it still hasn't changed color. *I could disappear this minute. Who would miss me? No one knows . . .*

When the green disk flashes on, she touches the gas pedal but does not gather great speed. She rolls past a Mobil station and pulls off the road against a stockade fence that is the boundary of a junkyard. She does not shut off the engine. She moves the shift knob to Park.

The phrase *No one knows . . .* runs around her brain

like a headline on the Times building. *No one knows . . . No one knows . . .* She folds herself over the shift panel and lays her head on cradled arms. Her sunglasses are askew on her forehead. The bandanna comes over her ear.

The soft drone of the motor dulls her mind. She is not asleep. She is not awake. The headline circles and circles to the hum of the motor.

The sun has brightened and risen almost to its highest point. A blue-and-white Suffolk County Highway Patrol car passes the Mercedes and continues north on Bay Road.

Marilyn cannot, will not, break the spell. Time has ceased to exist. She longs for the thrill of the saving. She is drawn to the empty hopelessness of losing everything, of not feeling, of not being. Aren't the two things one and the same?

The police car eventually returns from the direction it had gone. It parks across Bay Road. A spiffy patrolman steps out and looks both ways before crossing the road. He touches his holster as he approaches the car.

The policeman peers in. He sees a woman and taps on the window with his fingernails. Marilyn hears a muffled voice say, "Miss. Miss?" She doesn't move. She holds her breath.

He tries the door. It is locked. He walks around to the passenger side and raps hard on the window. "Miss. Miss."

Her face is buried in her arms. Marilyn is smiling.

CHAPTER THIRTEEN

Spiritual Nights

LIGHTS

HARVARD CRIMSON: When a person grows larger than life, as you have . . .

MONROE: Alas, alack.

CRIMSON: . . . as you have, whether you like it or not, there is a tendency for people to attribute powers to you no mortal should really have.

MONROE: Brother, ain't that the truth. (She giggles.)

CRIMSON: You're asked your opinion on everything from Sputnik and the Cold War to the G.N.P. and President Kennedy's performance in the White House.

MONROE: I know. Maybe, because the camera can make my face twenty feet long, people think my brain is multiplied fifty times too. It's one of the strangest things about being a celebrity. Although I can say unequivocally that President Kennedy has outperformed Sputnik.

CRIMSON: In staying with the delusion of omnipotence, though, we'd like to ask, just for the heck of it, if there really is a God.

MONROE: Are you really going to print this?

CRIMSON: Of course.

MONROE: Well, there is. Except that he has the power to make believe he isn't. And even when he's making believe he doesn't exist, he still has the power to make believe he does.

CRIMSON: Oh.

CAMERA

In mid-June, two weeks after her thirty-sixth birthday, nine days after shooting was broken off on Something's Got to Give, *Marilyn, alone in her Brentwood house, had not gotten dressed for three days. Fox was threatening lawsuits. Their flacks were already starting to go after her in the press. She didn't think she had the strength to fight back.*

Her body had never changed so quickly. On the set one

*week earlier, she was still pretty much Marilyn Monroe—a con-
cept made real; the jutting breasts, the remarkably contoured
rump, the reproductive display ceremony reduced to suggestive
body positions, eye, lip, and tongue signals. Marilyn, but not
quite the old Marilyn. Moving slower, too studied, almost consciously trying to be what she had already become.*

*Her bedroom was dark but luminous. Silver light from a
full moon filtered in through the French doors. In bed, wrapped
in a short pink terry-cloth robe, a black sleep mask on her forehead, Marilyn touched her flanks, squeezing fat she hadn't noticed before. Her upper arms, she knew, were plump, hatefully
so; she didn't touch them. She drew in her stomach and felt her
ribs while reaching her thumbs into the crevice below her suspended breasts. No fat on the ribs. But lower, below her navel,
there was no pulling in the bulge. She had seen very active,
beautiful women develop that protrusion; sit-ups didn't help. She
promised herself never to wear tight slacks again. She'd look like
one of those spunky middle-aged studio dancers.*

*From a drawer nearby she took an oval hand mirror, a
gift from Gable years before. A switch in the handle brought on
a ring of light from the mirror's rim, and she saw herself lighted
softly. Her pouting mouth revealed her disappointment.* Dead.
That's the only word for it. *Usually it took her skin two or
three days to revive from all the hours' cooking under makeup.
This was different. It seemed coated with powder, but there was
no powder on it. Wherever she touched it with her fingertips, it
yielded like cardboard. It looked ashen, but that was its reflection in the moonlight; it had no true color of its own.*

*Her insomnia had returned. Not the same wakefulness she
had when starting out on a project, the familiar voice in her
head giving way to dialogue and then a full, many-voiced discussion. Exhausting, but part of the process of invention. It was
normal; she got used to it. She usually got up, walked around,*

grabbed a book, a script, woke someone, anything. Eventually, without realizing how, she was wakened by her maid and eventually made her way to the studio. Late—on time for her.

This insomnia was different. It paralyzed her. There weren't other voices, only her own dullest self. Nothing to build on here. Just numb, wakeful depression. She never left her bed. She never read. She simply lay there waiting for sleep, calling it to her with a long sip of bourbon whenever she thought bourbon. *If sleep came, she was unaware of it; she lay dreamless until a sound or an excess of sleep woke her up.*

On the table near her bed were a touch-tone telephone, an uncapped bottle of bourbon, a dozen loose aspirins, two identical prescription bottles—Seconal and Dexedrine—both almost empty. In the headboard, a radio dial glowed amber; muffled sounds of conversation came from small speakers behind the bedposts.

ACTION

Marilyn hears the words "Son of God, that's preposterous." She reaches above her head and tunes the voice in more clearly.

The voice says, "I would not forbid those who want to, even though I think they're fools. I just don't want them imposing their beliefs on me, and they do that all the time. And I sure as heck don't want to be paying for their mumbo-jumbo through my taxes, while they, on the other hand, get away without paying any taxes at all. It's one of the biggest scandals in the history of our country. Any reasonable people wouldn't stand for it another minute."

Marilyn knows women with voices like this. When she was a girl, her grandmother's voice was exactly like this—

reliable, with a coloring of friendly midwestern twang, a no-nonsense voice that knew what it knew, that didn't have to get shrill or strident to make itself believed. Aunt Ana's voice was like that too. For Marilyn, this is precisely the way courage should sound.

Marilyn wanted to have a voice like this, wanted to be courageous. Maybe she didn't have the courage because she didn't have the right voice. She probably had his voice. Maybe that's why, she thinks, she went silent and then developed that breathy whisper. Went the other way entirely. Be unsure, vulnerable.

Still, she loved a woman who could say what she meant in that "bring in the wash" voice. *Bet anything*, Marilyn thinks, *she wears rimless glasses*.

The man's voice is deceptive. On the surface that standard, full radio vibrato, easily colored by changing tone and timbre, by plucking the vocal cords with different techniques and creating any effect—smiling, curious, probing, sincere. You name it. All of them phony.

Instinctively Marilyn dislikes the voice because it is so studied. She remembers Strasberg saying, "The hell with technique if it's gonna float like letters in alphabet soup." But there's something below the voice that draws her, the original voice, the original man before all the radio training. A rough, street quality that no amount of training can smooth, the consonants that linger at the ends of words. A nasal New York sound beneath everything.

"So what you're telling us, basically, Mrs. O'Hair, is that religion has no place in American life and that we should rise up and throw all the rascals out?"

"No. I'm telling you that I want the Church—which usually has very little to do with real religion—I want it off my back and out of the White House. I want it out of the Congress of the United States. I want it out of the schools.

I want it out of town halls. I want it out of everywhere it doesn't belong according to the Constitution of the United States. And I want it included in the one place it doesn't seem to want to be, namely on the tax rolls of cities, states, and the federal republic."

"My guest tonight is the outspoken and controversial Madalyn Murray O'Hair. I'm Ralph Norman. Our show is 'Night Voices.' We'll be here until 5 A.M. And the one person we'd like to talk to is, well, you know it's you. Our number is 388-3838. Our lines are open. And we'll be back after a word."

A hemorrhoid commercial is not a word, but Marilyn listens to the symptoms of discomfort, smiling for the first time all day, relieved at not having hemorrhoids and not having to leave the house and face a druggist to ask for this particular medication.

Marilyn wants to ask the woman about courage.

When the show comes back on, a female caller is already sputtering and fuming at Madalyn Murray O'Hair. ". . . like you and those Commies over there, nothing but a bunch of atheists and bums. Their word don't mean anything because they don't believe in God. They'll say anything and do anything because they don't believe in God. They want to enslave people because they don't value God's creatures. You know why? Because they set themselves up to be gods themselves. I swear I don't know why they put people like you on the radio."

"Do you have," asks Ralph Norman, "a question for Mrs. O'Hair?"

The caller has hung up.

"I'd like to say something, Ralph. If you listened carefully to that woman's voice, not especially to what she was saying but to the hysteria behind it, you get a sense of the true role of religion in the history of the world. It separates people, always has, always will. Separates the people who think Sunday is their Lord's day from the ones who think Saturday's the day; from the ones who salaam five times a day; from the ones who bow at the waist; from the ones who genuflect and throw water on their foreheads. Jonathan Swift saw how crazy it all was; he wrote satirically about a religious war where the people who break their eggs at the big end try to kill people who break their eggs at the small end.

"And it isn't so much of an exaggeration, really. True believers have been killing other true believers in the name of their gods since time immemorial. Trouble is, lots of just regular, innocent human beings get caught in between. And if you listened carefully, you could hear the old-fashioned hatred in her voice. That's the real voice of religion, and I hope you all heard it."

"I think," says Norman while clearing his throat, "you're generalizing a little too much there. All I heard was someone who got angry because you were attacking something she believed in deeply, not the voice of religious hatred throughout the ages. I wonder what you out there heard. Call us at 388-3838. And you're the next night voice on 'Night Voices.' "

"Yes, Ralph." The new voice is so impaired it's almost impossible to tell if it belongs to a man or a woman. "I wonder if your guest would be such a staunch atheist if she got the word tomorrow that she had lung cancer and had a few months to live?"

"You mean," says Mrs. O'Hair, "would the fear of death suddenly make me fall on my knees and repent? No, it wouldn't. I'm just like anyone else. There has been lots of tragedy in my life. And like everybody else, I've had to face it. I've faced it without any recourse to a god that does not exist, a fairy-tale god someone has had to invent so that we human beings can get through our lives without facing the pain or anguish of living. Personally, I think people who face life as it is live a lot more truly, more intensely, than what I like to call the mumbo-jumbo people."

The caller is talking gruffly when Marilyn reaches over and takes up the telephone. She's frightened. This woman's strength leaves dread in its wake. Even the caller is feeling it; she says, "You can say that, but they haven't told you you won't live out the year. Believe me, it's nothing anyone can face alone. Thank God . . ." The coarse voice begins to come apart. ". . . there's something to believe in . . . something beyond this world . . . to have faith in."

Mrs. O'Hair asks, "Have you been told that, sir?"

"I've been told. And I'm a woman."

"If it—believing in a god, in pearly gates, in a life forever after—if these make it easier for you, then why should it make a damn what some voice on the radio says? Live these days any way you want to. I like to believe I'd live them differently. I'd be with people, I think, doing what I could for them until the very last minute. And most of all, I'd be evaluating my life. Since I've known from a very young age that this single life is all I'll be given— nothing before it, and certainly nothing after it—I knew it was up to me, and to me alone, to live it well and to have as few regrets as possible at the end. And if I did, then I'd better damn well get out there and fill up these final days with some mighty strong living rather than slobbering and whimpering and praying for wings and a harp."

"But listen to yourself—you sound so heartless," the harsh voice contends. "Can't you see that we're all weak? We were born needing help, and we end that way too, no matter what it was like in between. And all around us nature doesn't even need us. It can destroy us without even blinking. The earth we're sitting on right now can start to tremble and swallow up the whole city of Los Angeles just like that. I mean, I'm not saying it will happen, but it could because God and nature are so powerful. And don't tell me you wouldn't be scared if it started to happen."

The atheist sighs softly. "I haven't come here to talk about death and destruction. I'm here to talk about the stranglehold religion has on this country, even though people seem to have forgotten that it was established to make sure everyone could believe whatever they wanted. Believers and nonbelievers. It just always seems to turn out that believers want everyone else to believe what they believe. This is supposed to be a country of limits. That's what makes freedom work. They never want to stay inside their limits."

The caller won't accept the change of subject. "It's just too heartless, like I said, not to care about dying. And I'm sorry, but I don't think you'd be so sure of yourself if you knew you weren't going to wake up tomorrow morning."

"I think I've got better things to do with my life than worry about leaving it. I will say, though, from what I know about priests and popes, it's no accident that they keep their flocks focused on death and misfortune."

Norman inquires, "And just why do they do that, Mrs. O'Hair?"

"They're in the fear business. Fear makes people humble and pliable. So they came up with a product almost everyone wants—eternal life. Best insurance policy you can have. Now, if only they'd pay their taxes like the other insurance companies do . . ."

Marilyn has the phone in her lap, squinting at the numbered buttons in the silvered dark. She misdials and must begin again. The voices coming from the headboard become background sounds. She listens to the pulsing busy signal in her phone for a very long while. She wants to talk to this woman about courage. She must talk to her.

Marilyn puts the phone back, slips out of bed, and walks toward the kitchen. The discussion of the tax-exempt status of the Church in America follows her into the hall and less distinctly into the kitchen, where her bare feet on the cold floor tiles have a sobering effect. She's forgotten about the sleep mask on her head. In the gloom, she flips on a small portable radio on the sill above the sink and runs up the dial until the voices harmonize with the ones in the bedroom. A man with an echoing brogue is saying, "Mother Church serves us so unselfishly, meeting the needs of the spirit—and those needs are as great, often greater, than those of the flesh—so ceaselessly that to ask the Church to render unto Caesar any of its meager resources would be an abomination."

"Meager resources. Hah. That's a good one. Have you visited the Vatican lately? I went last year with my son, and we couldn't believe our eyes. Jewels. Crowns. Precious metals. Paintings. Sculpture. The riches of the world. Riches beyond value. Priceless. Caesar was a pauper by comparison. And unless you've been absolutely brain-washed, when you see it, one thought has to pop into your head. If Jesus Christ came back to earth and walked into the Vatican and saw what has been done in his name, what in the world could he possibly think?"

"He'd know how mankind adores Him. . . ."

"Bunk. He'd look around and see that the moneylenders he threw out of the temple two thousand years ago were not only back but running the whole damn business. It would either break his heart or he'd shake the pillars of the place and bring it down in total ruin."

Marilyn can see the scene developing, can see the destruction. This is a very great woman. For the first time in days, Marilyn wants something healthy in her body. From a loaf in the fridge—the small bulb lights the room momentarily—she takes a single piece of whole wheat bread and places it in the toaster. She begins to boil some water on the stove and takes some herbal tea from a canister.

The atheist says, "Can anyone really believe all this pomp and wealth has anything to do with the poor ascetic who walked the desert, lived in tents, and spoke Aramaic and who just wanted us to treat one another a little better? If you can believe that, I'd just like to know by what mystical processes."

" 'Tis because you have no poetry in you, Miss O'Hair. Hence, no capacity to understand any of the invisible things that Mother Church offers a tormented soul."

"Such as?"

"Such as faith, such as hope, such as love."

"I've got a funny feeling. You aren't a priest, by any chance? I say that because clergymen are the only people I know who say the word 'love' and make it sound like it's got three or four syllables."

"No, I'm not a priest."

"I'm disappointed. In myself. Usually, I can tell."

"I am a brother in the Dominican order."

Madalyn Murray O'Hair lets out a howl of glorious triumph. "Good. I thought, Ralph, I was losing my touch."

Marilyn is smiling for the first time in days. She takes a lavender pill, a Quaalude, from a dark bottle in a drawer alongside the fridge. She holds it between her teeth and swallows it with grapefruit juice. Now her water is boiling. The radio voices become background as her tea steeps. She butters her toast. She carries the snack to her darkened bedroom. Smiling.

Propped up in bed, tea on the end table, Marilyn lifts

off her sleep mask and takes up a tortoiseshell hairbrush, the parting gift of Harlow's Mexican when Marilyn went to live in New York. She brushes her short hair straight back off her face. The brush is pliable yet able to engage the hair firmly. She tries not to count the strokes, but the habit is too familiar.

Again, she taps the number. On the first ring, an adenoidal voice says, "You got 'Night Voices.' If you're a first-time caller, I'll explain how the show works."

"No, I've never called before."

The breathless voice is so distinctively Marilyn Monroe's, the assistant producer becomes suspicious. "Look, when you get on the line with Ralph and his guest, don't fool around, just use your regular voice. Okay? We're on four-second tape delay, so turn your radio down when you get on, or you won't be able to make heads out of tails. Tell Ralph you're a first-time caller and give your first name only. Which is . . . ?"

"Which is what?"

"Your name?"

"Mickie."

"From?"

"Fontana."

"Okay. No profanity; we'll have to cut you off. What will you want to be talking about?"

What to say? Courage? Hope in a hopeless world? Belief when she is already far beyond belief? The fact that she feels more unconnected to anything than ever before? All she wants, really, is to have this woman talk to her, personally, exclusively, perhaps carrying her back to the strong women who preceded her generations earlier. Certainly to Aunt Ana. "I'd like to ask . . ." She realizes her voice is again too breathless. She cannot remember how she used to speak before she became a star. "I want to ask her where creativity comes from. If we can make our own miracles."

A snort at the other end of the line indicates disapproval. "Any way you can bring the Church in? Do you go to church yourself?"

"Sure. Don't you?"

"Also, Ralph likes it if you tell him how much you like the show when you get on. You'll be next."

Marilyn puts the receiver in her lap and sips her tea. It is almost 2:35 A.M. She is woozily excited about hearing her own voice on the radio. She has a sense that she will become a regular radio show caller.

Madalyn Murray O'Hair has dissected the Dominican brother, skewered him, and is serving him up as a well-meaning fool to the minute segment of the listening audience that is rational. She frightens Marilyn, who picks up her brush and feels her hair crackle beneath more vigorous strokes.

"Our next caller, I'm told, wants to ask Mrs. O'Hair why the church has become so uncreative. You're up, Mickey from Fontana."

Marilyn picks up the receiver and hears Ralph Norman say, ". . . takes a while for our signal to reach Fontana."

She says, "I'm a first-time . . ."

But the radio behind her repeats Norman's Fontana joke.

She repeats, "I'm a first . . ."

"Turn your radio down, Mickey. You can't listen to the radio and talk on the phone without a lot of divine intervention."

Marilyn turns the volume knob behind her head. "I'm a first-time caller, Ralph."

"That's better. But you're not Mickey from Fontana."

How did he know? "I am."

"A lady Mickey?'

"That's right. I'm a M-i-c-k-i-e Mickie."

"I'll buy it, but I won't buy that voice, Mickie from Fontana. That can't be your natural voice. You're doing your Marilyn Monroe impersonation for some friends."

She tries to put stress on words where she normally doesn't and to alter natural rhythms. "No I'm not. This is how I speak. My friends all know I speak like this. And I am a Marilyn. But they call me Mickie for short."

Ralph Norman has become more curious. In trying to change her rhythms and timbre, she has led him to suspect the true music beneath. "Well, Mickie, Marilyn, whoever you are, we're awfully pleased you've called 'Night Voices.' What do you want to talk to Mrs. O'Hair about?"

"I guess about . . ." She has not shut off the radio in the kitchen, and the distant out-of-sync babble is slightly disturbing. ". . . about where human creativity comes from."

O'Hair says, "Well, honey, one thing's sure—it doesn't come from the Church. They're the sworn enemies of anything creative, original, unique, whatever you want to call it. They don't want anybody or anything unconventional, except as they define it and can make all the sheep believe it. When they do it, it doesn't matter how crazy it is. Like a virgin who has god's baby. If they can get you to believe something as crackpot as that, they've got your mind forever. That's why they put so much emphasis on faith: if you can't understand it, you've got to believe it anyway— by faith. That's just their way of saying your own mind doesn't count for anything whatsoever. You know the story of Galileo?"

Marilyn has gotten that piece of history from Miller, but she says she doesn't. She needs time to compose herself.

"Well, Galileo was a scientist, and darned if he didn't prove with his telescope that the earth really did revolve around the sun. Up till that time, the Church was teaching the earth was the center of things—made god and the priests a lot more important in the scheme of things that way. Well, Galileo is brought before the pope to tell him what he just saw through his telescope, and the pope tells him, 'You didn't see any such thing.' 'But I did,' he swears. 'No you didn't,' the pope says. And they go on that way till the pope throws him in jail until he takes an oath saying he didn't see what he actually saw. . . ."

Ralph Norman interrupts: "Mickie, and all the rest of our listeners, let me just say that this is a very special O'Hair version of what really happened back in the sixteenth century."

"Actually, it was the seventeenth century, Ralph. And I'm just trying to lighten the story up a little. All my facts are dead accurate. You can check them out. In fact, I hope you all will—it'll get you on the path of using your own minds. Anyway, the pope made poor old Galileo recant. That's where truth and reason and facts get you with the hocus-pocus people. They're as intolerant as they can get when their power's at stake, because power's the name of their game. So, no, to answer your question, they don't tolerate creativity, unless it's their own."

"But," says Marilyn in her own voice, "where do you think creativity comes from? I think it's from our sexuality. Connected to it in ways we don't even understand our-selves."

"Personally, I think it comes from our brains, if our brains are allowed to travel wherever they like and think whatever they can. Rationalists put no restrictions on think-ing, other than that it be logical."

"That's quite a restriction right there," Norman jumps

in. "This caller is talking about sexual impulses. They sure aren't the most rational things in the world, yet they're what make the world go round. Aren't they, Mickie?"

Marilyn's unerring sense of an interested man, which flickered earlier, flashes stronger. "I guess what I was wondering was whether God could be our sexuality. People used to believe that in ancient times. After all, if we didn't reproduce, didn't carry ourselves into the future the way we do . . ." Earlier, Marilyn slipped her hand under the bodice of her dressing gown and cupped her breast. She is drowsy now and fingering her nipple as she speaks.

"We don't," insists Mrs. O'Hair. "We don't live on in anything. Maybe a few old photographs and in the memories of relatives. If you call that 'living on,' you sure aren't very hard to please."

"But that's so . . . literal-minded."

"Where does it say truth isn't allowed to be literal? Seems to me that's exactly the way it usually is. Literal and harsh. And harsher." Her laugh is demonic.

"You know," Marilyn says, "it's almost like you purposely make it hard for someone to believe in what you say. Instead of saying things that will bring us along with you."

"Why in the world would you think I'd be interested in that! Gawd, that's the worst thing anyone could do. Those kinds of people are dangerous. They're the ones I'm trying to stop. And one way to do it is for me to try to make anyone capable of it into a free thinker. And, yes, there's no two ways about it, it does take some courage. At least at first, at the stage you're at."

"What stage is that?"

"I call it 'the tweens.' You're honest enough to figure out there's no sense to all the magic tricks, but you still aren't brave enough to cut loose and follow things to wherever they take you. In between. Lots of folks are 'tweeners' and stay that way, unfortunately."

"What you're really saying is I've got no courage."

"Seems to me, you're the one who just said that."

Marilyn has a pang of pure, intense feeling—part fear, part desire, a large part doubt. Does she really lack courage? What about supporting Miller against that Un-American Committee stuff? What about leaving Joe? Taking on the studio? Of course she has courage. She does. No, not always; not when she went to New York. She didn't do *Rain* or anything else on Broadway. She didn't stay and test herself. Bailed out. She . . . she . . . Courage was something you didn't really know about yourself definitively, that's why the pang. "Maybe," she says, "that we are so cowardly is the reason so many of us believe in God in the first place."

At the studio, Norman and O'Hair face each other across a low table. Large earphones squeeze their faces, great overhead mikes block their vision. He can see part of a large freckled forehead, a clear, unblinking blue eye, a bulldog mouth and chin. Through her tortoiseshell glasses, she sees a long oval face, thinning light brown hair, dark darting eyes behind thick glasses, a chin that quivers when he speaks. He scans papers on the table while Marilyn's voice fills the studio. She knits and reknits her fingers.

O'Hair says, "If you're looking for help out there somewhere, out in the ether, you won't find it. And if you think you'll get it from a man who dresses up like a woman and speaks Latin, you're in even worse shape."

Norman looks up, shaking his head slightly. "We're really beating this thing to death, I'm afraid, but at least we always know where Mrs. O'Hair stands. I hope that answers your questions, Mickie Marilyn."

"I've got one more. If life's so harsh and there's nothing for us to believe in, why don't we all just kill ourselves?" She adds, not fully realizing the intensity of the feeling welling up within her, "I'm not . . . I'm not connected to anything." She stifles a yawn.

Madalyn Murray O'Hair knows that truth has broken through mere talk. She makes a decision to maintain her honesty. "Religions tell you you don't have the right to do away with yourself. Why? Because if you did, it would mean you were taking charge of your own life, even to the extent of ending it. And such taking charge, such independence, is the one thing above all others they cannot tolerate. It seems to me that when Shakespeare wrote, 'To be or not to be . . . ,' he was talking about the ultimate choice each of us has in life—to live it or to end it. It's a choice I believe every one of us has, and no one can tell us it's immoral."

Ralph Norman squeezes his eyes closed with thumb and forefinger. He must step in and minimize the effect of this too-free speech. His boss's wife committed suicide two months ago. "I'm sure Mrs. O'Hair isn't advocating suicide as a solution for people with personal problems. My feeling is . . ."

"Mrs. O'Hair," says Mrs. O'Hair, "is saying that free people have the right to make up their own minds about anything and everything—about whether or not there is a god, about whether to have a baby or not, even about whether to live or to die."

Marilyn has not taken her fingers off the tip of her breast. Her thumb rolls small circles over the rough areola surrounding the soft nipple.

Mrs. O'Hair says to Marilyn, "If I was right before, and you are a 'tweener,' you don't sound like someone who's going to be thinking about suicide. You sound like someone who's starting to get real smart."

Norman cuts in. "What do you do, Mickie? For a living?"

After a pause that's a beat too long, Marilyn says, "I'm a waitress."

"Well, if you're not happy with the way your life's been going, there's a much simpler solution." He leaves a pause.

She must ask, "What's that?"

"You pick up a newspaper tomorrow morning and look for a brand-new job. Something you may not be sure you can do, something that will stretch you in a new way."

"What if I find out I really can't do it? I'd be in an even bigger fix than I am right now."

"You know something, Mickie? You're right. I should have kept my big mouth shut. Just hang on a minute, Mickie, and my producer will be on the line. You're listening to Madalyn Murray O'Hair espousing her philosophy of free thinking, or godless atheism, depending on your point of view. And we're 'Night Voices.' I'm Ralph Norman, your late-night transmediator. My number is 388-3838. If you can't sleep, call."

The nasal voice of the producer is back. "Just hold, okay? Ralph Norman wants to say a few words soon as we go to commercial. We're almost there."

At precisely the moment a jingle about borrowing money begins in the kitchen, Ralph Norman says hello to Marilyn. "You know, it's uncanny, your voice. I'm a betting man, and I'd bet anything you're her. You're not really in Fontana, are you?"

"Depends." In spite of herself—rather, a great part of herself—she is in character, teasing, coaxing, baiting. It is as though she had never spoken to the atheist about courage.

"Depends on what?"

"On why you're asking."

"Truth? What you said tonight was one of the most interesting calls we've had in weeks. I want to talk to you more about it."

"Sure. Because you're so concerned about me."

"Actually, because I *am* concerned about what I heard you say."

"No, I don't live in Fontana."

"And are you her?"

"I'm myself. But I've got a question to ask you."

"Sure. Quick, though."

"Are you Jewish? Are you thin?"

Ralph Norman must calculate an answer quickly. He thinks about Miller. Remembers she became a Jew when she married him. But the answer lies in the question itself, that she even asked it. "Ralph 'Skinny' Nadelman, P.S. 54, Borough Park, Brooklyn."

"Good for you, Ralph 'Skinny' Nadelman."

"I've got a question too. Are you your basic blond California *shiksa* with freckles?"

"I've got some freckles."

"So tell me, where do you live?"

Marilyn Monroe tells Ralph Nadelman.

"I'm done here at five."

"I know."

With difficulty, Marilyn brings her cup and plate to the kitchen. She struggles not to lose her balance. The atheist is talking. Marilyn hates her logic. Despises her lonely strength. She pours bourbon into a crystal glass.

Mrs. O'Hair's voice is distant but distinct: "What about the animals? Don't they accept their deaths as the most natural thing there is? They even go off alone to die in dignity. Very few human beings have such good luck."

"In some ways," says Norman as Marilyn feels the warmth of the bourbon in her chest and its radiance in her stomach, "the animals are more fortunate than humans. We know we're going to die. Maybe that's why we have the need for a God."

"That's just like fainthearted man. Look at the advantages we've gotten all our lives through knowledge—we know pleasure, we anticipate, we plan, we arrange, we try to shape things to our liking. You would think a mind that could do things like that would be enough of a gift. But not for a two-face like mankind. No, he's got to use his mind—his knowing and his imagination—to invent an easy way to get out of life too. Never mind that it takes all the savor out of his living. I mentioned Shakespeare before. Well, he had it right. He wrote, 'When we are sick in fortune, we make guilty the sun, the moon, and the stars,' never ourselves. In other words, always trying to get out of his simple human responsibilities. If there's got to be a bible, we couldn't do better than the complete works of William Shakespeare, believe me."

Marilyn's resentment is so strong she tries to imagine some way to spite this knowing voice. She could, of course, simply turn the knob, only inches away. She pours herself another drink. If she lived through this phase of her life and became an older actress, she'd never play a woman like this. Never.

Marilyn tosses down her drink and takes the bottle back to her bedroom. Through the French doors she believes she sees the sky lightening in false dawn. The faint song of a bird is undeniable.

Marilyn pours another drink. She pulls the black sleep mask over her eyes and slips under the covers. Madalyn Murray O'Hair has never really spoken to her. Marilyn drinks the forgetting warmth. There is no Madalyn Murray O'Hair. There never was. Marilyn has almost reached a stupor.

Ralph Norman drives an azure Thunderbird, drives it proudly and, this morning, with a sense of anticipation and well-being rare even for Ralph Norman. He parks under a large palm on the silent Brentwood street. It is 5:25. A soft breeze promises warmth. Bird songs promise bliss.

He tosses away a cigarette and walks up the driveway. Across the patio. The house is small, but he's sure it's hers. At the front door, a bell produces vibrating chimes within. His heart beats strongly, his balance is a bit off. His excitement is extreme. He knows the atheist is wrong. There must be a God.